BRIAN FLYNN
THE FIVE RED FINGERS

BRIAN FLYNN was born in 1885 in Leyton, Essex.
He won a scholarship to the City Of London School,
and from there went into the civil service. In World
War I he served as Special Constable on the Home
Front, also teaching "Accountancy, Languages, Maths
and Elocution to men, women, boys and girls" in the
evenings, and acting in his spare time.

It was a seaside family holiday that inspired Brian
Flynn to turn his hand to writing in the mid-twenties.
Finding most mystery novels of the time "mediocre in
the extreme", he decided to compose his own. Edith,
the author's wife, encouraged its completion, and
after a protracted period finding a publisher, it was
eventually released in 1927 by John Hamilton in the
UK and Macrae Smith in the U.S. as *The Billiard-
Room Mystery*.

The author died in 1958. In all, he wrote and published
57 mysteries, the vast majority featuring the super-
sleuth Antony Bathurst.

D1453563

BRIAN FLYNN

THE FIVE RED FINGERS

With an introduction by
Steve Barge

DEAN STREET PRESS

INTRODUCTION

"I believe that the primary function of the mystery story is to entertain; to stimulate the imagination and even, at times, to supply humour. But it pleases the connoisseur most when it presents – and reveals – genuine mystery. To reach its full height, it has to offer an intellectual problem for the reader to consider, measure and solve."

THUS WROTE Brian Flynn in the *Crime Book Magazine* in 1948, setting out his ethos on writing detective fiction. At that point in his career, Flynn had published thirty-six mystery novels, beginning with *The Billiard-Room Mystery* in 1927 – he went on, before his death in 1958, to write twenty-one more, three under the pseudonym Charles Wogan. So how is it that the general reading populace – indeed, even some of the most ardent collectors of mystery fiction – were until recently unaware of his existence? The reputation of writers such as John Rhode survived their work being out of print, so what made Flynn and his books vanish so completely?

There are many factors that could have contributed to Flynn's disappearance. For reasons unknown, he was not a member of either The Detection Club or the Crime Writers' Association, two of the best ways for a writer to network with others. As such, his work never appeared in the various collaborations that those groups published. The occasional short story in such a collection can be a way of maintaining awareness of an author's name, but it seems that Brian Flynn wrote no short stories at all, something rare amongst crime writers.

There are a few mentions of him in various studies of the genre over the years. Sutherland Scott, in *Blood in Their Ink* (1953), states that Flynn, who was still writing at the time, "has long been popular". He goes on to praise *The Mystery of the Peacock's Eye* (1928) as containing "one of the ablest pieces of misdirection one could wish to meet". Anyone reading that particular review who feels like picking up the novel – out now from Dean Street Press – should stop reading at that point, as later in the book, Scott proceeds to casually spoil the ending, although as if he assumes that everyone will have read the novel already.

It is a later review, though, that may have done much to end – temporarily, I hope – Flynn's popularity.

"Straight tripe and savorless. It is doubtful, on the evidence, if any of his others would be different."

Thus wrote Jacques Barzun and Wendell Hertig Taylor in their celebrated work, *A Catalog of Crime* (1971). The book was an ambitious attempt to collate and review every crime fiction author, past and present. They presented brief reviews of some titles, a bibliography of some authors and a short biography of others. It is by no means complete – E & M.A. Radford had written thirty-six novels at this point in time but garner no mention – but it might have helped Flynn's reputation if he too had been overlooked. Instead one of the contributors picked up *Conspiracy at Angel* (1947), the thirty-second Anthony Bathurst title. I believe that title has a number of things to enjoy about it, but as a mystery, it doesn't match the quality of the majority of Flynn's output. Dismissing a writer's entire work on the basis of a single volume is questionable, but with the amount of crime writers they were trying to catalogue, one can, just about, understand the decision. But that decision meant that they missed out on a large number of truly entertaining mysteries that fully embrace the spirit of the Golden Age of Detection, and, moreover, many readers using the book as a reference work may have missed out as well.

So who was Brian Flynn? Born in 1885 in Leyton, Essex, Flynn won a scholarship to the City Of London School, and while he went into the civil service (ranking fourth in the whole country on the entrance examination) rather than go to university, the classical education that he received there clearly stayed with him. Protracted bouts of rheumatic fever prevented him fighting in the Great War, but instead he served as a Special Constable on the Home Front – one particular job involved warning the populace about Zeppelin raids armed only with a bicycle, a whistle and a placard reading "TAKE COVER". Flynn worked for the local government while teaching "Accountancy, Languages, Maths and Elocution to men, women, boys and girls" in the evening, and acting as part of the Trevalyan Players in his spare time.

It was a seaside family holiday that inspired him to turn his hand to writing. He asked his librarian to supply him a collection of mystery novels for "deck-chair reading" only to find himself disappointed. In his own words, they were "mediocre in the extreme." There is no record of what those books were, unfortunately, but on arriving home, the following conversation, again in Brian's own words, occurred:

> "ME (unpacking the books): If I couldn't write better stuff than any of these, I'd eat my own hat.
>
> Mrs ME (after the manner of women and particularly after the manner of wives): It's a great pity you don't do a bit more and talk a bit less.
>
> The shaft struck home. I accepted the challenge, laboured like the mountain and produced *The Billiard-Room Mystery*."

"Mrs ME", or Edith as most people referred to her, deserves our gratitude. While there were some delays with that first book, including Edith finding the neglected half-finished manuscript in a drawer where it had been "resting" for six months, and a protracted period finding a publisher, it was eventually released in 1927 by John Hamilton in the UK and Macrae Smith in the U.S. According to Flynn, John Hamilton asked for five more, but in fact they only published five in total, all as part of the Sundial Mystery Library imprint. Starting with *The Five Red Fingers* (1929), Flynn was published by John Long, who would go on to publish all of his remaining novels, bar his single non-series title, *Tragedy At Trinket* (1934). About ten of his early books were reprinted in the US before the war, either by Macrae Smith, Grosset & Dunlap or Mill, and a few titles also appeared in France, Denmark, Germany and Sweden, but the majority of his output only saw print in the United Kingdom. Some titles were reprinted during his lifetime – the John Long Four-Square Thrillers paperback range featured some Flynn titles, for example – but John Long's primary focus was the library market, and some titles had relatively low print runs. Currently, the majority of Flynn's work, in particular that only published in the U.K., is extremely rare – not just expensive, but seemingly non-existent even in the second-hand book market.

In the aforementioned article, Flynn states that the tales of Sherlock Holmes were a primary inspiration for his writing, having read them at a young age. A conversation in *The Billiard-Room Mystery* hints at other influences on his writing style. A character, presumably voicing Flynn's own thoughts, states that he is a fan of "the pre-war Holmes". When pushed further, he states that:

> "Mason's M. Hanaud, Bentley's Trent, Milne's Mr Gillingham and to a lesser extent, Agatha Christie's M. Poirot are all excellent in their way, but oh! – the many dozens that aren't."

He goes on to acknowledge the strengths of Bernard Capes' "Baron" from *The Mystery of The Skeleton Key* and H.C. Bailey's Reggie Fortune, but refuses to accept Chesterton's Father Brown.

> "He's entirely too Chestertonian. He deduces that the dustman was the murderer because of the shape of the piece that had been cut from the apple-pie."

Perhaps this might be the reason that the invitation to join the Detection Club never arrived . . .

Flynn created a sleuth that shared a number of traits with Holmes, but was hardly a carbon-copy. Enter Anthony Bathurst, a polymath and gentleman sleuth, a man of contradictions whose background is never made clear to the reader. He clearly has money, as he has his own rooms in London with a pair of servants on call and went to public school (Uppingham) and university (Oxford). He is a follower of all things that fall under the banner of sport, in particular horse racing and cricket, the latter being a sport that he could, allegedly, have represented England at. He is also a bit of a show-off, littering his speech (at times) with classical quotes, the obscurer the better, provided by the copies of the *Oxford Dictionary of Quotations* and *Brewer's Dictionary of Phrase & Fable* that Flynn kept by his writing desk, although Bathurst generally restrains himself to only doing this with people who would appreciate it or to annoy the local constabulary. He is fond of amateur dramatics (as was Flynn, a well-regarded amateur thespian who appeared in at least one self-penned play, *Blue Murder*), having been a member of OUDS, the Oxford University Dramatic Society. Like Holmes, Bathurst isn't averse to the occasional disguise, and as with Watson and Holmes, sometimes even his close allies don't recognise him. General information about his background is light on the ground. His parents were Irish, but he doesn't have an accent – see *The Spiked Lion* (1933) – and his eyes are grey. We learn in *The Orange Axe* that he doesn't pursue romantic relationships due to a bad experience in his first romance. That doesn't remain the case throughout the series – he falls head over heels in love in *Fear and Trembling*, for example – but in this opening tranche of titles, we don't see Anthony distracted by the fairer sex, not even one who will only entertain gentlemen who can beat her at golf!

Unlike a number of the Holmes' stories, Flynn's Bathurst tales are all fairly clued mysteries, perhaps a nod to his admiration of Christie, but first and foremost, Flynn was out to entertain the reader. The problems posed to Bathurst have a flair about them – the simultaneous murders, miles apart, in *The Case of the Black Twenty-Two* (1928) for example, or the scheme to draw lots to commit masked murder in *The Orange Axe* – and there is a momentum to the narrative. Some mystery writers have trouble with the pace slowing between the reveal of the problem and the reveal of the murderer, but Flynn's books sidestep that, with Bathurst's investigations never seeming to sag. He writes with a wit and intellect that can make even the most prosaic of interviews with suspects enjoyable to read about, and usually provides an action-packed finale before the murderer is finally revealed. Some of those revelations, I think it is fair to say, are surprises that can rank with some of the best in crime fiction.

We are fortunate that we can finally reintroduce Brian Flynn and Anthony Lotherington Bathurst to the many fans of classic crime fiction out there.

The Five Red Fingers (1929)

"Hard luck to be murdered just after your horse has won the Derby! Don't you think so, Doctor?"

IN 1929, Brian Flynn switched publishers from John Hamilton to John Long, his initial contract for five books having finished. However, this title, the first John Long book, is the fifth Anthony Bathurst tale, with *Invisible Death*, the final John Hamilton book, the sixth, not just by publication date, but also chronologically for Bathurst – a passage in the latter book refers to this mystery as one of the five cases that Bathurst has solved. John Long went on to publish the remainder of Flynn's Bathurst mysteries as well as those written under his short-lived pseudonym, Charles Wogan. John Long primarily published for the library market, which may be another reason why people have neglected Flynn's work over the years, but they proved to be steady partners over the next thirty-plus years.

The Five Red Fingers highlighted one of Flynn's great loves – horse racing. One chapter contains quite a lot of cricket as well, but horse racing is the over-riding theme as we meet Julius Maitland, the owner of multiple horses, but in particular Red Ringan, a genuine contender for the Epsom Derby. In fact the only serious rival for the race is Princess Alicia, a horse from the same stable, but owned by his wife, Ida.

A word of explanation is in order for one aspect of the plot. Flynn makes the horse racing terminology and rules clear even for the novice, but one example has fallen out of common usage over time, namely the Calcutta Sweep. This is a high money sweepstake, linked to important races, where, for a significant sum of money, a ticket is bought that is randomly assigned to one of the horses. The money is put into a prize pot, but then the tickets are potentially auctioned off, with that money also going into the pot. The prizes are then apportioned between the owners of the tickets for the first, second and third horses. This was a significant event tied to the races at the time, with the winners of the sweep often being announced in the national press.

There is a second piece of horse-racing trivia that may come as surprise to the reader, namely that if the registered owner of a Derby-winner is dead when the race is run, the horse is disqualified. This becomes crucial when the owner of the winning horse is found murdered soon after the race finishes, but was he killed before or after the race takes place? Despite only having worked with him twice before (*The Mystery Of The Peacock's Eye* and *The Murders Near Mapleton*), Commissioner of Police Sir Austin Kemble immediately suggests calling in Anthony Bathurst – this is by no means the last time that Sir Austin shows a complete lack of confidence in the abilities of his own force of investigators – who soon finds a complex case to solve that is right up his street.

The Five Red Fingers, like the books before it, was well-received by the critics who took a look at it. The *Bystander*'s review referred to it as "undeniably exciting and mysterious", the *Aberdeen Press and Journal* "a well-told tale of crime and detection" and the *Northern Whig* praised the way that "the detective interest and the sporting interest are skilfully interwoven."

One small piece of trivia about this one – Charles Wogan gets mentioned. Wogan was a Jacobite soldier of fortune in the eighteenth century, famed for many exploits, eventually being rewarded by the Pope with the title of Roman Senator. More significantly, it is also the pseudonym that Flynn adopted for his short series of books concerning Sebastian Stole.

The Five Red Fingers was first published in the UK in 1929, but it was not until 1938 that it saw publication in the US. Macrae

Smith chose not to publish it for unknown reasons when it was released, but it appeared a decade later, along with later titles *Fear and Trembling* (as *The Somerset Murder Case*) and *Tread Softly*, published by Mill. At the same time, it was among the first Flynn titles to receive a UK paperback release, alongside *Murder En Route*, *The Fortescue Candle*, *Cold Evil* and *Tread Softly* as part of the Four Square Thriller range. It was rare for any Flynn title to get a paperback reprint, so it such a pleasure to be able to add to that list with these titles.

Steve Barge

CHAPTER I

WHEN JUNE chooses to be at its beautiful best, this England of ours wants a tremendous amount of beating, for the month of roses is the queen month of them all. There is a fashion among scholars and men of understanding to give a sex to each of the months—some seem to be masculine and some feminine. Certain it is that this month of June always must be placed in the latter category just as surely as March, the rude and rough, the bombastic and boisterous, would take its stand with the mere males.

On the particular day upon which this story opens June had chosen to give to its adoring subjects from the fullness of its two hands as lavishly as it ever knew how. For the day was perfect. For the hyper-critical, perhaps a trifle too hot. Or, on the other hand, not hot enough. It must be remembered that the hyper-critical are always with us, and though their purpose may be obscure, no doubt they serve it with a due measure of faithfulness. To the man and woman in love with life and one another, it was a day for which to thank Almighty God; to the man and woman in love with life only, a day for which to thank Him even more. The shimmering sunshine flamed about the cheeks and hands and arms, and a gloriously cool breeze, wafted across the roll of the Berkshire Downs, was sufficiently active to bring a cold comfort that for once at least, despite its paradoxical nature, was both eagerly desired and certainly welcomed.

It was the Thursday of Ascot week. Cup day! The course looked parched and rather yellow, its condition being a heritage of the fine summer that had commenced during the second week in May, had survived, surprisingly, the customary challenge of Whitsun, that menace of so many summers, and had courageously endured for just on twenty days of imperious June itself. The distant woodland was hazy with hanging heat and there was that indescribable hum of insects vitalizing the heavy and drowsy air as they winged on their way to worship. The royal inclosure was already more than comfortably full. Lovely girls passed with lovely women who once had been lovely girls and who were trying to be lovely girls still. The frocks were suitable to the occasion—one cannot say more.

Suddenly there came a roar of cheering down the course, and then it began to come from those who had gathered at the gates of the inclosure and along the railings. It was for the coming of the King. The few that had remained behind stood up. The men among them removed their hats as the strains of the national anthem, played by the distant band, floated down the course toward them. Thus they stood until the flash of the red and the gleam of the grey, jaunty postillions and eagerly quivering team swept the royal carriage into the inclosure.

"That's a fine sight, Pauline!" exclaimed Sir Matthew Fullgarney. "That and the trooping of the colours, I don't know which impresses me the more—there's nothing to touch 'em."

Lady Fullgarney smiled mischievously, the imp dancing in her violet eyes. They were a happy hunting ground for him.

"I could name several other sights that leave you far from unmoved, Matthew. In fact, I could assert that some of them rival the two you have just named. Your susceptibility is much keener than your memory, I fear."

Her husband evaded the controversy. His eyes had caught sight of a familiar figure. He fled down the welcome way of escape.

"By Jove," he declared, "there's Sir Austin! Look—just over there! I haven't seen him for months."

"Neither have I," replied Pauline.

"Not since I saw him just after the Mapleton murders. Is he alone?"

"You bet he isn't. You won't make a safer bet than that to-day. He's very well looked after. But your friend Bathurst isn't with him."

The commissioner of police certainly seemed to be the centre of attention. Mr. Bathurst therefore could not possibly be with him. As far as Sir Matthew could see, he was one of a large party. A heavily built man of about five feet ten, superbly dressed, whose face seemed vaguely familiar, was engaged in animated conversation with him. Sir Austin Kemble was smiling and jerking his head in the way that was peculiarly his own. The speaker stopped his conversation fairly regularly to frown. Every time he frowned Sir Austin smiled. On their left stood a woman—young, charming and sweet, dainty elegance. Her frock was simple, but very beautiful. It was of *crêpe de Chine* with an exquisitely pretty pattern of wild roses, the flowers being repeated in the embroidery on the white georgette sleeves and vest. Across her shoulders and falling round her figure in graceful folds was a decorative wrap of silk *côtelé*, for although the day was hot, the lady was inclined to feel the cold. She also realized (which is probably very much more to the point) that these wraps had a mysterious charm in themselves and that the proximity of "mysterious charm" served to enhance her own seductive and appealing beauty. Her sweeping lashes—ash-gold like her hair—fringed eyes of glorious blue, and her lips and mouth held that demurely challenging curve that seems to invest feminine loveliness with that last alluring touch that renders it completely irresistible.

In an instant the trooping of the colours and the royal procession were ingloriously relegated to the background of Sir Matthew Fullgarney's discerning mind. Lady Fullgarney, fully conscious of the truth of her recent statement, could see the manner of their submerging. Her eyes followed his and understood the reason very thoroughly. As she did so, Sir Austin Kemble's glance was arrested by hers and, having come racing in mufti, he gallantly removed his silk hat in swift recognition and acknowledgment. Sir Matthew waved a social hand, towards which the commissioner directed a sharp look and then suddenly beckoned.

"We will walk over, Pauline," announced Sir Matthew.

"You'd like to, my dear," returned the lady, "but you won't. It won't be an easy matter like that. I will wager very confidently that there will be many other runners for that particular handicap." Laughter came from her lips.

Sir Austin walked a few steps to meet them and bowed over Lady Fullgarney's hand.

"Let me introduce you," he urged. "This is Mr. Julius Maitland—and Mrs. Maitland. Sir Matthew and Lady Fullgarney. Sir Matthew is Lord Lieutenant of Westhamptonshire."

For the fraction of a second the commissioner looked at the two ladies and contrasted their different types of beauty. Ida Maitland had created something akin to a sensation in society when it had first been called upon to welcome her.

Sir Matthew Fullgarney knew now the identity of the man to whom he had been introduced. Julius Maitland was reputed to be the richest man who had ever left the shores of South Africa for the homeland. Of his antecedents not too much was known, and rumour had whispered more than once that this reticence was a kindness to him. His friends used to say that his telegraphic address was "Diamonds, S. A." At the present moment he was in the late sixties and, as far as the shrewd Lady Fullgarney could judge upon so slight and recent an acquaintance, somewhere about thirty-five years senior to his delightful young wife. She was his second wife, and Maitland had always bitterly resented sneering suggestions that coupled May with December. "I don't mind them calling us April and October," he had been heard to say, "because that's nearer the truth. And if people love each other—as we two do—what are the odds, anyway?" Anyhow, Julius Maitland, the man who had been alone for nineteen years, had met, loved and married Ida Greatorex in a whirlwind escapade that had lasted a mere matter of months, and if she had not been received too kindly or graciously by Maitland's daughter and the younger of his two sons, nevertheless, as far as her husband himself was concerned nothing had happened to occasion her to regret very much the union that she had made.

She had gone to South Africa at the age of seventeen upon the death of her parents. An uncle had sent for her from sheer kindness of heart and had taken the place of her father, his dead brother. Maitland had first encountered her in Durban.

During the fashionable winter season, between May and September, visitors swarm to Durban in thousands, for as a resort it equals in the strength of its appeal many of the popular watering places of Europe. Its prosperity is at the same time its power—and its charm lies in its variety. In West Street the raw Kaffir girl in beads and blankets rubs brown shoulders with the lady gowned from the Rue de la Paix. A Mohammedan in brilliant robe and garish turban passes with Zulu house boy in tunic and knickerbockers close upon his heels. A dusky Indian woman, bare of feet, will avert her languorous eyes as you gaze in barely disguised amazement at the wealth of golden trinkets at her neck, wrists and—nose, and hard by, as you turn quickly and with eagerness that you may miss nothing, there glides gracefully by an Eastern lady of high rank, very dignified and excessively stately, clad in the traditional splendour of her exalted caste, and her male escort follows her in close and unwearyingly vigilant attendance. Across the way a Kaffir chieftain on one of his infrequent excursions to the town recalls the strange ancestry of his civilization, and the Zulu and Basuto "rickshaw" boys, strong, supple and speedy, darting hither and thither in the irresistible impetus of industry, seem in their gorgeous and violently coloured trappings more like monstrous birds than human beings.

It was in this shopping centre and business thoroughfare of Durban that Julius Maitland and Ida Greatorex had first met, and five months subsequent to the encounter saw them on their honeymoon trip. For Julius Maitland was not a man who lets the grass grow under his feet. He vowed that he would show her every beauty that his own South African country possessed, and according to his own statement it possessed myriads. She had not been disappointed, for he had more than kept his word. The Paarl with its excursions as far as Ceres and over Blainskloof; Worcester and the Hex River Pass; the famous Cango caves on the brink of Oudtshoorn and the Zwart-Berg and Montagu Passes; the Knysna Forest, Port Elizabeth and the Zuurberg. All these she visited and loved, for their natural beauties were enhanced by the excitement in the eyes through which she saw. But most of all she loved the Orange River Falls near Uppington and the falls at Umlass in Natal, for running water always had attracted her.

They had finished their wedding trip in the picturesque neighbourhood of Cape Town, that rivals the south of France along its coast, and when Julius Maitland set foot upon the boat that was to bear his bride, his family and himself to England, there were those that said mordantly that he was taking I.D.A. away and leaving I.D.B. behind. Damned good-natured friends every one of them. But among these could not be numbered Patrick Wogan Dillon, for he was only concerned with the first. The latter troubled him in no way whatsoever. Therefore he turned away cynically in the full measure of his bitterness and determined to forget. Three years had made little difference to Ida Maitland, as she stood and bowed to the parties of the introduction.

"This is Sylvia," she said in her turn, "my husband's daughter. And these are her brothers—Valentine and Vivian. This gentleman is Captain Nigel Lumsden."

Sir Matthew Fullgarney fluttered heavily through the overture of these further introductions, but his wife was supremely at her ease. She could give him points at most things.

"Of the Worcestershire Lumsdens?" she asked sweetly of the young officer who stood at the side of Sylvia Maitland.

"Why, yes, Lady Fullgarney. My people live between Kinver and Kidderminster. Do you know them by any chance?"

She smiled her most angelic smile.

"Ever so well, Captain Lumsden. I went to school with your sister Evelyn—she would be your eldest sister, I think—so we can call our two selves the oldest of old friends, can't we? Your eldest brother is—?"

"Vicar of Talehurst," replied the young officer.

Sylvia Maitland smiled prettily. She was a very fair, slender girl, with perhaps something un-English about her.

"Like her mother, I expect," commented Lady Fullgarney inwardly.

"Of course you can claim to be friends," said the girl. "I suspect Sir Austin Kemble must have known something of the kind when he introduced you to us. Or else he had an inspiration."

"Inspirations are very costly things at such places as Ascot," put in Vivian Maitland. "Well I know it, to my cost."

Pauline Fullgarney put him down at two or three and twenty and his brother Valentine at about a year older. The latter was tall and fair. Vivian was a complete antithesis—short and dark, and, like his sister, to a certain extent exotic. He proceeded to enlarge upon his last remark.

"I had an inspiration for the Hunt Cup yesterday. I backed Valiant Mandarin because it happened to have the same initials as I have. Well bred, too—by Kwang Su out of Plucky Liège. It ran nowhere, of course."

His brother laughed: "You omit the most important part of the story. You don't tell them you got me to lose money on the wretched animal as well, because my initials were the same as yours."

He laughed again and showed a row of perfect teeth. All the others laughed an accompaniment.

"Never mind, Val," said his father. "You'll get it all back this afternoon, barring accidents, of course." He turned to Sir Austin and Sir Matthew Fullgarney. "There's a dark two-year-old of mine running in the New Stakes. Cruden thinks very highly of him. He's answered a very big question set him in a trial. If it's any good to you, I'm having a good bet. Cruden tells me I can with confidence, and he's not a man who mixes geese with his swan. Still, please yourself."

Sir Matthew frowned, as he always did when he endeavoured to remember anything. "Up against something pretty stiff, aren't you? You've got to beat Excalibur, one of the best Gay Crusader colts I've ever seen. I saw him win the Woodcote Stakes three weeks ago at Epsom in a common canter. Made hacks of his field."

Maitland nodded. "Quite true. I'm aware of all that. I know very well that my horse has got his work cut out and that he'll have to be a rare good 'un to win. All the same, my trainer's confident, so am I. Good enough for you?"

Sir Austin glanced at his race card. He turned to the long and imposing list of entries for the New Stakes. Half way down the list of two-year-olds he paused. "Mr. Julius Maitland's ch. c. Red

Ringan by Buchan—Scarlet Shoon (petunia and cream hoops, petunia sleeves, apricot cap—Cruden)."

"I like all Buchan's get," he announced, "always have done. He was a game little horse himself—none gamer ever looked through a bridle—and he seems to have the knack of passing his courage on to all his offspring."

"The numbers are going up for the first race, Julius!" cut in Ida Maitland.

"All right dear. Don't be reckless, though I suppose you will be to the end of the chapter. Why don't you wait for the good things?"

His wife grimaced and Captain Lumsden and the two boys laughed boisterously at her apparent discomfiture.

Maitland turned away from his family group again and for a moment or two seemed to be turning something over in his mind very carefully. Pride in his horse was warring with his natural inclination to reserve. The former conquered in the struggle.

"Look here, Sir Austin," he said with sudden impetuosity, "Red Ringan's a smasher. We've proved that conclusively down at Queensleigh. I hope to get fives or sixes about him this afternoon, but take it from me, we shall be very lucky to get anything like that price again. My wife has a two-year-old filly in my stable that won the Cotton Stakes at Manchester on the second of the month. She won by a street. In the ordinary way we should feel very proud to own her, but Red Ringan can lose Princess Alicia. Every gallop down at Queensleigh tells us the same story. We've clocked him a certainty, too."

Sir Matthew had listened to this eulogy with rapt attention, for it had a most pleasant sound. He felt that he wanted to lick his lips.

"If he can do what you say with Princess Alicia, I begin to understand your optimism, Mr. Maitland," he observed.

As he spoke, his wife and Ida Maitland rushed to meet them.

"We've got tens about The Wheelsman for the first race," said Lady Maitland. "Of course it ran second! The number of seconds that I can unfailingly find is positively—"

"Why on earth didn't you do it each way?" interposed her husband.

"But I did," she expostulated, round-eyed.

He laughed good-humouredly. "Then what in thunder are you grousing at? You've made a bit on the first race," he returned. He called back to all the others: "Back your fancies for the Gold Cup and then let's come and have some lunch. That's a much safer and infinitely more attractive proposition than trying to find winners—or even seconds." He added the last three words slyly, glancing sidewise at his wife.

Lunch proved all that he had claimed for it—the time passed as rapidly as enjoyment always makes it—and Sir Matthew and Lady Fullgarney, who had been invited to join the South African millionaire's party, were very soon on the best terms not only with themselves but with all the others.

"I'll take you two men across," said Maitland eventually. "You shall see the colt before the numbers go up for the New Stakes. Cruden will be putting the finishing touches on him. He's a beauty, I can tell you! You won't wonder that I'm so proud of him." He paused and looked round at his two sons. "You two boys coming?"

"Yes, dad." Vivian spoke for himself and for his elder brother.

"You, too, Lumsden?"

The younger officer grinned. "No thanks, sir," he sallied back. "If it's all the same to you, I'll stop and look after Sylvia."

Maitland's heavy underlip curled sarcastically as the men set off.

Humphrey Cruden—the wizard of Queensleigh, as the sporting press described him—was superintending the final preparations of a handsome chestnut colt that stood placidly in a corner.

Sir Matthew ran his eye over him critically. It would have been difficult to fault him. The June sun gave his chestnut coat a glittering sheen that only served to intensify his beautiful symmetry and perfect balance. There was abundant promise of both power and speed. Sir Matthew, however, was at least a keen critic and he flattered himself that he knew the points of a horse with anybody.

"A trifle on the leg perhaps just at present," he murmured half to himself, "but with ample scope both for growth and improvement. Another year will work wonders for him." He turned to the owner. "A beauty," he declared. "Whom are you putting up?"

"Remington," said Maitland laconically. "Here he is."

The jockey was a bigger man than is usual for a fellow of his profession, although dry biscuits and cold toast figured largely in his diet. He had long, thin legs that contrasted oddly with his dark, saturnine countenance. They gave him a spidery appearance. But both Sir Austin Kemble and Sir Matthew Fullgarney knew that no jockey in the land had "nicer" hands for a two-year-old that was not too sure of his business, and might have a tendency to run "green" first time out. Remington's hands were beautiful and his handling of a two-year-old worthy of Fred Archer, Mornington Cannon or "Brownie" Carslake at their best. The commissioner and the Lord Lieutenant of Westhamptonshire decided there and then to let Red Ringan carry their maximum.

Cruden called Remington over to him.

"Ride him in your own way," he said. "You know what I've told you. If you can't win, don't press him unduly, and on no account punish him."

Remington nodded and swung himself lightly into the saddle, and a few moments later the gratified owner could hear the murmurs of undisguised admiration for a beautiful horse as the colt cantered down to the starter.

"If you tell me what you want," said Maitland, "I'll put yours on with mine."

"I'm casting caution to the winds," declared the commissioner. "I've caught something of your optimism. It must be infectious. Put me on a cool hundred to win."

Sir Matthew was guilty of a hasty and probably inaccurate calculation.

"I'll have the same," he declared, "and Lady Fullgarney can have what she wants of it—before the race."

Maitland pushed his way into Tattersall's, but was back before the start, which was delayed by more than one of the big field.

"Excalibur is favourite at five to two. There's a dark Beckhampton colt second favourite at fours. I got sevens about mine. But nobody else will," he added grimly.

The three seniors listened to the shouts of the bookmakers as they came across to them.

"Each of you boys is well on," continued Maitland, "and you won't have to pay me if you lose. But you *won't* lose."

"Thanks," they chorused, "it's no end good of you—"

But Maitland had no ears for their reply. He was listening to the roar of the ring.

"Red Ringan's down to fours," he said quietly. "I told you so."

"They're off!" came the cry.

In the group five pairs of glasses went to five pairs of eyes.

The race needs little description. Remington took things very comfortably to the distance and kept a place within a length of the speedy Excalibur. He was sitting still on Red Ringan, who was travelling smoothly and easily. At the distance he commenced to ride. The bookmakers and the clever race readers shouted him home long before the finish. The son of Buchan flashed by his rivals with devastating strides and won easily by three lengths.

Maitland put his glasses down. His hands were shaking a little. He was quiet, but his eyes were the true index to his mind. They gleamed with exultant triumph.

"I told you he was a smasher," he said quietly. "Now I'll tell you something else, gentlemen. You've seen next year's Derby winner. There won't be a three-year-old to touch him! And I shall gratify what has been my lifelong ambition, one of the reasons that brought me to England. I shall lead in the Derby winner—Mr. Julius Maitland's Red Ringan!" His voice rang with the timbre of overwhelming excitement as his sons, full of congratulations, caught his hands in theirs.

Sir Matthew thought of his stake and the price and became mathematical. These were the only occasions upon which he did—that is to say, with any degree of accuracy.

A quiet voice sounded behind Maitland. Its owner had heard what the millionaire had predicted.

"Perhaps, Mr. Maitland, but don't be too sure, sir. A lot may happen in twelve months. And remember, too, that they are all triers in the Derby."

His mouth twisted into a cynical smile. It was Humphrey Cruden who spoke. But Cruden had already trained five Derby winners, so he was entitled to speak.

CHAPTER II

TOWARDS THE end of July, about five weeks later, Julius Maitland made up his mind to run down to Queensleigh to have a word or two with Cruden. He decided, after some consideration, to travel by train and, when he alighted at the station of the tiny Wiltshire village nestling at the foot of the downs and famous only for the racing stable two miles away, he found the trainer's limousine awaiting him. A quick dash through leafy lanes brought him to Queensleigh, the stable with a record second to none in the history of the English turf. Two foxhound puppies frisked and gamboled about his legs as he crossed the yard to meet Randall, the head lad.

"If you're wanting the master, sir," said the latter, pulling at his cap and hastily removing the inevitable straw from the side of his mouth, "he's indoors with Mrs. Cruden. Shall I tell him for you, sir, or will you go along to him yourself?"

"Don't you trouble, Randall, I'll go up to the house. I'm not in such a hurry that I can't do that."

Maitland leisurely crossed the stone-flagged yard and made his way to Cruden's apartment.

"Good morning, Mr. Maitland! This is rather unexpected. I sent the car for you directly I heard that you were coming. I wasn't altogether expecting to see you, though, before Goodwood."

The clean-shaven face of the Queensleigh trainer betrayed none of the feeling that he mentioned. It was a face that had been schooled by its owner to be expressionless whenever he so desired, which was very often. Imperturbable and immobile before the two supreme impostors, triumph and disaster, neither the winning of a Derby nor the losing of an insignificant handicap was ever reflected upon it.

Although Humphrey Cruden was intensely interested in the question he was going to put, it would not have appeared so to the casual hearer. Cruden loved a good horse better than most men and even better than most trainers and in Red Ringan he knew that he stabled one, but the man's natural disinclination to show others the real state of his mind was always dominant. His father had been at Queensleigh before him, and he had carried on his father's traditions. Besides being a clever trainer, he was a clever man. It seemed that you never knew what he was thinking, but that he always knew exactly what you were; therefore he always seemed to meet you at an advantage. His staff took their cue from him, and whispers of Cruden's "good things" never leaked out, for touts got short shrift if they ventured near Queensleigh. His most optimistic declaration during his lengthy career, according to a leading London sporting journalist, had been: "My horse *may* win—if nothing beats it." The journalist had replied out of his cleverness: "Under those conditions, '*will* win' surely." Cruden had turned on his heel but remarked: "You forget the existence of the objection room."

Maitland had selected him as trainer with definite purpose. He was renowned for his reliability, and in the racing game this quality goes a very long way. Julius Maitland desired the best from life in every direction, and as Cruden put the question to him, he found himself more satisfied than ever that he had made a wise choice.

Maitland had laughed at Cruden's greeting, then said: "Cruden, I had an hour or two to spare, so I came down to have a chat with you about my horses. How's Red Ringan? Fit?"

"As fit as the proverbial fiddle, Mr. Maitland. Better than that, in fact. As fit as my hands can make him. What's his future program? Have you settled it yet?"

"Not altogether," Maitland replied. "I prefer to be guided by you. Your judgment should be sounder than mine. What about Goodwood?"

Cruden thrust his hands into his pockets before replying.

"Correct me if I'm wrong," he said at last. "Red Ringan is engaged in the Molecomb Stakes next week, the Champagne Stakes at Doncaster in September, and in the Middle Park and Dewhurst at Newmarket at the back-end. That's his lot, isn't it? Or is it the Criterion and not the Dewhurst?"

Maitland showed agreement with a quick nod of the head.

"That's quite right, Cruden. He's in the Dewhurst. Now, what do you think about it? As a matter of fact, it's the very question about which I came down to see you."

Cruden knocked the ashes from his pipe slowly and deliberately.

"Well, Mr. Maitland, if you're willing to be guided by me, as you say you are, and if you have implicit confidence in my judgment, as you say you have, I'll tell you what I should do if the horse were my own. He's a grand colt and he thrives on hard work. But I'm a firm believer in not overdoing a two-year-old. He may run up against a hard race and never recover from the effects of it. Another thing, I should like to see him muscle up a trifle more and, as a result, get greater power behind the saddle." He paused here as though carefully considering a special something, and then turned to Maitland again: "I suppose your primary objective's the Derby?"

"It is. All the rest can go hang for all I care, I'm prepared to sacrifice anything for it. Work toward that end all the time."

"Very well then, Mr. Maitland. If you take my advice, you'll let Red Ringan have a couple more outings this year and no more. Let him go to Doncaster for the Champagne and then to Newmarket. Let him go for the Middle Park Stakes there. Then, barring accidents, once again Queensleigh will stable the winter favourite for the Derby, which is as it should be."

"That means him giving Goodwood a miss, then?"

"Why not? The going's bound to be very hard, all this dry weather. I can see no sign of rain. Send Princess Alicia for the

Molecomb instead. She's engaged, and, believe me, she has an excellent chance."

"Anything else for Goodwood?"

"Well, as to that, Finnan Haddie ought to win the Gratwicke Stakes and Old Vendetta has more than a sporting chance in the Stewards' Cup. If she gets off well, she may easily run into a place. I shouldn't advise you running anything else. Not if you're out to win races."

"That's a bargain then, Cruden, and a bargain to which we'll stick. Now take me down to have a look at the horses."

The two men strolled down to the stables. The July sun was blazing from the sky with almost tropical intensity, and to Maitland, South African as he was, the day seemed almost perfect.

The first of his horses that he greeted was the mare Old Vendetta by Spoin Kop out of Retribution. It was strange that, sired by such a true stayer, she herself had followed her dam and had proved successful over short cuts only. On Cruden's advice she had been entered for the Stewards' Cup, possessing what he had described as more than a sporting chance. Her conformation was good and, what was perhaps more important, she was of good disposition, a child could handle her. Maitland was more than ordinarily fond of her. Especially as she nuzzled against him to receive his customary greeting and the usual piece of sugar.

"I shall retire her, Cruden, at the end of the present season. She's certainly earned a rest, and I hope, with judicious mating, she'll throw something pretty good. She ought to make an excellent brood mare."

"She should do. There are two Derby winners in her pedigree, as close as they can be. But breeding's a curious business, Mr. Maitland—you never know your luck. The highest priced yearlings have a knack of turning out the most abject failures. It must be the inevitable law of compensation in operation—but come and have a look at our two stars—Red Ringan and the Princess."

Maitland gave the mare a pat and passed on to reach the filly first. Princess Alicia was another aristocrat, for her owner was a strict devotee of what is known as "fashionable breeding."

She was by Gainsborough out of Cos, and as Maitland had said at Ascot a month or so back, would have held higher reputation and distinguished the stable more had it not housed such a smashing colt as Red Ringan. She was a shapely bay filly with most blood-like quarters and perfect action. At the same time she was just a little temperamental, and Cruden knew that she had two ways of going. A lot depended on how she felt and the mood in which she found herself. But she was coming to hand nicely now, and the trainer was beginning to have high hopes of achieving what he had so far always failed to accomplish. His turf triumphs had been innumerable, but he had never yet brought off the most desired of all "doubles"—the classic double of "Derby and Oaks." The pair of beauties that his stable sheltered at the present time had sown the seeds of this hope in Humphrey Cruden.

"She's making exceptional progress, Mr. Maitland," he commented. "In my opinion you can safely leave the Molecomb Stakes to her. Tell Mrs. Maitland what I say. I know she's fond of her."

Maitland laughed—perhaps at the trainer's uncharacteristic note of optimism.

"We'll see if she proves equal to the task. As a matter of fact, I don't know whether I've ever told you, she actually belongs to my wife. I gave her to Mrs. Maitland as a birthday present— the day that I bought her happened to be my wife's birthday. I got her at the Doncaster sales. She was a Sledmere yearling and made an unusually big figure for these days."

Cruden's face twisted into one of his rare smiles.

"I hope then that next year we shall witness yet another record."

"In what way, Cruden?"

"That we shall live to see the Derby and Oaks won by husband and wife."

Maitland rubbed his hands as the full mental visualization of the unprecedented triumph came home to him. But Cruden spoke again before he could reply in words.

"But as I hinted before, Mr. Maitland—*l'homme propose*— Come and see Red Ringan."

As he looked at his two-year-old champion, Julius Maitland's eyes gleamed with pride, satisfaction and what was perilously near arrogance. He was proud to possess Red Ringan, but he considered in the inner recesses of his mentality that Red Ringan in his turn should be equally proud to be possessed by Mr. Julius Maitland. After all, there should be give and take in all matters. He looked the colt over.

"The filly is entered for the Derby, too, you know, Cruden. The nomination belongs to my wife. I'm pleased at that. It's always as well to have two strings to your bow. Especially two strings of the calibre of these two."

"Every time, Mr. Maitland—I thoroughly agree. And of course the form of horses constantly changes from time to time. Some make abnormal improvement from two to three years— and others don't. They don't grow much, they don't develop as they should, and consequently fail to hold their place. As a trainer I've seen extraordinary things happen in this respect."

The two men walked slowly back to Cruden's quarters. On the way Randall, the head lad, stopped them and asked Cruden's permission to speak to him. The trainer drew Randall to one side. As they talked Maitland saw a frown appear and deepen on Cruden's face. Randall seemed to be arguing a point with his master, stressing something which Cruden appeared ill-disposed to accept. Maitland looked away for a moment, and, upon looking back again, found Cruden's eyes watching him. The trainer left Randall and joined Maitland once more.

"You will have lunch with me here, of course, Mr. Maitland?"

"Thank you, Cruden. I shall be very pleased to accept your hospitality. I want to get back to town, though, by tea time."

"Going by train?"

"Yes—same way as I came down. There's one about twenty to three, isn't there?"

"Two forty-three. I'm catching it myself as it happens. I have some rather important business to see to in town, that I must attend to to-day. We can travel together—but we'll discuss some lunch first. You must be hungry."

Maitland had been entertained at Queensleigh before and had formed the opinion upon these occasions that Mrs. Cruden was an admirable hostess, who had grown white-haired in the service of Queensleigh's distinguished guests. But on this occasion she did not seem entirely herself. Unfailingly courteous as always, eagerly apprehensive concerning her guest's personal comfort, she nevertheless gave him the impression that her thoughts were not entirely centered upon her immediate task. They seemed to be far away, and more than once he stole a glance at her covertly to see a distant look in her eyes, and made a quick remark that served to awaken her and bring her back to reality. Cruden did his best to cover her temporary embarrassment on two or three occasions, and when he and Julius Maitland, lunch over, commenced upon their journey to the station, he volunteered the information to his companion that the state of his wife's health was giving him a considerable amount of anxiety. To Maitland's idea, the trouble, whatever it was, was certainly not entirely physical, but he judged it discreet to make no comment upon the trainer's remarks.

As they waited upon the platform a tall, heavily built man came toward them, who, as he quickly passed, nodded somewhat off-handedly to Humphrey Cruden, and raised his hat to Maitland. The latter frowned as he attempted to identify the acquaintance. For the moment the memory eluded him.

"Who was that, Cruden?" he questioned. "I know his face quite well, but I'm hanged if I can place him."

Cruden smiled whimsically: "That's Alec Pollock, the Baverstock trainer. Fancy you forgetting him! He usually travels from here. The Queensleigh station is almost as near for him as Baverstock." Cruden rubbed one hand within the other. "He's worried is Master Alec. He'd give his ears to know how good Red Ringan and Princess Alicia really are. He's afraid they're going to prove troublesome to him. But I calculate he'll still have his ears when next Derby Day comes. But he's a cute 'un for all that."

"Is he likely to be dangerous to us, Cruden?"

"He's always liable to upset calculations. He doesn't always give you a straight run. He doesn't mind them running down the course a bit the first two or three times out. It fattens the price when they do click, and in handicaps helps to get the weight off. Of course a bit of information leaks out now and then as between one neighbouring stable and another, as it's bound to, and I'm told one of Sir Thomas Rotherham's two-year-olds is pretty good. Present intentions, I believe, are to run it in the Gimcrack. Sir Thomas, by the way, fancies himself as an after-dinner speaker." Cruden s eyes twinkled for the first time that day. "But he's no speaker at all. He's an M.P."

Maitland smiled at the trainer's sally as the train ran in promptly to scheduled time. Cruden stood back to let Maitland enter in front of him and was able to notice as he did so that Pollock and a woman boarded the train much lower down.

In less than half an hour the gossamer-like spire of Salisbury Cathedral showed shimmering in the afternoon sun. Cruden was very silent, and although Maitland was inclined to conversation he was able to make little headway. The Queensleigh trainer sat in his corner seat and smoked pipe after pipe of tobacco. Eventually his fellow-traveller fell back for entertainment upon the liberal supply of periodicals with which he had supplied himself. One by one he scanned them perfunctorily, to toss them down in succession upon the seat beside him.

Through half-closed eyes Cruden regarded him lazily and puffed away at his pipe. He had his own problems to solve, and he had to bring the best of his brains to bear upon them—problems beyond the problems of his stable. Suddenly he was intensely surprised to see Julius Maitland change colour. The whole thing was the work of a moment, of less than a moment—almost, it might be said, instantaneous. The South African millionaire had been carelessly scanning an illustrated weekly when his eyes left the printed page to wander idly toward the corridor of the train. A stout, florid-faced, rather over-dressed man was proceeding along the corridor in the direction of the refreshment car, and a handsome dark woman of very uncertain years was following him. Cruden saw Maitland's eyes almost start from his head and there came an involuntary parting of his lips. At the same time Cruden saw him partly avert his face and pass his hand across his eyes.

Whether it was the man or the woman that had caused his attention to be thus attracted, Cruden found it impossible to say, although he fancied that it was the latter. Whatever or whoever it was, there was no denying the fact that Maitland had suffered a severe shock. The incident had made him a changed man. He sank back into the soft seat of the carriage with his face an ashen pallor and an unpleasant greyish colour tingeing the corners of his lips. As he sat there, he appeared, for a short passage of time, to be completely oblivious of his companion's presence. Cruden watched him intently to see if he gave any sign or ventured any explanation. But neither came. The trainer determined to put a question.

"Somebody you know?" he enquired coolly.

Maitland started with annoyance and the colour began to well slowly back into his cheeks.

"No," he muttered. "No. Where?"

Cruden nodded toward the corridor.

"Thought you recognized somebody," he declared airily, "and it upset you."

"Oh, no, I had a bit of a heart twinge—that was all. I've had them before, but they pass off after a time. My doctor tells me I shall always be subject to them. Bad luck, isn't it? I'm better now."

Maitland made the announcement confidently, but he was unable to tell from the expression on Humphrey Cruden's face if the explanation were accepted, as the trainer had relapsed again into his impassive taciturnity.

When the train reached Waterloo, Cruden noticed that Maitland seemed very disinclined to hurry from the compartment, and when they made their way down the long platform, very slowly, they were well in the wake of the crowd. Cruden could see Pollock's burly figure looming some distance in front of them.

CHAPTER III

PRINCESS ALICIA went to Goodwood at the end of July and duly won the Molecomb Stakes from eleven others. This victory over six furlongs drew attention to her stamina. Red Ringan took the Champagne Stakes at Doncaster from a big field and followed up this success with a handsome victory at Newmarket on very heavy going in the Middle Park Stakes at the "back-end." In this race he had a smashing Papyrus colt, Sacred Beetle, trained at Whycombe, two lengths behind him, with Excalibur, his old Ascot opponent, a neck away, third. Thus, according to plan, Cruden, the "wizard of Queensleigh," once again harboured the winter favourite for the Epsom Derby.

But Alec Pollock of Baverstock had other views. Cortina, the winner of the Gimcrack, by Feather Bed out of Loud Speaker, besides being responsible for an outburst of his owner's oratory, was the best colt he had trained for years, and who knew what might happen in seven months' time? He was experienced enough as a trainer, both here and in the colonies, to know that "three-year-old form" has a habit of completely upsetting what happened when the same animals met when they were a year younger. He was content to wait and to bide his time.

That winter and spring the rains were heavy—abnormally heavy even for England. The result was that the majority of the provincial stables failed to have their horses anything like ready. Queensleigh and Baverstock, tucked away down in Wiltshire, were no exception to the general rule. But when the weather began to get better, as it eventually did toward the end of March, one fact became very apparent to the habitués of Queensleigh. Princess Alicia had made tremendous improvement from two or three years, and Cruden, as he looked at her, remembered her illustrious lineage, thought particularly of her sire and muttered to himself in his more garrulous moments that he had another "top-notcher."

With Red Ringan he was perhaps not quite so pleased. The colt had wintered well, it is true, and had thickened out nicely, but the critical eye of Humphrey Cruden decided that his pasterns were not all that could be desired, and his hind joints were possibly a trifle on the weak side. But all the same he was a beautifully handsome horse and a grand mover, and Cruden knew that if he could give him a little more strength and power behind the saddle, it would take a very exceptional animal to beat him. It had been obvious in his three races as a two-year-old that Red Ringan was a rare battler, and the trainer fervently hoped that the sun on his coat would bring him along nicely and help to eradicate his little physical weaknesses. When that happened, Cruden considered that he would have a world-beater.

Maitland came down to Queensleigh on several occasions to have a look at the gallops and on two of these occasions Ida Maitland accompanied him. She was intensely interested in her Princess, as she called her horse, and laughingly proposed to her husband one evening in early April that their two horses should be matched over a mile. Julius Maitland scouted the suggestion.

"Nice thing for the papers to get hold of, that would be. They'd know as much as we know. That would never do. Take it from me, Ida, Red Ringan will always beat her. A good horse will always beat a good mare. Cruden considers him among the first half-dozen he's ever trained, and he's trained some stuff, too."

As she crossed the paddocks a few minutes after her semi-humorous challenge to Julius Maitland had been turned down, she heard a quick step a few yards behind her. Turning quickly, she was somewhat surprised to face Remington the jockey. She had met him before, of course. He raised his cap.

"Pardon me intruding upon your time, Mrs. Maitland, but I wanted a word with you. Is it convenient? I wanted it with Mr. Maitland, as an actual fact, but he seems to have disappeared for the moment. I expect he's gone down to the gallops with Mr. Cruden. So you mustn't mind me approaching you in his stead. Have I permission?"

Ida's eyes flickered over him for a brief moment before she replied.

"Why, certainly, Remington. What is it you want to say to me?"

Remington's teeth flashed in a smile and Ida realized for the first time the undeniable fascination of the man. He was popular wherever he went—among his patrons, his peers and his parasites, for the man possessed a natural integrity. There was that indefinable touch of "character" about him. When you spoke to him or merely looked at him, you became immediately conscious of its presence within him. You could not escape it—there it was! His Irish father had married his Scotch mother and Remington had proved a son of whom any parents might well be proud. He himself, like most Irishmen, had found it very much easier to make love than money and equally impossible to retain either.

"I couldn't help overhearing what you said to Mr. Maitland just a few minutes ago, and I was very interested in it."

"What about, Remington?" Ida frowned. It was never a pleasant thought to her that any of her conversation had been overheard.

"About matching Princess Alicia against Red Ringan over a mile."

Ida continued to frown. Remington's recalling of the matter annoyed her.

"The idea's all off, Remington. My husband won't hear of such a thing, so it's no earthly use discussing it."

"That may be, madam, but I'm not exactly concerned with that as it stands. Not altogether, that is. I've come to tell you something rather different, although it touches upon the point in a manner of speaking." He paused to watch the effect of his words upon her before proceeding. "Have you ever heard of Bend Or and Robert the Devil?"

She wrinkled her brows again. "I think I heard them mentioned once at Newmarket. I believe that they were famous race horses, weren't they, but I couldn't say anything beyond that. What's the point?"

Remington warmed to his work, for he was on congenial ground.

"You are right—they _were_ famous horses. Bend Or won the Derby in 1880, I fancy, and Robert the Devil was his great contemporary. I've heard old stagers tell how the two used to meet and beat each other almost alternately. It was a remarkable thing, however, but whichever horse Fred Archer rode beat the other. In other words, they were so close that jockeyship turned the scale—every time! Interesting, don't you think, Mrs. Maitland?"

"Interesting, certainly," conceded that lady, "but I fail to see the application."

The jockey looked round carefully to see that no one was near. In one thing at least he was like Ida Maitland. Satisfied with the conditions as he found them, he sank his rather cultured voice to what bordered upon a whisper.

"The curious story of Bend Or and Robert the Devil has its modern counterpart, Mrs. Maitland. The position has arisen again—here in Queensleigh—to-day. Whichever I ride—Red Ringan or Princess Alicia—each beats the other—every time. As in the days of the 'Tinman,' jockeyship tells! Your mare, Mrs. Maitland, can beat Red Ringan—with Remington up." His face flushed with the egotistical pride of his last words.

Strangely, Mrs. Maitland's face flushed too, but for another reason.

"Do you know, Remington," she said, "I'm very gratified to be told that, more gratified than you perhaps realize. I am proud of the Princess—and prouder that my pride in her looks likely to be justified."

"That's all I had to say to you, madam," declared Remington. "I consider that you should know. The mare belongs to you. Perhaps you will be good enough to tell Mr. Maitland what I have told you. For some reason or other"—here he lowered his voice again—"Cruden's kept it very dark. Good afternoon!" He gave her a glance of frank admiration and strode quickly away.

Ida Maitland watched his retreating figure before going to find her husband. She found him with Humphrey Cruden and, as it was her method to move straight to her objective, she saw no reason to alter her habit upon the present occasion. She at once outlined to her husband what Remington had told her. Maitland raised his eyebrows in obvious cynicism.

"I've heard some of these jockeys and their opinions before. But very often they're the worst of judges. They've a tremendous belief in themselves and in their horsemanship. When they win a race, it's jockeyship; when they lose, the excuse is always: 'I'm sorry, sir, but I couldn't come without the horse.' It's never because they've ridden a bad race."

Cruden smiled a smile of tolerant understanding. But Maitland went on impetuously, without giving his trainer a chance to speak:

"What do you know of this tale of Remington's, Cruden?"

"Remington has certainly got into his head exactly what he has just told Mrs. Maitland. It has happened as he says. I must give the man his due. Each horse goes a lot better for him than for anybody else here. But what he forgets, I think, is that down here he's usually up against stable jockeys. You can't place any of them in his own class. There might be a different story if he were opposed to, say, 'Brownie' Carslake, Gordon Richards or Steve Donoghue on the course, for instance. Still, there's an element of truth in what he says."

Cruden shrugged his shoulders and Ida formed the impression that for some reason he did not intend to be too communicative. Maitland also gave no indication of desiring to pursue the subject any further, and although his wife made one or two attempts to reopen it in the car on the homeward journey, she was unsuccessful and began to realize very thoroughly that her husband's pride and belief in Red Ringan were so firmly rooted and established within his mind that he resented even the idea of Princess Alicia being regarded as anything like the colt's equal. His conversation on the way home was scanty, and eventually Ida gave the matter up as a bad job and pursued it no further. Maitland's mind was completely made up as it had been for many months. Red Ringan would win the Epsom Derby and Princess Alicia would take the Oaks. Rigid adherence would be kept to the original campaign as mapped out by the Queensleigh stable.

Through an oversight, and much to Maitland's indignation and annoyance when he had first discovered it, Red Ringan had not been entered for the Two Thousand Guineas, his only engagements before the Derby being in the Craven Stakes at Newmarket and in the Chester Vase at Chester. Princess Alicia, on the other hand, was only entered for the first of the ladies' classics, the One Thousand Guineas, prior to the Derby and Oaks. Maitland, with Cruden's full agreement and entire support, intended to run his colt at Newmarket and Chester, and Ida Maitland, as was very natural, was dead set upon capturing the One Thousand. Easter, the queen of seasons, bright although unstabilized, brought the sunshine as it so often does, and Red Ringan relished the climatic change and revelled in it. But Remington, who rode him in most of his spins, had the leg up on the mare one morning and beat him in a rough gallop a good half-length over a mile, Red Ringan showing nothing like his real form in the hands of one of the stable lads. The crack jockey smiled cynically as he dismounted and made an eloquent gesture with his shoulders as Cruden came up. The trainer had watched the final stages of the gallop with great interest and most careful observation.

"You weren't riding a trial, you know, Remington," he said, "although you rode as though you imagined you were. If you had been, I should have had Old Vendetta to jump in for the final five furlongs. The lad wasn't putting the work in that you were."

Remington's smile broadened as he ignored the trainer's implication.

"What I ride beats the other. Don't forget it, Mr. Cruden. And the Princess is a beauty—aren't you, old girl?"

He patted the superb creature's neck as he led her away.

Three or four lads at work in the stables grinned cheerfully at him as they took the mare into their keeping. They knew Michael's whims and idiosyncrasies.

The Craven Stakes that year was due to be contested on April 18, and Red Ringan, although nothing like cherry-ripe, was sent to Newmarket from Queensleigh with every confidence, for the probable opposition was not of much account. This confidence he fully justified. Without taxing him at all, Remington, riding a beautifully judged race, had him perfectly balanced throughout and, with never a moment's anxiety, won comfortably by a length and a half. Black Liquor, a nicely molded Captain Cuttle colt, was second, with a Lemonora dark colt, Lemon Curd, well behind the others, third.

After this victory Red Ringan went to threes for the Derby, and with some bookmakers it was difficult to trade at half a point less. Unbeaten as he was and apparently travelling from strength to strength, the best and most reliable of the sporting writers told the world that the great race was well within his compass, and that nothing could defeat him. In fact, it looked uncommonly like lying at his mercy. Julius Maitland felt nay, knew—that these vaticinations were true and rubbed his hands in the exquisite relish of delightful anticipation. Sacred Beetle, the second in the Middle Park Stakes of the Autumn before, won the Two Thousand Guineas with ease, putting up a remarkably smooth and stylish performance, and as a consequence was established as a firm second favourite for the Epsom Derby.

Ida Maitland went down to Newmarket on the Friday following the Papyrus colt's victory in the Two Thousand and saw Princess Alicia—Remington up—score a ready victory in the One Thousand. The cheers that greeted her as she led the Princess in were genuinely warm and appreciative. The mare had started a well-backed second favourite, and her victory was immensely popular with almost everybody. Ida was the only lady owner running anything in the race, and it was felt by many that the success was both happy and appropriate. More than one clever reader of races put down his glasses as the daughter of Gainsborough romped away with the race well in her keeping, and made the mental reservation that she must be backed every time she was saddled, no matter in what company.

"A true stayer, with enough speed for anything," was the verdict of Sir Matthew Fullgarney, who regarded himself, since last year's Ascot meeting, as possessing an especially intimate interest in the fortunes of the Maitland stable.

"Winner trained by H. Cruden, Queensleigh," once again appeared beneath the result of a classic race, and it was whispered very freely now that the famous trainer was confidently expecting to experience the most glorious season of his already distinguished career. At any rate, Dick Cruden, his only son, ne'er-do-well and scapegrace and, naturally, the whole orchard of his indulgent mother's eye, had a good bet on Princess Alicia in the One Thousand and took what was in the circumstances a really good price about the "Queensleigh Derby and Oaks double" to a sum of money many times greater than he could afford. But not with his father's knowledge or consent.

Chester came. Red Ringan and Remington travelled up to the world-famous Roodee, the course of the tantalizing twists and turns, and the horse, although badly drawn, which means a great deal at Chester, started an odds-on favorite for the Chester Vase. The only other horse backed in the race was Pollock's Cortina, the winner of the Gimcrack Stakes of the previous year. The bookmakers had a good time that lovely afternoon in early May. Unable seemingly to negotiate the turns, Red Ringan suffered the first defeat of his career, being beaten easily by the Baverstock colt to the tune of six lengths. Julius Maitland and Cruden were staggered at the result. They met Remington after the race.

"What's amiss with him, Michael?" demanded the trainer, every word vested with anxiety.

"Never got going properly, Mr. Cruden. He was badly drawn, as you know, for one thing, and the course didn't suit him. It happens like that sometimes. Also Cortina's a nailing good horse."

Maitland's left hand caressed his chin.

"I'm thinking of the Epsom course, Cruden. If Red Ringan can't act at Chester, how will he negotiate that damned Tattenham Corner? The Derby is so often decided round there. Steve Donoghue's bound to tide Sacred Beetle. You know how he'll ride the race—the same way that he always does. Sacred Beetle's a Papyrus colt too. Papyrus won at Chester and Epsom, and Donoghue rode him."

"Come, come, sir," interjected Remington. "Red Ringan's not beaten yet. I'm convinced to-day's result will prove to be quite unreliable. The form's too bad to be true. Horses are like human beings, you know. They're not machines and some days come along when they don't feel like it—just as we feel off colour sometimes." He flicked his heel with his whip. "There are three weeks yet to Derby day. Those three weeks'll make a big difference to Red Ringan. You see if I'm not right." He smiled and turned away. "All the same," he said over his shoulder very quietly, "take my advice and run the two. And let me choose my mount on the Wednesday morning of the race itself. That is, if you want to make sure of the race coming to Queensleigh."

His eyes met the frown on Julius Maitland's heavy face fearlessly, but the latter made no reply. The jockey walked swiftly away and the owner of the beaten colt turned disconsolately in the direction of Humphrey Cruden.

"He's a good horseman is Remington, but he knows too much and he's a darned sight too free with his tongue for my liking. He's got a regular bee in his bonnet over my wife's mare, and he loses his sense of proportion when he discusses the matter. It tends to become an obsession with him. Unless something very untoward happens, our plans remain as they were. Mrs. Maitland's mare will not run in the Derby. She will be kept for the Oaks. Don't you agree, Cruden?"

The trainer's long, thin fingers moved to his forehead.

"You must please yourself, sir, of course. I am entirely in your hands. Personally, were the two of them mine, I should do what Michael Remington suggests—run 'em both. Horses are kittle cattle, and they have their ups and downs. In a fight two weapons might be better than one."

Maitland made an impatient movement with his mouth.

"If we do decide on that, Cruden, there's one thing that I shall certainly settle myself, one thing over which I will not give way. Remington rides Red Ringan that's a certainty—and the sooner he understands so the better. There'll be no picking and choosing as far as that gentleman's concerned. I run horses to suit myself, not to pander to the whim of every damned jockey who thinks he knows everything. But he doesn't—not by a long chalk! There's one thing, everybody will see then that the colt's the better of the two, which will be something at least for which to be devoutly thankful, unless, of course, they put it down to Remington's jockeyship." The sarcasm cut into his words.

Cruden glanced curiously at him. He sensed the feeling in what had been said. Julius Maitland, it was evident, did not relish the idea of being beaten, even though the victor might prove to be his wife.

When the gentleman in question reached home at the conclusion of the Chester meeting, he told Ida in very plain terms what he had decided. She heard him very quietly and without interruption. When he had finished she spoke to him as she considered she should.

"I know you're quite within your rights, Julius, in putting Remington up on Red Ringan, but all the same I think you're making a mistake, if, say, he wishes to ride Princess Alicia. If I'm not deceived, it will be a very big mistake."

He looked at her with some surprise and not a little annoyance.

"Why? What do you mean? I like that! In what way am I making a mistake?"

"Well, I look at it like this. I think Remington's the wrong kind of man to offend, to cross in any way. Why not let him choose his mount as he wishes. Supposing you upset him?"

A flash of indignation crossed Maitland's face.

"Why the hell should I? For goodness' sake, Ida, answer me that. I want to win this Derby. It's been my pet ambition for years. Take Remington and the two horses at his own valuation! 'Whichever,' mind you. Very well then, Red Ringan's my horse. Let him ride Red Ringan and win."

"As you wish, dear. It must be a matter for you to determine, of course. But I can't help thinking that no good will come of it. I've a feeling in my bones."

Maitland laughed intolerantly and boorishly.

"Rubbish, Ida! Utter drivel! The Oaks for you and the Derby for me—and a double for Cruden and Remington. What more do they want—or we either for that matter?" He filled a champagne glass for her and then proceeded to do the same for himself. "Here's to it!" he cried.

Their two glasses met and tinkled and his eyes looked across them into hers.

CHAPTER IV

JULIUS MAITLAND put down the letter that he had been reading with what sounded suspiciously like an oath.

"What an extraordinary thing!" he muttered. "Ah well, it might have been worse—a lot worse." He replaced the letter in his pocket and, walking across the room, rang the bell. "All the same," he muttered, as he returned to his seat, "it's a most extraordinary coincidence. Copeland," he said a moment later, in answer to the butler's appearance, "tell Mrs. Maitland I want to speak to her. Ask her to come at once. It's important. Be quick."

The butler bowed his obedience and withdrew unobtrusively.

"Ah, Ida! Good morning, my dear! You're looking charmingly fit. Something very remarkable has occurred. The draw for the Calcutta is known. It was drawn over the week-end, as usual, and most of the numbers are known. Dawson had an early cable last night, and, as he promised, at once sent me the information that I wanted. It's most kind of him. Who the devil do you think has drawn Red Ringan?"

Ida Maitland shook her head blankly. "Anybody I know?" she inquired.

"The last person you'd think of, my dear. Alec Pollock of all people! The Baverstock trainer!"

"The trainer of Cortina, do you mean?"

"No less." His fat face wreathed in smiles. "Extraordinary when you come to think of it, isn't it? I'm offering him twelve thousand pounds for a half-share of the ticket. Do you think he'll take it? He'll be a mug if he doesn't."

She shook her head again. "I couldn't say, I'm sure. What a funny position for him to be in!"

"Extraordinary, as I said! Dawson also says that Pollock is very annoyed that the information should have leaked out as it has. He has tried his utmost to keep it dark, but it's pretty common knowledge by now. Some ultra-enterprising and inordinately curious journalist got on the track of the lucky ticket and ran it to earth at Baverstock. After all, you can't blame a trainer for having a flutter in the Calcutta."

"Who's drawn Princess Alicia?"

Maitland laughed carelessly: "Ask me another, sweetheart. I've only got the names of the holders of the more important tickets here, although no doubt many small people have backed her. But the Princess isn't regarded by the *cognoscenti* as having any chance at all. Putting Remington up on Red Ringan has silenced all the rumours that were flying about and has now shown the public what we think and what we expect. We've shown our hand, you see. I got sevens on Saturday night at the club, and I hope to make another bet tonight at the call over. That defeat at Chester has lengthened the price. It may turn out to be a blessing in disguise."

Ida made no reply and he watched her closely as she gazed out of the window. He coughed and cleared his throat and something in the way that he did it made her await his next words with a strange expectancy and perhaps some curiosity.

"By the way, dear, while we're on the subject, I've got something to tell you. I've made up my mind today finally not to run Princess Alicia on Wednesday. Red Ringan is as fit as can be. Let's keep her fresh for Friday."

Ida frowned and her foot began to tap imperiously on the carpet.

"Why, may I ask? What's the reason for this sudden new decision. I thought we agreed that they should both take their chance."

Maitland moved uneasily in his chair at the pointedness of his wife's question.

"It's not exactly a sudden decision, my dear. Or, even, as you say, a new one. As a matter of fact, it has been in my mind from the first, only I allowed myself to grow sentimental and to listen to Cruden and the others. And—er—of course, to yourself. Now, come, be guided by me. I'm too old a hand at the turf game to make any particularly big mistakes. Rest assured that I know best. Besides, she's no chance with young Gillman riding against Michael on Red Ringan. Let her be as fresh as possible for Remington to ride on Friday."

Ida stood stock still for a moment, and then her half-rebellious mood suddenly changed. With an impulsive gesture of submission, she crossed to where her husband was sitting and put her hand with a caressing movement upon his broad shoulder.

"Very well, Julius," she said. "I'll do exactly as you desire. I'm sorry if I appeared to resist your decision. You'll tell Cruden, of course?"

"Naturally, my pet, naturally. Leave all that to me. I must run down to Queensleigh to see Cruden some time this afternoon."

She bent down and kissed him lightly on the forehead. As she did so, a tap sounded on the door. Copeland entered at Maitland's call. He placed another letter in his master's outstretched hand.

"For you, sir. Just left by a messenger. I was requested to hand it to you at once, if you please, sir."

Maitland glanced at the exterior carefully before tossing it temporarily on one side. Ida waved her hand to him.

"I'll leave you to it for a little while," she announced cheerfully. "I know you've tons to do, and so have I. I've got to get ready for to-morrow night."

Her husband smiled back at her and watched her out. He felt in a better mood than when she had entered. But he took his handkerchief from his sleeve and wiped the beads of perspiration from his forehead. Picking up the letter that Copeland had just brought in to him, he opened it mechanically. As he did so, the envelope fell from his trembling hand and fluttered slowly to the ground. Julius Maitland did not trouble to recover it. Copeland entered again and he answered the butler almost absent-mindedly. After an appreciable time, he tore the letter into very small fragments and dropped them slowly into the wastepaper basket. His face was very white as he leaned over to his telephone and unhooked the receiver.

After her guests assembled on the following night for Julius Maitland's much-heralded eve of the Derby party, Ida Maitland as hostess, faithfully acting upon instructions she had received, made apologies on behalf of her husband and their host. She told them what she herself had been told. Julius Maitland most unexpectedly had been called back to South Africa upon business of the most extreme urgency and importance—business that would not brook an instant's delay. But she hoped that it would make no difference to their enjoyment.

The great crowd at Epsom seethed with excitement, for the Derby this year was considered to be as open as it had been for many years. Such was the consensus, and it was proved by the roar in the ring. Sacred Beetle, ridden by Steve Donoghue, was now a firm favourite at fives. His victory in the Two Thousand Guineas, coupled with the abject failure of Red Ringan at Chester, was responsible for his commanding position in the market. There was the prowess of his jockey, too, to be considered. Red Ringan held his position comfortably as second favourite, being quoted at thirteen to two. Cortina, his Chester conqueror, stood firm at eights, with Black Liquor, Excalibur and Lemon Curd ranging from tens to a hundred to six.

The early events proved commonplace and there came the usual lull in the racing prior to the big contest. The Maitland contingent, somewhat chastened in spirit at the unexpected absence of the head of the family, presented to an unprejudiced observer strange contrasts. Sylvia was plucking nervously at her race card and her heavy eyes spoke of a personal worry possibly unconnected with the result of to-day's great race. Captain Lumsden, her escort, had already discovered that it would pay him, to ensure a completely happy day, to mind his p's and q's. Three times at least he had committed follies of the tongue for which he had been soundly censured. They had taught him that to-day he could not be too careful. Val Maitland, as usual, looked the picture of cheerfulness; he, it may be said, never carried his heart on his sleeve. But the younger and darker Vivian frowned uncompromisingly upon friend and foe alike. Vivian had bad days and black moods. In Ida's eyes there danced anxiety, emotion and excitement. She was very pale and a red spot showed in each of her cheeks.

"Sylvia," she said, "if Red Ringan wins, I want you to lead him in. I think it would be very popular if you did so. I think perhaps your father would like it. What do you say, you two boys?"

Valentine assented graciously, but from his brother there came no ready response.

"All right," he conceded eventually. "If you wish it, Ida. Did my father express that wish when he said good-bye to you. Or is it—?"

"No, Vivian. The last time that I saw him I was not aware that he was going away so quickly. We had no time to talk horses. If we had, I have no doubt that he would have expected me to act for him in every way. You can guess what it cost your father to miss to-day. He's lived for it. What he will say if Red Ringan does really win—" She shrugged her shoulders helplessly.

"The numbers are up, Sylvia," said Captain Lumsden, using his glasses on the number board.

The girl to whom he spoke flushed and, excited at the request that her stepmother had just made to her, looked eagerly in its direction.

"They're all running—all the probables," she remarked quietly, checking her card. "Nothing important missing."

"Hullo!" cried Vivian. "What's that going up? A chalk jockey, by Jove! That's unusual surely for the Derby."

The others followed his eyes, when suddenly Valentine Maitland let fall a sharp but smothered exclamation.

"Number twenty-two!" he cried. "Gillman."

They could see the name of the unknown jockey chalked up, white and distinct from the names of the other riders in the frame, and turned instinctively to their cards.

Vivian Maitland swore indiscreetly under his breath.

"What's this?" he demanded. His finger pointed to No. 22. "'Mrs. Ida Maitland's b.f. Princess Alicia by Gainsborough—Cos—apricot jacket, parma violet sleeves and cap—Cruden.' What's the idea, Ida?" His dark eyes held more pertinent query than even his words or voice. "I thought the Governor and you had agreed to run Red Ringan only? Why the change of policy?"

Ida Maitland's jaw set rigidly and courageously. She smiled a half-smile.

"It means just this, Vivian. I'm taking advantage of dad's absence to have my own way. That's a lot to a woman, you know. I have always wanted to run the Princess, so did Remington, and I can't see it will do anybody any harm. Your father will forgive all right when he hears Red Ringan has won."

It was easy for all of them to detect the slightly imperious note in her voice, a note which was obviously meant to put a closure upon any more discussion. But there was also a note of anxiety. She proceeded:

"I have given Cruden my instructions and I have had a talk with Gillman. He's immensely bucked at getting an unexpected Derby mount."

"Are you backing her, Mrs. Maitland?" put in Captain Lumsden cheerily. "Because if you are—"

"I have backed Princess Alicia each way. I managed to get twenties. I think I was lucky. I don't think you'll do as well as that. Still, try. But I warn you—I don't expect her to win. Don't find fault with me if you lose your money. Remington rides Red Ringan. Don't forget what he always says. What he rides beats the other. I have no reason to expect a different result this afternoon."

Nigel Lumsden laughed. "I'll toddle off at any rate for a nice little each way. What about you others?"

Sylvia went across and whispered something to the young officer, but the two boys shook their heads.

"Val and I will stand by what we've already done," affirmed Vivian. "Remington will lose Gillman over this course. If the jockeys were transferred now, I might consider—" He shook his head again in refusal. "All the same, I don't think it's altogether fair to father to run her. It would have been different if he'd been here."

"That's right, Vivian," interjected Ida, "be loyal. I admire you for it. I have always admired loyalty. One meets it so very seldom."

His dark eyes flashed back at her as he caught the bitterness in her voice, but he said nothing. He gave his attention to the parade.

The fact that Mrs. Maitland had unexpectedly decided to run Princess Alicia at the last moment had been the cause of much excitement and speculation—excitement and speculation in which the whole Queensleigh Stable staff had joined. As the filly went down to the post, she was watched by all eyes. Remington, controlling Red Ringan in his own masterly manner, flung a glance over his shoulder at his Princess, as he always called her to himself, and had a difficult job to conceal his personal bitterness.

"What's the game now?" he queried savagely to himself. "Damned funny work I call it, after what I understood. Why did Cruden—?"

But the other work that lay just ahead cut out all surmise and put an end to all introspection. He had a job of work demanding all his best attention.

The starter got them off to a nice level, even start—almost a perfect start. None got a flier. Ida Maitland put the glasses up and watched the race with an almost tragic intentness. An outsider from the Sharebridge Stable made the pace a cracker and led the others at a merry trot for more than five furlongs, and it could be seen that of the more fancied horses Excalibur had been chopped for speed. The field flew along and Remington could see that Donoghue, well drawn on the rails, meant to have that much-cherished lead and position at Tattenham Corner. And he got it. Sacred Beetle thundered round Tattenham Corner in the lead, but Red Dingan was at his withers. Cortina, with his jockey riding him hard, lay a length behind and the apricot jacket with the parma violet sleeves of Princess Alicia was a good half-length behind him. Thus they ran to the distance, when Gillman, seizing an opening, got through and moved up third, with the Baverstock colt beaten and the rest of the field strung out. The favourite and leader, beautifully handled by Steve, settled down to put the issue beyond doubt, but Remington and Red Ringan inexorably refused to be shaken off. Every effort put forward by the Papyrus colt was answered in like manner by the beautiful son of Buchan. As Cruden had always maintained, Red Ringan was a bonny fighter.

Neck and neck they raced, stride countering stride, the petunia and cream hoops side by side with the green and white. Each name was shouted alternately, for the most experienced watcher could not be sure. "Sacred Beetle!" "Sacred Beetle!" "Come along, Steve!" "Steve!" "Steve!" "Sacred Beetle wins!" "Red Ringan!" "Red Ringan!" "Red Ringan!" "Red Ringan wins!" First one and then the other appeared to hold the mastery, and still the most astute race readers watched with judgment suspended. Then the incomparable Steve was seen to use his whip and the Beetle received two sharp reminders. Remington watched him keenly, eager to seize his chance. There were less than a hundred yards to go and he knew that only a supreme effort would turn the scale and land him first past the post.

But Ida, watching the precociously indefatigable Gillman, could see that the Princess was now traveling better than anything else in the race, although she had a lot of ground to make up. But would she get up in time? The distance to go was cruelly short. Gillman sat quiet, had the sense not to use the whip at a critical moment like this, and began to ride with the genius of inspiration. The parma violet sleeved jacket grew nearer and nearer—inch by inch—to the two mighty leaders fighting each other for the mastery.

Suddenly the frenziedly cheering mass of onlookers saw Michael Remington at his inimitable best. At the psychological second his iron arms with the velvet hands gave Red Ringan the streak of stimulus that he needed and, almost lifted into his final strides, he flashed past the winning post a head in front of the second. Remington's eyes, strained and surprised, shocked and startled, saw the second's jacket a moment afterward—apricot and parma violet—not green and white—Princess Alicia had passed and beaten Sacred Beetle in the last few strides—to be herself beaten a head—by Red Ringan—Remington up! Winner and second trained by Cruden, Queensleigh.

Ida's lips opened, but no words came, and as the horses pulled up within a few yards of each other past the winning post,

Remington leaned out of the saddle and stretched his hand out toward the Princess's neck and patted it. His touch held affection as well as admiration and perhaps Princess Alicia knew it.

"If only I had ridden—" Then his eyes caught Gillman's. "Well ridden, youngster!" he said chivalrously. In his ears surged the muffled roar of the mighty crowd. But Michael Remington hardly heard it.

CHAPTER V

"Go on, Sylvia! Lead Red Ringan in! To please me—I want you to." Ida Maitland's voice came quietly insistent, although still quivering a little with the excitement of the race.

The three young men supported her request.

For a moment the girl seemed disinclined to accede, then she pulled herself together and went out to meet Remington on Red Ringan.

There was no doubt of the popularity of the result, for Red Ringan had been a popular fancy and well backed by all classes of people. The cheering crowds gathered round her and showered their congratulations upon herself, the horse and the rider; they seemed to be like a vast army of strangers trying to become fast friends all in a fleeting moment. She led the chestnut into the unsaddling enclosure, glad to be free from that vast sea of faces. Gillman on Princess Alicia entered the one adjoining. If only her father had been there to enjoy his success to the full! That was her dominating thought. It was the day for which he had lived, to which he had looked forward so long and so eagerly. Remington passed into the weighing-in room. The "all right" was called and one more Derby was now history and its story being flashed round the world, not only to the homesteads near at hand but to the far-flung outposts of the British Empire.

Less than half an hour later, just as the numbers for the next race were going up, the police station at the very select seaside village of Friningham was roused from its afternoon sleep and stung into semi-wakefulness by the insistent ringing of the telephone. As a rule it experienced very little postprandial excitement, for Friningham was excessively law-abiding. Sergeant Mansfield picked up the receiver very lazily, sprawled himself on the table, and prepared to listen to the harrowing tale of a lost Pom from a lachrymose spinster. His yawn expired at birth. At the same time his official eyes nearly fell from his official head. A voice, labouring under unmistakable physical agony, cried:

"Help! Help! Police! Police! Come to Ravenswood, Pine Hole Way, at once! I'm being murdered."

The sergeant caught his breath and strained his ears to hear more. In doing this he was rewarded. There came the sound of a heavy object falling to the accompaniment of overturned furniture. What seemed to be a man's voice could then be heard, a different voice from the voice that had just appealed for help, but the sergeant was unable to catch what was being said. Then there came the noise of loud laughter, followed by the strains of a violin. Suddenly—just as suddenly as the interlude had commenced—silence intervened. Dead silence. Mansfield, although he continued to listen intently, was unable to hear anything more.

"Damned funny thing," he muttered to himself. "Maybe a hoax, of course, but I'd swear that that cry for help was genuine enough. I reckon I can recognize the real thing when I hear it. I ought to be able to by now." He rose from his desk and, walking into the charge room, called the constable on duty there to his side. "Tell Markham to come in here, Drummond, will you? You yourself come along with me."

Constable Drummond looked questioningly at his superior.

"Don't stand there gaping, Drummond. Just do as I say and come along with me. I'll wait for you on the sidewalk outside. I'm going to borrow a car from somewhere."

Constable Drummond realized that Sergeant Mansfield was serious, and within the space of two minutes joined him as he had been directed.

Sergeant Mansfield drove the car a short distance in silence before he told his story. Drummond listened to his sergeant's account of the extraordinary incident.

"Mighty queer!" he contributed at length. "Mighty queer, when you come to think of it. Like what you see on the movies. Still, we'll be going down to have a look round, eh, sergeant? That's the idea, isn't it?"

"That's it, Drummond. There are times when you've almost human intelligence. I can't ignore the fact that I may have listened to a person's last despairing cry for help. I can't turn a deaf ear to anything like that now, can I? Supposing the whole affair is genuine, and, thanks to my negligence, the guilty party or parties get away, I should never forgive myself. On the other hand, it may be a hoax, a practical joke of some kind."

Drummond nodded: "Naturally, sergeant, naturally. If it's any help to you, I know Ravenswood in Pin Hole Way. It's the big bungalow standing semi-detached on the left-hand side going down to the seafront. A very fine place, indeed, with a laid-out garden. Almost at the bottom it stands. My missus does a bit of dressmaking for the young lady that lives in the next bungalow to it—Beau Geste, they call it. According to my missus, who got it from young Miss Collingwood—that's the young lady I spoke about—Ravenswood is seldom occupied these days. The folks it belongs to believes in a breath of the briny very few and far between, according to her."

"Who are the people at Ravenswood, Drummond? Do you know anything about them—their name, for example?"

Drummond shook his head with disappointment at his failure to satisfy the sergeant.

"Can't say as I do, sergeant. I've heard the missus say more than once that it belonged to a middle-aged couple—posh people from London or somewhere. Turn down here, sergeant—you'll find it's the quickest way down there. Go straight along to the dairy, turn to the right and Pin Hole Way lies almost bang in front of you."

A couple of minutes more brought them outside Ravenswood. It was one of a number of modern bungalows within the reach of only the very well-to-do. Semi-detached, replete with every modern convenience and labour-saving device, they also gave a magnificent view of a splendid stretch of sea. Friningham prided itself—and it can be said, prided itself justifiably—that it had not only set a high standard but that it had also strained every effort to maintain it. Pin Hole Way was the avenue that contained the pick of the basket. In every handbook and official guide issued by the Friningham authorities photographs of Pin Hole Way occupied a prominent place. A famous actress was only one of several distinguished persons who had transferred some of their own distinction to the little town in general and to this avenue in particular. In fact, Pin Hole Way to many people meant Friningham, and visitors who came to the clean little seaside place for the first time were considered by the best judges to have missed everything if they had but missed Pin Hole Way.

Sergeant Mansfield strode to the front door and rang the bell in a businesslike manner. Drummond looked at his watch and instinctively felt in his pocket to see if his money had survived the hasty car ride. His mother had been a Macgregor! The time was exactly ten minutes to four. There was no answer to Mansfield's summons. He rang again, promptly. Again he obtained no response.

"What about it?" said the constable. "How about trying one of the windows at the back?"

"Looks to me as though we shall have to, Drummond. Come along and give me a hand."

The two policemen made their way to the back and Mansfield went up to the main window. It occupied his attention for a couple of minutes, then he was surprised by an exclamation from Constable Drummond.

"No need to worry about the window, sergeant. This door's open."

Mansfield clicked his tongue as Drummond proceeded to explain matters.

"I tried the handle of the door, sergeant, as anybody might have done, just carelessly like, and the door opened. It wasn't locked."

Mansfield suddenly felt himself growing uncomfortable and apprehensive. It was quite possible, he concluded, assuming the affair to be serious, that the murderer or murderers might still be on the premises, whilst Drummond and he were unarmed. What a fool he had been not to have considered the possibility! The fact that his ringing of the front door bell had elicited no reply he regarded as beside the point. That might very well prove to be a question of tactics on the part of the persons concerned. Against that, however, there was the fact of the telephone message.

For a while he made no reply to Constable Drummond. He was trying to think what his best plan would be. At length he decided that he must take the risk.

"We shall have to go in this way, Drummond," he declared. "There's nothing else for it, I'm afraid. Let me go first, but keep your eyes open to get busy if required."

Drummond squared his shoulders and signified his approval. One of his ancestors had fallen on Flodden Field. He determined, if necessary, to do justice to that ancestor's memory.

Mansfield opened the door and the two entered an apartment that obviously was used as a kitchen. It held nothing to excite comment. They passed into a corridor that led into a sumptuously furnished dining room. The door of this dining room was slightly ajar. Mansfield followed Drummond's example. This time it was his turn to square his shoulders, although his only fighting ancestor had been an unhappily mated grandmother.

He slowly and carefully pushed open the door of the room. To his great relief, nothing happened. Then he entered. Drummond, much more phlegmatic, followed him at a respectable distance. A shocking sight met their eyes. On the floor lay the body of a man—undeniably dead. From the position and appearance of the body there was no mistaking the fact. He had been shot through the throat. He lay on his back with his right leg drawn up and the foot twisted strangely and almost under his body. A chair lay overturned at his side and the receiver of the telephone was not hooked up, but hung trailingly over the edge of the table, as though the last person who had used it had been summarily interrupted. In a recess stood a magnificent Chesterfield. On this lay a violin, bow and violin case.

"I was right, Drummond," said Mansfield laconically. "I thought I was. Murder, Drummond—no doubt about it—but how on earth the poor devil managed to get to the phone to—" He broke off and bent down to look at the dead man. "Drummond! Phone for Doctor Forsyth at once. Stay, though. Don't. Don't touch that telephone at all. I forgot. It's just been used. It may prove a gold mine to us. Come over the rest of the place with me. Let's make sure of things."

They quickly covered the whole of the establishment. But they discovered nothing. The place was empty—deserted.

"Now, Drummond," said Mansfield, "get along up to Doctor Forsyth's in the car and bring him back here as quickly as you can. I'll remain on guard in the dining room where the body is. And for goodness' sake look slippy, Drummond. Don't waste a moment. If the doctor's not in, find him by hook or by crook. This has given me a nasty turn. I think it must be through getting that ghastly telephone message as I did. Fair knocked me off my balance."

Dr. Forsyth, the police doctor of Friningham, by a stroke of luck, happened to be at his office, and shortly was kneeling beside the body of the man. His autopsy was brief, but convincingly clear.

"Shot in two places," he observed. "One bullet has lodged somewhere near the clavicle—in one of the humeral bones, I think. The clavicle itself is splintered. The other bullet has severed the carotid artery and passed right out. It should be somewhere about here. The bullet through the carotid artery, of course, has caused death. Hallo! What's this?" He looked intently at the knuckles of the dead man's right hand. They were cut and slashed as though with a sharp knife and the blood had dried upon the top of each knuckle. "See that, sergeant?" he asked, holding up the dead man's hand. At that moment his eyes caught sight of something else. Clutched tight between the fingers were four or five strands of long, raven-black hair. "Go through his pockets, Sergeant Mansfield," said Dr. Forsyth. "See if you can find any clue to his identity."

The sergeant felt in the pockets of the dead man's coat. Every one of them was empty save one—the right-hand breast pocket. From this pocket he extracted a letter. On the envelope there was printed a name—in capitals—nothing else. Mansfield looked at the name and whistled in astonishment.

"Good Lord," he cried, "look at this! Look at this, Doctor Forsyth! We've made a find here and no mistake. I fancied when I first clapped eyes on him that his face was familiar to me. This is Julius Maitland—*the* Julius Maitland!"

"What!" yelled Drummond, his interest getting the better of his discretion. "You don't mean—not the—"

"Yes, I do," replied Sergeant Mansfield. "The owner of to-day's Derby winner, Red Ringan, and no other. Gad, hard luck to be murdered just after your horse has won the Derby!"

CHAPTER VI

DOCTOR FORSYTH regarded the sergeant with amazement written upon every line of his features.

"What on earth are you talking about, Mansfield?"

This time it was the sergeant's turn to show surprise.

"Why, doctor, what do you mean? If this is the famous Julius Maitland, as I think it is—"

"Yes, yes, sergeant, I'm quite prepared to accept all that. I'm not alluding to that part of your statement at all. What I'm referring to is your remark about the man having been murdered after his horse had won this afternoon's Derby. You're talking through your hat, sergeant. You're gibbering, my dear man. This man's been dead a couple of days or thereabouts."

"But, Doctor Forsyth," gasped Sergeant Mansfield, "that's impossible. The dying man called me here a few moments before he—"

"Rubbish, sergeant! Don't you imagine I know what I'm talking about? Your story won't hold water for a minute. Are you going to suggest that I don't know how long a man's been dead? This man's been dead for a good couple of days—more in all probability. When you say he called you a few moments before he died—I imagine that was the gist of what you were about to say—you're talking sheer rubbish. It's absolutely physically impossible that such a thing could have happened. What in the name of goodness gave you such an extraordinary idea? His ghost may have done."

Sergeant Mansfield looked at Dr. Forsyth and then back at Constable Drummond, as though he were on the point of awakening from a most unpleasant dream and, obtaining no satisfaction from another look at the face of the police doctor, fixed his gaze again upon the somewhat forbidding countenance that belonged to Constable Drummond. Drummond seemed as flabbergasted at the doctor's remarks as the sergeant himself, so the sergeant made a big attempt to collect his scattered wits and to pull himself together. He had to make some attempt to justify himself. As far as he could remember, he recounted to Dr. Forsyth the telephone call that had been the means of bringing him and the constable to the scene. Forsyth furrowed his brow and looked at him critically, completely incredulous.

"You say the message asking for help came to you over the telephone—at some time this afternoon? That you heard the chair overturned?"

"No, doctor, I didn't say that. I said I heard the noise of a heavy object being overturned. The chair would fit the case." He looked at the chair in question and proceeded: "I have no doubt it was this chair. The noise of a chair overturning would be exactly similar to what I heard."

"Then you heard another person speaking?"

"Yes, a man, I should say, from the depth of the voice."

"What did he say?"

"Couldn't catch it. I tried hard to, but I didn't succeed in defining a word. It seemed fainter than the other."

"Then what do you say happened? Tell me again."

"Somebody burst out laughing—and peculiar laughter it was at that. Almost demented—more like what I should call a cackle than an ordinary, honest laugh. Anyhow it made my blood run cold for a minute or two—and I'm not a particularly nervous man. Then I heard the music of a violin, which stopped most suddenly—most abruptly would be an even better way of describing what happened. It was broken off like, as though a string had snapped. And I should say that there's the violin, doctor. But the strings are all right." Sergeant Mansfield indicated the instrument on the Chesterfield standing in the recess.

Doctor Forsyth shrugged his shoulders.

"I'll give you the chair, sergeant, and I'll throw you in the dead man, and even the violin, but I can't allow you the fact that this man was being murdered when you are trying to say he was. There's something wrong somewhere. You've turned psychic or something like it."

The sergeant reddened and shook his head obstinately, almost with a touch of defiance.

"I'm sorry, doctor, but I know what I heard. You can say what you like. I'm not romancing—I give you my word."

"Damn it all, sergeant, and neither am I! I know what I know! This man was dead on Monday some time, and this happens to be Wednesday afternoon. Use your common sense, man. Look at the condition of the blood on the knuckles and round the throat. It's dried—congealed. It's passed from the fluid to an almost solid state. Look for yourself, man! Use your eyes and see that it's hard, cold truth that I'm telling you. Whatever fantastic telephone message you received this afternoon didn't come from him. More likely from his murderer, I should say."

Sergeant Mansfield started and considered this new aspect of the case. Then an idea struck him and he pointed to the dead man's hand, where the few strands of raven-black hair showed clutched between the stiff fingers.

"I should say then that he was murdered by a woman, doctor—from the evidence down there!"

Doctor Forsyth knelt by the body again and looked very carefully at the hair.

"Looks like a woman's hair certainly, sergeant. I won't touch it. Cleverer eyes than mine may read something important from it. I suggest you get into touch with the dead man's relatives at once and also get somebody along from Cobbleton. There's sure to be ructions if you don't."

Sergeant Mansfield looked undecided for the moment. There was a lot in what Doctor Forsyth said. Then a new thought presented itself to him.

"Where's that bullet that you say did the damage, doctor? The fatal one."

"What do you mean, sergeant?"

"You said a bullet had severed some artery and passed out. You said it ought to be here somewhere."

"Yes, quite true, I did. What of it?"

"Well, doctor, where is it?" The sergeant indicated the expanse of the room. The room as it stood gave no sign of the missing bullet or its passage.

"Was that window open when you entered, sergeant?"

"No, doctor, it was shut—as it is now. Nothing has been touched. You can bet I was as careful as careful about that. I warned Drummond here, especially about touching the phone. If that was used, as I know it was, whatever other people may say, it might yield a clue of some sort. We shall have to pay great attention to it."

"I quite agree, sergeant. Take my advice and test it for finger-prints. Meanwhile, do as I say. Send along to Cobbleton." Doctor Forsyth paused—to proceed again immediately. "And you'll have the doubtful privilege, sergeant, of giving the public one of the greatest shocks of the century. I'm speaking apart from the question of the murder, of course."

Sergeant Mansfield showed some signs of bewilderment, but eventually light seemed to break in upon him.

"You mean about the Derby, doctor, I suppose?"

"I mean this, Sergeant Mansfield, that Julius Maitland, having been dead many hours before the Derby was run this afternoon, his horse, the winner, *ipso facto* will be disqualified, as his nomination would have become void, and as a result his horse had no right to run in the race at all. I imagine that the news will come, as I said, as a shock." He smiled. "To others, with an entirely selfish outlook, it may come as a relief. It's an ill wind, you know, sergeant. I backed Sacred Beetle myself, so it won't affect me. Let me know when Inspector Garth from Cobbleton wants me and I'll come along. And don't delay in sending for him." He put his hat firmly on his head. "I should imagine he'd be rather interested in your famous telephone story, Sergeant Mansfield, when you tell it to him. I've been hung up a devil of a time over a call before now myself, but a couple of days for a local call—well, it's a bit too thick, Mansfield. It is really! Even for the telephone service."

CHAPTER VII

THE ASTOUNDING NEWS of the murder of Julius Maitland hit the sporting public with the violence of a bombshell. It was a shock entirely unprecedented. It created something very much like chaos. Awaiting formal identification of the body by his two sons and the testimony of Doctor Forsyth that death had taken place at some time on the Monday previous, the racing authorities disqualified Red Ringan and awarded the race to Princess Alicia, placing Sir John Douglas's In-Swinger third. Alec Pollock, the Baverstock trainer and the man who had been publicly placarded as the winner of the famous Calcutta Sweep, saw his anticipation of a newly acquired fortune disappear with the disqualification and the public prepared to welcome a new prize winner. But Pollock shook hands with himself heartily for having had the good sense to take the dead man's offer of £12,000 for a half-share in Red Ringan. He did not expect that Ida Maitland would reopen the question of the validity of his sale. To think that the transaction had taken place but a few hours at most before Maitland's murder! Pollock shrugged his massive shoulders and determined to accept the changed situation as philosophically as he knew how. At the same time he wished the lucky holder of the Princess Alicia ticket every success, whoever it might be. There was at least one other feature of the affair for which he could feel some degree of thankfulness. This new shadow hanging over both Red Ringan and Princess Alicia would give Cortina a much better chance of carrying off the St. Leger at Doncaster in September. In this transitory life of faiths, hopes and fears, he concluded it was incumbent upon one to be thankful for small mercies. He determined to get into the market for the St. Leger and back Cortina as quickly as possible in order to make his intended coup as effective as he could. But he was of course outside the dead man's intimate circle.

When Ida Maitland received the news from the bungalow at Friningham she collapsed under the shock. Why had she been informed, she asked, that her husband had been suddenly summoned to South Africa?

The two boys, stunned by the loss of their father in such circumstances, put the question to her in their turn again and again. What did she think? Did their father intimate in any way what it was that had caused such a sudden change in his arrangements? Had he received a message or call from anybody? But she could tell them nothing beyond what she had already told them and could only shake her head blankly at their repeated and despairing inquiries.

Sylvia Maitland seemed perhaps less obviously affected than any. She bore her grief dry-eyed and was able to draw upon some big reserve of courage. It was plain to the most discerning that she was deeply distressed by her father's death, but she was able to fortify herself with an almost unnatural calmness. Captain Lumsden, young and irresponsible though he was, watched her with extreme concern, because he flattered himself that he understood her rather strange nature. He found himself wishing that she would show her grief more, give way to it more. He felt that to do so would be much better for her, and that this strange external tranquillity boded ill for the future. There would be a reckoning—there must be a reckoning—to think anything else was absurd.

In the Cruden household down at Queensleigh there reigned a dull sense of tragedy. The whole training establishment appeared to be affected by it. Humphrey Cruden himself felt that he was living in a dream, but at any rate consoled himself with the satisfaction that he had done his duty both to the dead man and to the dead man's wife. Their horses had run first and second in the greatest race the world knows, and the fact that this unexpected calamity would actually prevent Princess Alicia from running in and winning the Oaks on Friday was no fault of his. He was also unconcerned—professionally—with the fact of Red Ringan's disqualification. In the circumstances it was inevitable. He had other worries of his own besides the anxiety of other people's misfortunes. His much-desired double, after all, had not materialized. It was a shrewd blow of fate for him, but he had taken buffets of this kind before and, please God! would take them again. His wife had been cast in a different mold and there was another matter also upon her mind. The Sunday night before the Derby Queensleigh had received a surprise visit from her son. Dick Cruden found very little time to visit his parents in the ordinary way, which was a source of much tribulation to his mother. To his father it was a matter of undisguised relief and sincere congratulation. When he arrived on the Sunday for a week-end, as he put it, his visit brightened and coloured his mother's entire world.

His father received him very diffidently. His many wild escapades, forgiven by his father time after time, had ultimately effected an estrangement between them, and as a result of this rupture Queensleigh saw little of Dick. But it was the oldest of old stories and, like all sons of this calibre, he was well aware that his mother's heart was always open to him, no matter what he did or undid, and at all times he was sufficiently clever to take advantage of this fact. His position as managing clerk to a firm of London solicitors, Barraclough, Laurence & Tolworthy, often hung on a thread, and at the time of his surprise visit to the home of Red Ringan and Princess Alicia the thread was more delicately fragile than ever. Monica Cruden heard the news of Maitland's death stoically. Her thoughts were more on her son and her son's employment. Michael Remington was unapproachable. To have had the Derby at his mercy, had he been allowed to follow his own bent, to have actually won the race against the force of his inclinations, and then to have had the honour snatched from him relentlessly and mercilessly—these things tried him sorely.

At eleven o'clock on the morning following Sergeant Mansfield's discovery in Pin Hole Way, Sir Austin Kemble's car drove up in front of the Maitlands' town house and came to a standstill. Sir Austin emerged, spoke a few peremptory words to his chauffeur, as befitted the commissioner of police, and went on to ring the bell. A few minutes later saw him bowing over Ida Maitland's hand with gallant sympathy.

"At moments like this, Mrs. Maitland, mere words are inadequate. Let me assure you, however, of my most heartfelt condolence. I will not say any more—I am sure you will understand."

Ida, white-faced and heavily ringed beneath her blue eyes, murmured something and motioned him to a chair.

"All the facts that have come to light so far, Mrs. Maitland, are in my hands. As soon as I heard the identity of the murdered man"—he went on quickly when he saw the distress surge into her eyes, resolved to bridge the details of the case as quickly as possible—"I determined that the Yard should immediately take charge of the case. It was the very least I could do, considering that I know you as I do. And, of course, your husband has been extraordinarily kind to me on many occasions. Sergeant Mansfield, the man at Friningham, and Inspector Garth, who had gone along there from Cobbleton, are hardly—well, you can guess what I mean—hardly the right type." He shrugged his shoulders. "Very decent people for the bread-and-butter species of case, such as usually comes their way, but totally unfitted to tackle a case of these dimensions and—er—national importance." Sir Austin wiped his forehead with his handkerchief, sincerely glad that the opening was over, and watched the bereaved lady as he gave vent to these opinions. He continued almost at once. "That brings me, my dear Mrs. Maitland, to the real thing that I wish to say to you, the real object of my visit. I have a proposal to make to you, a most important proposal."

Ida's blue eyes sought his questioningly.

"I don't quite—"

"I've not expressed myself too well, I'm afraid. What I mean is this. Have you ever heard of Anthony Bathurst?"

"Anthony Bathurst?" She repeated the name after him, but meaninglessly.

"A friend of mine, Mrs. Maitland, and a man whom I hold in the highest possible regard. A brilliant man, Mrs. Maitland—Uppingham and Oxford—a man who has helped Scotland Yard more than once when it has confronted very grave difficulties. Candidly, now that I'm becoming conscious of Anno Domini, I don't know his equal. I suggest—with your permission, of course—that I ask Bathurst to handle the case. I feel sure that he will—if I ask him personally. Believe me, you couldn't possibly do better. He's most discreet and most tactful."

For a few moments Ida made no reply. Then she shook her head.

"It's very, very kind of you, Sir Austin, and I appreciate your intentions intensely. But it's all so horrible—and so sudden—and so much in the nature of an upheaval—that I can't—"

Sir Austin broke in again with a full measure of sympathy.

"Of course, of course. I realize all that you're trying to say. I understand that thoroughly. You feel that, as matters now stand, you can't wax enthusiastic over the qualities of my protégé. I can well realize how you feel."

"No, no, Sir Austin." She laid her hand impulsively on the sleeve of his coat. "It isn't that at all. You misunderstand me. I am sure that this Mr. Bathurst is all that you claim for him. I was just thinking of something quite different. It's just this—I'll tell you—I don't feel that anything matters now that my husband is dead—killed in the way that he has been. To find his murderer, to try him, and to hang him possibly, won't bring my husband back, and won't do me or anybody else any good that I can see at the present moment. That's what I was feeling, as well as I can explain to you."

Sir Austin leaned back in his chair, at a loss momentarily to frame an adequate reply. He had had that type of reasoning put to him before during the course of his long career, but never had it sounded to him so convincingly simple. After all—he found himself asking the question—what was the good of revenge to this woman whom destiny had used so cruelly? But at length the traditions of his profession reasserted themselves and he leaned forward again to clasp her hand in his with a gesture of almost old-world courtesy. Sir Austin prided himself upon the fact that every situation found him prepared.

"My dear Mrs. Maitland, I know exactly how you are thinking. If I may say so, the sentiments do you tremendous credit. Any person would agree with me. They indicate the depth of your feeling. But there is the question of your duty to the dead, besides your affection. Look on that side of the picture for a moment. I feel personally that we should leave no stone unturned to discover the perpetrator of this awful crime, that we should be remiss in our duty as citizens if we did not. Surely you will agree?"

Ida's quiet sobbing brought him to a sudden stop. He had the sense not to interrupt it, to let it come to completion. The feeling came to him that he was an intruder in a shrine that he should never have approached, let alone entered. It was an unusual feeling for him. Suddenly Ida's sobbing ceased and she looked up at him with a curious touch of quiet dignity.

"I suppose you are right, Sir Austin. I should have understood the real meaning of your kindness before. Forgive me. No doubt I appear to you to be dreadfully ungrateful for the way in which I received your offer. It was most ungenerous of me—churlish almost. Please forgive me. I shall be very grateful if your friend, Mr. Bathurst, could see his way to take over the case. Whatever fee he charges will be—"

"There will be no fee, Mrs. Maitland. Bathurst is not a professional investigator. He has a fair competence of his own and indulges in this work occasionally as a pleasure."

She looked up with a quick light showing in her eyes. Sir Austin corrected his choice of words with embarrassed haste.

"As a hobby, I should have said. After all, somebody must—"

She accepted the amendment silently.

"I will bring him along with me this afternoon to see you—unless he wants to run down to Friningham first. He may do, you know. You never can tell with Bathurst. He makes up his mind quickly and always moves straight to his point. I remember down at Seabourne, when he was looking into that little problem of the peacock's eye, that more than once he astonished me with his absolute—"

She intervened quickly, feeling that she was in no mood at the moment to listen to a recital of this Mr. Bathurst's triumphs in other murder mysteries, no matter how brilliant they might have been.

"Valentine and Vivian, my husband's two sons, have gone down to Friningham, Sir Austin. If your friend wishes to go down, he will find them down there. They may be able to help him. If, on the other hand, he wishes to start here and to come here to see me, he will be welcome. I shall remain here with Sylvia until after the funeral. That is to say, I shall be here over the week-end. I may even stay for a week or so later than that."

Sir Austin bowed.

"Would you like Lady Kemble to come to see you? Friends in time of trouble, you know, can do a rare lot towards softening—"

"She will be welcome the same as Mr. Bathurst, and it's most good of you, Sir Austin, to suggest it. But don't worry about me, Sir Austin. I shall be all right. I'm not a baby and I don't think I'm a coward. Captain Lumsden—that's Sylvia's fiancé, you met him at Ascot last summer, do you remember?—has been awfully kind. He's been like a big brother to me. It's a great comfort to have men friends handy at a time like this. Let me know when to expect you again. Good-bye, and thank you." She gave him her hand as bravely as she could.

Half an hour later Sir Austin Kemble was seated very comfortably in the most luxurious armchair that Mr. Bathurst's flat possessed. He had made his usual beeline for it. Mr. Bathurst himself was dexterously manipulating a siphon of soda.

"Just a spot, Bathurst," said the commissioner. "That's just right. Two fingers! Good health, my boy! Sit down there opposite to me and listen for a few minutes. Listen—and don't interrupt."

"Charmed, Sir Austin. To what am I indebted for the honour of this visit? Is it the—shall I say Red Ringan sensation? I can imagine no other case taking up your own valuable time." He sank into the depths of a second armchair.

Sir Austin drained his glass and filled it up again.

CHAPTER VIII

SIR AUSTIN laughed at Mr. Bathurst's nod of approval perhaps just a trifle nervously.

"Well—er—as a matter of fact, it *is* that extraordinary affair that brings me here, my boy. I have a special reason for being interested in the case. You see, I was by way of being a friend of the murdered man."

"Really?" said Bathurst. "Please tell me more. You sound as though you have something particularly interesting to tell me. I should have thought that the mere fact of his friendship with the commissioner of police would have been better than a life insurance policy for him and would have tied the hands of the Ku-Klux Klan itself. I regard it as most inconsiderate on the part of the criminal, Sir Austin. Most uncomplimentary to you! Help yourself to the Scotch."

His keen grey eyes twinkled humorously and his mouth took the twist that Sir Austin had seen at its corners many times before. The commissioner could see it over the rim of his glass.

"Well, my boy, whether you consider it in that light or whether you don't, Julius Maitland, whose dead body was found yesterday afternoon, was a man I regarded as a friend and a man in whose company I have recently spent a great deal of time."

"South African, wasn't he?"

"Yes. But I never knew him before he came to this country. My acquaintance is of about a year's standing. I met him for the first time at the banquet to the Spanish Ambassador at the

Guildhall somewhere about the April of last year. Yes, it was, about a fortnight after Easter. He was what I should call an extremely companionable man. He had a particularly charming wife, and we found that we had many tastes in common."

"Including the charming wife?" murmured Mr. Bathurst nonchalantly.

Sir Austin glared: "It is not my habit to—"

"Habits have to be formed, Sir Austin. You never know when one may start growing. Still, I accept the disclaimer. I beg your pardon. Please overlook the suggestion." He waved Sir Austin on.

"The tastes to which I referred were such things as racing, polo at Hurlingham, a little rubber now and then, and—"

Anthony looked significantly at the tantalus.

"I think I know the other, sir. Don't trouble to inform me. So you want me to help you find out who murdered Comrade Maitland, eh?"

Sir Austin nodded and helped himself to his fourth Scotch.

"If you could see Mrs. Maitland's distress, my dear Bathurst, I'm perfectly certain you would have no option but to help her in her trouble. As a gentleman, you would be bound."

"When did you see it, sir?"

"I came straight from her to you to enlist your services."

"At her request?"

Sir Austin hesitated for a moment. How should he put it now he had had the direct question?

"Well—er—almost. I told her that I would do all in my power to assist her. I mentioned your name. I told her that as a detective you were unequaled. That is why I am here now." He continued before the smiling Anthony could speak. "My dear Bathurst, you couldn't be impervious to beauty in distress?"

Mr. Bathurst smiled satirically: "Beauty is a relative term, sir. It does not exist of itself, remember, but only in the abstract. Beauty lies in the eyes of the beholder. To some even, for example, you might appear beautiful."

"Look here, Bathurst," exploded Sir Austin, "I don't altogether appreciate your—"

Anthony waved a deprecating hand.

"Don't misunderstand me, sir," he said cheerfully. "You didn't let me finish what I was about to say. *You* might appear beautiful—*I* might appear beautiful—any one of us might! Speaking personally, 'I ne'er could any lustre see, in eyes that would not look on me.'" He helped himself to a cigarette and pushed the case over to the commissioner. "Tell me as many details as you know, sir. I promise to listen to you most carefully."

"I'm not strong on the details of the case at all, my dear Bathurst. All I know is that the body of Maitland was found in a bungalow at Friningham yesterday afternoon by a member of the local police force—a Sergeant Mansfield, I believe. The doctor who conducted the autopsy states that the man was murdered some time on Monday."

"Has the body been identified as that of Maitland?"

"Yes, it's Julius Maitland all right."

"Identified by whom?"

"The dead man's two sons—Valentine and Vivian Maitland. According to what Mrs. Maitland just told me, they are down at Friningham now. They went down last night."

"H'm! Been dead since Monday, you say? Shot, wasn't he?"

"Yes, through the throat."

"Any revolver there—on the premises or round about?"

"Nothing. At least I haven't heard of any being found."

"To whom does the bungalow belong?"

"Can't answer that either—or what took Julius Maitland down there. Nobody seems to know that. I've simply been put into possession of the bare facts."

"When did Mrs. Maitland see him last? By the way, Sir Austin, this Mrs. Maitland—what's her Christian name? I like to know these things."

"Answering your first question, Bathurst, I believe she last saw him early on the Monday in question. After that she got a message that he had been suddenly called to South Africa upon most important business. With regard to your second question, the lady's Christian name is Ida. Why do you ask? It's not important surely?"

Mr. Bathurst smiled.

"I have a little theory of my own, Sir Austin, regarding the bestowal of Christian names. I rather fancy the fairies have a judicial and discriminating hand in it and cause the majority of us to be named moderately happily. For example, consider the Reginalds, Raymonds, Normans, Gordons and Roys of your acquaintance, mentioning a few of our own wretched sex. The handicap is invariably too much for them—it's inevitable. Only occasionally does one rise above it. So the dead man was supposed to have gone to South Africa, eh? Had he any immediate business in South Africa?"

"Don't know. That is what he told his wife."

"And he's found dead down at Friningham! An interesting little problem, without a doubt. By the way, Sir Austin, there's one feature of the case as I've heard it so far that strikes me very forcibly. How was it the police found Maitland's body in the bungalow during the afternoon?"

Sir Austin gazed at him with seeming failure of comprehension.

"I don't quite—"

"In the afternoon, sir, in the afternoon! What took the police to this bungalow during the afternoon? I understood you to say now that it was unoccupied save by the dead man himself. Who gave the alarm? Or did the police happen on the crime by chance? Curious thing, if they did."

"I see your point, Bathurst, of course. But I can't answer it. I really can't say. Of course the point struck me—"

"Yes, sir, I noticed that it did. All the same, it puzzles me, that does. It seems to me to require a deal of explaining."

"What will you do, Bathurst? Come to Friningham with me, or see Mrs. Maitland first?"

Bathurst considered the questions for a moment. "Where is Mrs. Maitland now?" he asked.

"In town. Her house is in Carlton Terrace. You will see her?"

"I shall see her, Sir Austin, most certainly, but after I've been to Friningham, I think. Let me glance at the ABC. I don't think, taking everything into consideration, that we should lose any time whatever in getting down there. After all, it's where the murdered man is. There's a two fifteen from Liverpool Street, Sir Austin. What do you say? Suit you all right?"

"A little light lunch, my dear boy, and the two fifteen will suit me very nicely. And I've no doubt on those conditions that it will suit you too."

"I don't know about the 'light' part of it," replied Anthony, putting on his hat, "but, after all, that can be easily remedied. Come with me. Like Harris—or was it George?—I know a nice little place round the corner."

The two fifteen ran into the peculiar one-platformed station at Friningham soon after five o'clock, and Sir Austin, who had partaken of tea in the restaurant car attached to the train, and criticized the service somewhat strongly, was gratified to find that his peremptory message relative to his intended arrival had received prompt attention. Sergeant Mansfield, together with two plainclothes men, was waiting on the platform, secretly delighted to have the honour of working in such eminently distinguished company. To work on a murder case under the direct eye of the commissioner of police himself was a privilege for which he had never bargained. For all he knew, it might be the turning-point in his career. He looked rather inquisitively at the tall, lithe man with the athletic carriage and the determined swing of the shoulders who immediately ranged himself at his side. He was not the first man to feel the force of Mr. Bathurst's personality.

"We will walk up," said Sir Austin, "if it's not too far. Send the car away."

"One question I very much desire to ask you, Sergeant Mansfield," said Mr. Bathurst after the introduction by Sir Austin, "what was it took you to this bungalow where the dead man was yesterday afternoon? I can't quite understand that."

Sergeant Mansfield seized the opportunity to tell his story once again, and with avidity. He welcomed every possible opportunity for justification. His recital afforded his listener both amazement and pleasure.

"Really now, Sergeant Mansfield," he rejoined, "that interests me tremendously. I'm beginning to understand something that puzzled me quite a lot. I was unable to deduce satisfactorily how it was you got to the bungalow when you did." He turned to the commissioner. "What do you make of the sergeant's story, sir? I should value your opinion."

"Very unusual, Bathurst. Very extraordinary in every way. Who gave the alarm? Is it possible that the doctor who made the examination may be mistaken? That's a point, it seems to me, that will have to be considered and thoroughly threshed out."

Mr. Bathurst pursed his lips critically: "One other point, sergeant, while I think of it. The two sons of the murdered man—are they still down here in Friningham?"

"Yes, sir. The two young Mr. Maitlands arrived here late last night and have naturally seen to some of the arrangements. They're staying at the Majestic. That's the hotel just by the golf clubhouse. I've arranged that they shall meet the commissioner at the bungalow this evening. We are not far off now, sir. This is the main road from London. It leads through Friningham to Nazing. Pin Hole Way is on the left. It's the best avenue in Friningham. It leads down to the sea."

"I suppose the murdered man wasn't a familiar figure in these parts, sergeant, was he? He wasn't known to you physically, for instance, when you discovered him?"

"No, sir, not at once. I identified him from a letter I found on him. His name was on the envelope. But I'd like to make this plain, sir. Although the man wasn't known to me as a local resident or anything like that, his face seemed familiar to me when I first saw him. When I found the letter with his name on the envelope, I knew why. I had seen his photograph in some of the papers. It was the famous Mr. Maitland."

"One thing you haven't told me—nobody has told me so far. What was the nature of this letter you found?"

"Simply a business letter, sir. From a firm of solicitors—making an appointment with Mr. Maitland."

"When?"

"In the afternoon of last Monday, the day Doctor Forsyth states that he met his death."

"Where is the letter, sergeant?" put in Sir Austin.

"Everything is at the bungalow, sir, under supervision."

"Good! What's the trouble, Bathurst?"

Mr. Bathurst's face had assumed an interested expression.

"No trouble, sir. That happened to interest me, that was all." He pointed to the beautifully even top of the clipped hedge in the front garden of a bungalow which they were on the point of passing.

Sir Austin frowned in the direction of Mr. Bathurst's indication.

"I don't quite get you, my boy," he observed.

Anthony smiled good-humouredly.

"No? Look on the top of the hedge, then, sir. Don't you see what I mean?"

Sergeant Mansfield and the two plainclothes men halted a few yards in advance as Mr. Bathurst and Sir Austin walked toward the carefully trimmed hedge. Judging by the commissioner's silence, he did not see what his companion meant.

"On top of the hedge, sir! Don't you see them?"

"The two hedge cuttings, do you mean, Bathurst? What on earth interests you about them?"

He scanned Anthony's face searchingly, as though about to find there the answer to his question. But Mr. Bathurst's face remained impassive. Sir Austin proceeded to fortify his statement:

"Surely you could find nothing more natural or more totally in keeping than hedge cuttings on a newly trimmed hedge?"

"I'm not sure, sir! Let me look again," said Bathurst. The two twigs that had occupied his attention were crossed and one was much longer than the other. Mr. Bathurst rubbed his hands.

"No, Sir Austin. I'm almost certain of my ground. It's a message from little Ursula."

Sir Austin's frown deepened.

"Another of your riddles, I suppose, Bathurst. That's the worst of—"

"Don't get impatient, sir. Perhaps if I'm able to show you something else a little later on, as I fully expect to be able to, you'll find it in your heart to forgive me."

"Get along, sergeant!" said the commissioner. "I'm anxious to reach our destination."

In a few moments they turned into Pin Hole Way, crossing an open field that lay at the end of it. Suddenly Mr. Bathurst caught Sir Austin by the arm. The latter turned to find Anthony pointing triumphantly to the ground.

"*Plus ça change, plus c'est la même chose.* Not twigs this time, Sir Austin, but a mere handful of grass. Yet, in combination with the twigs, more than sufficient for those to read who can. For that too is telling Ursula's story. I'll tell you what, Sir Austin. I'll bet you the price of to-night's dinner that there will be a couple of twigs very close to the outside of the bungalow known as Ravenswood?"

"I'm not betting with you, Bathurst. I've found that a proposition far too expensive in the past," returned Sir Austin, somewhat stiffly, "but don't be too certain of yourself, my boy. Pride goeth before destruction, remember. The twigs you're so anxious to bet on might turn out to be grass—like this little lot."

Mr. Bathurst laughed. "They might, sir, but they won't. And even if they were, I should consider that as equivalent to winning the bet. It's a million to a soused mackerel on it. But you haven't long to wait—we shall be there in a moment—and seeing will be believing." Four minutes later they stood in front of the bungalow. Mr. Bathurst impetuously pushed open the front gate. As he did so he stopped with an eager suddenness. He waved Sir Austin to the grass bed of the front garden. There again lay the two twigs—a replica of those on the hedge top that they had just passed—the longer one lying on top and pointing in the direction of the front door of Ravenswood.

"*Voilà!*" murmured Mr. Bathurst. "I'll suggest we have oysters, thick white soup, whitebait, saddle of—"

"I didn't bet," returned Sir Austin curtly, "so you needn't mention the other courses."

CHAPTER IX

Sergeant Mansfield rang the bell and the stolid Constable Drummond admitted them.

"Inspector Garth has been down, sergeant," he announced, "and was going to make arrangements for the removal of the body. But when he heard that Sir Austin Kemble would be along here later, he gave orders that everything was to remain as it was. I understand that the inspector will be returning here to-morrow."

"That's excellent," ventured the commissioner. "That's excellent, eh, Bathurst? Better than our usual experience."

"Very true, sir. We may be able to pick up something. It's a great help to know that nothing at all has been touched."

They made their way into the room in which was the body of Julius Maitland. Mr. Bathurst walked up to it and removed the white covering from the face. He looked intently at the features. Then he caught sight of the slashed knuckles on the right hand. He held up the hand and carefully examined the thumb. Unclasping the clenched fingers, he removed the strands of black hair that they held so tightly. To the surprise of both Sir Austin Kemble and Sergeant Mansfield, he put the hair to his nostrils and sniffed at it. He turned toward his watchers and smilingly explained the reason of the procedure:

"You will very often find a perfume clinging round a woman's hair, and I have little doubt that this came from—" He paused abruptly and sniffed at the hair again. "Now that's very strange," he muttered. His eyes contracted as though he were pursuing a line of thought based upon an elusive memory, but his face quickly reverted to the normal. "Take charge of this hair, sergeant," he said. "I may want to have another look at it—or smell."

Stooping suddenly, he went on one knee beside the body, examined the two wounds, and then picked up the damaged hand again. He followed this up by carefully examining the dead man's shoes and turning out the permanent turn-up of his trousers. From the latter he took a small piece of straw. He appeared to obtain but small reward from this, for the onlookers were again mystified to see him bend down even farther and sniff at the shoes, socks and also at the cuffs of the trousers.

"Quite what you might expect," they heard him whisper, seemingly to himself, "but where? That's the question."

He straightened himself and looked carefully round the apartment. It was a typical modern dining room, and it was extremely well furnished, he decided. The Chesterfield in the recess, the dining table and sideboard, the chairs and the appointments as a whole were excellent, both in taste and quality. The two or three pictures were extremely artistic. A gramophone of the latest pattern stood on a table in the corner by the window, a radio and loud speaker were on the top of a bureau at its side and a bookcase crammed with what looked like the most popular novels of the day occupied a good space opposite them. The occupant, whoever it might have been, lacked no creature comforts. Mr. Bathurst walked slowly across to the Chesterfield and picked up the violin.

"The door of this room was ajar when you arrived yesterday, I understood you to say, sergeant, didn't I?"

"Yes, sir. Quite right, sir."

"And this violin is presumably the instrument which you heard being played? Although you heard nothing like a revolver shot, I suppose you are certain in your mind that it was a violin that you heard being played?"

"No doubt at all, sir. I heard no shot, but I heard the violin. I know the strains of the instrument too well not to recognize it when I hear it. As a matter of fact, both my daughters are what you might call musical, sir. One plays the violin and the other's by way of being an elocutionist, as well as very handy on the Joanna. To hear her do—"

"Quite so, sergeant, I understand." Mr. Bathurst held the instrument away from him on a level with his eyes and let the rays of the sun through the window rest upon its surface. He then picked up the bow from the Chesterfield and drew it across the strings of the instrument. "What shall I play you, Sir Austin?"

he observed with a humorous twist of his mouth. "Have you any particular penchant?"

The commissioner shook his head with a tinge of impatience. He was anxious to get to closer grips with the affair.

"The immortal Holmes," continued Anthony, in his lightest mood, "was a devotee of Sarasate, if you remember. I rather fancy, if my memory be correct, he allowed that genius to freshen his mind whilst engaged upon that fascinating little problem that Sir Arthur has handed down to us under the somewhat bizarre title of 'The Red-Headed League.'" He fiddled a few more notes of uncertain music before wagging his head doubtfully.

"Put it down, Bathurst," ventured the commissioner testily. "Playing the violin is evidently not one of your strongest points."

"You judge me too harshly, Sir Austin," replied Mr. Bathurst. "Possibly, I admit, because my own standard in other directions runs moderately high. At the same time, if you only knew—" He replaced the violin together with the bow on the Chesterfield. "What was the quality of the music you heard, sergeant? Are you any judge?"

"The goods, sir, absolutely the—"

As Mansfield spoke there came a sharp ring at the bell of the front door of the bungalow.

"See who it is, Drummond," called out Sergeant Mansfield, breaking off in his reply. He looked inquiringly at Sir Austin. "What do you think, sir? Shall we—?"

"Better go to see who it is yourself, sergeant. Then you can decide at your discretion."

"Mr. Valentine Maitland, Mr. Vivian Maitland and Doctor Forsyth," said Mansfield a moment or two later.

"Come this way, gentlemen. This is—"

Sir Austin bustled forward and abbreviated his form of introduction.

"I am Sir Austin Kemble from Scotland Yard, commissioner of police. This gentleman here with me is Mr. Anthony Bathurst, a friend of mine. We are looking into this very, very sad case because it is felt at the Yard that it presents a number of undoubted difficulties. But first of all to you, Mr. Maitland and to you, Mr.—er—Vivian Maitland, please let me convey my most sincere condolences on your heavy loss."

The tall young man was about to reply when his dark and more impetuous brother entered into the breach.

"Thank you, sir. To lose one's father is a heavy blow under any circumstances. Under conditions like this, it is—well—" He gestured helplessly and turned to his brother, apparently more for corroboration than from any appeal for support.

Valentine Maitland spoke in a soft, low, pleasing voice.

"Doubly hard to lose him when we did, Sir Austin. I am looking at it from my poor father's own point of view, too, although the remark may appear strange and perhaps foolish. To have been stricken down on the eve of the Derby—"

Here Mr. Bathurst interposed: "Was your father intensely keen to win the Derby, Mr. Maitland? Think over my question carefully before you answer it. Any man, I suppose, would be keen to win the race. But was Mr. Maitland intensely keen?"

"Mr. Bathurst," answered Vivian, to the fore again, before his brother could reply, "my father was living for the day. It was another case of *Der Tag* with him. Even the expression 'intensely keen' wouldn't be an adequate index to his feelings."

"Do you subscribe to that opinion, too, Mr. Maitland? I should like to hear what you have to say." Mr. Bathurst put the question to the elder brother, the man to whom he had actually put the question which Vivian had taken upon himself to answer.

Valentine nodded emphatically: "Most certainly, Mr. Bathurst. I thoroughly confirm my brother's statement. Anybody living with my father must have been certain of it. He didn't try to hide it. He was so keen that he didn't like the idea of his wife even having a chance of winning the race and beating him."

"Thank you. You would not countenance then the idea of suicide?"

"I can't think of it in connection with my father," urged Vivian, but his brother did not reply for a moment or two.

"It would be very hard to believe, Mr. Bathurst," he returned at length. "But, of course, sometimes—"

Sir Austin Kemble turned to Doctor Forsyth.

"What is your opinion, doctor? Did your examination lead you to suppose anything of the kind?"

Mr. Bathurst awaited the doctor's reply with interest.

The doctor screwed his face up in consideration of the latest suggestion.

"Well it didn't, to be quite candid. I presumed that the absence of the weapon with which the crime was committed disposed of—"

"Naturally, doctor," intervened Anthony. "But putting aside that particular point, don't you think that the condition of the wound near the clavicle points to the bullet having been fired at very close quarters? There is a most distinct blackening—"

"Undoubtedly, Mr. Bathurst," returned Doctor Forsyth. "I am in entire agreement with you. It was fired at very close quarters. Here is the bullet that had splintered the bone." He put his fingers into a pocket of his waistcoat and extracted something which he handed over to Anthony.

Anthony looked at it somewhat critically and then passed it over to Sir Austin.

"Fired from a smallish revolver of some kind, I should say, sir. Nothing particularly distinctive about it. Everybody seems to own a revolver nowadays."

"That was my impression, Sir Austin," put in Doctor Forsyth, "when I extracted the bullet this morning. I should say a thirty-eight Colt automatic. The puzzle is, where's the other one—the fatal one? It's not in the throat—there's not a trace of its presence there, but of course plenty of its passage. The carotid artery was severed and the bullet has passed out through the neck on the other side. My point is, where is the bullet?" Mr. Bathurst looked carefully round the room.

"An excellent point, doctor. But bullets find strange billets upon occasion. Have I ever told you, Sir Austin, of a little problem I was called upon to solve at Assynton Lodge, in Berkshire? On that occasion I discovered a missing bullet embedded within the pages of a book."

"I remember that you have mentioned it to me, Bathurst." Sir Austin looked round the apartment critically. "I can't suggest a likely hiding place in here, my boy. It will be another problem for your ingenuity. What do you think, doctor?"

"I entirely agree, Sir Austin. Truth to tell, I've given a lot of thought to the question, because I found it worrying me."

"The bullet might have gone through the open window," ventured Vivian. "It's quite a possibility, I should say. It's June. It's almost certain that one of the windows of a living room such as this appears to be would be open at this time of the year."

"As to that, sir," said Sergeant Mansfield, "when I entered on Wednesday, all the windows of this room were shut."

"To whom does the bungalow belong? Does anybody know? I understand that it was not your father's?" Anthony looked inquiringly at the two brothers.

"To a Mr. Ponsonby," replied Vivian Maitland quickly.

Valentine darted a quick glance at his brother, which Mr. Bathurst happened to be in a position to intercept. He decided that the elder Maitland was either annoyed or surprised at the answer Vivian had given. Vivian met his glance temporarily and then avoided it.

"The manager of the Majestic gave me the information this morning," he added. "I asked him. I was trying to account for my father's presence here. I have been puzzled as to what it was that could have brought him down here. I have never heard him even mention the word Friningham. So I've been putting a few inquiries round. The manager was able to help me."

Anthony nodded in acceptance of his explanation.

"Who is this Mr. Ponsonby?" he questioned. "A local man?"

"I wasn't able to discover. The manager couldn't tell me. He said he didn't know."

Sergeant Mansfield came forward.

"If my information is of any use to you, sir, the name is unfamiliar to me in these parts. I know of no local man of that name."

"Ah, well, it's of small consequence," said Anthony. "It will be a comparatively simple matter to find out." He turned again to Doctor Forsyth. "The dead man, doctor," he asked, "was he in pretty good condition for a man of his age—physically, I mean?"

"Nothing much wrong with him. I should say that he enjoyed his life, liked plenty of good food, wasn't a teetotaler, generally used to having just what he wanted and very fond of what he liked. Still, there are few signs of anything like serious intemperance in any direction."

"Thank you, doctor. One more question. You have given an unshakable opinion, I understand, that death took place some time on Monday. Against that I have heard a most extraordinary story from Sergeant Mansfield, who has told me of the circumstances under which he was summoned here and found the body. Do you still maintain that opinion of yours? You realize its importance?"

Doctor Forsyth permitted the vestige of a smile to flit across his features. It was almost contemptuous.

"Mr. Bathurst," he rejoined, "you can take it from me as absolutely certain that, when I was called to this bungalow yesterday afternoon, the man whom I found here had been dead something like forty-eight hours. I have now made a further examination. You can put it at a couple of days at least and you won't be far out. That's as certain as my name's Alexander Forsyth. As to Sergeant Mansfield's story"—he paused for a moment and shrugged his shoulders—"well, I'll put it like this, because I'm not doubting the sergeant's sincerity for a single moment. The man he heard on the telephone being murdered, if you like, the man who sent him the message for help, was certainly not the man whom I found in here dead."

Sergeant Mansfield's face flushed as he listened to Doctor Forsyth's statement. It seemed to him that his veracity was being doubted, and his bona fides questioned, despite the doctor's denial. But he was sufficiently sensible to remain silent. He felt that to challenge the medical man's declaration at the moment would fail to strengthen his own standing and perhaps do more—weaken it. He had had an old schoolmaster who had taught him that there were two qualities of silence, the golden, and the leaden one of ignorance and lack of understanding. Silence could be golden—and it could be guilt. Forsyth looked at him as though he anticipated that the sergeant would attempt to justify himself, but the self-vindication not being forthcoming, the doctor addressed himself again to Anthony Bathurst.

"My solution of the mystery, Mr. Bathurst, is that there is probably a second dead man lying somewhere else, probably not very far away, and his was the voice that Sergeant Mansfield heard."

"That is a possibility, Bathurst," put in Sir Austin. "As a matter of fact, it had occurred to me. What do you think about it yourself?"

"Candidly it hadn't struck me, sir. I was toying with another possible situation. Tell me, doctor, do you think each wound was made by a bullet from the same revolver?"

"It is hard to say. The throat wound is torn so."

"I see." Anthony turned again toward Mansfield. "By the way, sergeant, have you been all over these premises? I should like to run over them with you, if you don't mind."

"Certainly, sir. As a matter of fact, I have been over them. There's nothing of any importance that I can see, or that I've been able to see. Perhaps that would sound better."

"May we accompany you, Mr. Bathurst—my brother and I?"

The question came from Vivian Maitland, and Anthony gave a quick nod of assent.

The tour produced nothing whatever to excite Mr. Bathurst's interest, and as the company returned to the dining room, he could be seen to be stroking his chin very carefully. The darkness of the problem seemed to him almost impenetrable, but he made an examination of the letter found upon Maitland and noted the address of the firm from whom it had come.

That night in the smoking room of the second-best hotel in Friningham, the Queen's, Mr. Bathurst took Sir Austin into his confidence.

"Before I return, sir, to interview Mrs. Maitland, there are two things I want to do in Friningham."

"And what are they, Bathurst? Say the word and we'll do them. Search for that missing bullet and—"

"No, sir. There's no bullet to be found in Ravenswood. You can take that from me. No, I want to have a chat with the telephone girl that put the message through to the police station and then I want to stroll up to the Majestic."

"To see the Maitlands again?"

"No, not that exactly. To have a word with the manager."

"Why? What does—"

"Concerning a Mr. Ponsonby, the owner of Ravenswood. Don't you remember what Vivian Maitland told us?"

CHAPTER X

ON THE following morning Mr. Bathurst was up betimes. He slipped out of the hotel. The coast air, fresh, buoyant and vivid, tempered the heat of the morning sunshine and he was able to understand readily why Friningham had unblushingly appropriated to itself the title of "Queen of the East Coast." He intended to put in a couple of hours' hard thinking before breakfast; that is to say, before he saw Sir Austin Kemble again. Before that gentleman questioned him again he wanted to have certain ideas that had come his way neatly docketed and put in order. Careless in some things, mentally he liked everything properly tabulated. He communed with himself as he traversed the stretch of cliff that swept toward the neighbouring seaside resort of Magthorpe.

"One extraordinary feature of this case," he thought, "is that so many of the important pieces of evidence remain uncorroborated. First, we have Sergeant Mansfield's story of the telephone message, purporting, so the sergeant says, to come from the murdered man. A story which Doctor Forsyth flatly contradicts as being absolutely impossible, the man having been killed two days previously, a fact which certainly makes the doctor's evidence pretty conclusive. I have been able to get the fact that the message was sent confirmed, but I am doubtful if I shall get corroboration of the actual terms of the message. That will probably prove to be impossible."

Anthony proceeded to fill his pipe with extreme care, for he always found tobacco a stimulant to mental activity. "Second, the fact that Julius Maitland is found in this bungalow at Friningham hasn't a link or connection that we have so far been able to ascertain which I may regard as a corroborative link. So far as any one of us knows, he has no relationship whatever with the place. Strange—very strange. Third, what was it that Julius Maitland regarded as of such paramount importance that he disappeared on the eve of the enjoyment of his triumph in the Derby? A triumph which had meant so much to him that each of his sons states he was living for the day. His wife is informed that he has been called to South Africa very suddenly on business of extreme urgency and yet at some time on the very same day, so we are assured by Doctor Forsyth, he meets his death in a bungalow at Friningham." Mr. Bathurst frowned and made a mental reservation. "In this particular connection, note one thing: Mrs. Maitland's story that her husband was called away to South Africa is also entirely uncorroborated."

"Remarkable how that kind of evidence keeps cropping up everywhere. In this respect there are two possibilities to be considered. Julius Maitland may have told a lie as to where he was going—she may have told a lie about what he said to her. Latter possibility remote, but certainly worth consideration. But I must obtain full details of that going-away story." Mr. Bathurst selected a seat on a cliff overlooking the sea and puffed steadily at his pipe. "No bullet to be found inside the bungalow—no weapon of any kind. A man speaking, gibbering kind of laughter heard, a violin being skillfully played, and all the accompaniment of sound that goes with a physical struggle, except the sound of the actual shots. Mansfield could never imagine such things. Yet when he gets there, all is as he expects to find it, save the most important part of all—the dead man won't fit. He's an anachronism by two days. Why therefore—?" Anthony paused and his brows contracted. "Then we have the Borrow touch which I was fortunate enough to detect, and which I am moderately certain has something to do with the crime. For whom was that message intended? I wonder if that was the—"

Mr. Bathurst rose from his seat and retraced his steps to the hotel, to meet Sir Austin Kemble on the threshold of the coffee room.

"I've ordered your breakfast, Bathurst. I've learned to respect your powers at the breakfast table. There's never any morning after the night before about you. I've ordered you grapefruit, a nice sole, bacon and eggs, with a kidney, if you'd like it—"

"I am abashed, Sir Austin. You humiliate me. I stand aghast at my flagrant animalism. Can I really manage as much as that? Still, while we're waiting, come and sit down over here. I want to ask you something. Perhaps you will be able to throw a ray of light on my darkness. This telephone message that Mansfield swears he had—from whom did it come? Consider all the possibilities before you commit yourself, Sir Austin."

Sir Austin leaned back in a very comfortable chair and replied immediately.

"I have considered them, my dear boy. There are three definite possibilities with regard to it. It came from one of three people—one, the murdered man, two, the murderer or three, the murderer's confederate. The struggle may have been taking place while the last of the three was doing the telephoning."

Mr. Bathurst looked at Sir Austin: "That's an extraordinary suggestion you're making, sir. Why on earth should a murderer or his confederate, as you call him, acquaint the police of all people of his crime and set them immediately upon his track? Surely they would be the last—"

Sir Austin, far from being taken aback, chuckled. "That isn't what you asked me, Bathurst. You asked me to discuss the 'possibilities' of the case. Possibilities aren't probabilities. I considered everything purposely, but I'm not prepared to advance coherent reasons for all of them. Come on, let us eat."

"I accept your point, Sir Austin," said Bathurst, when they were seated at the table. "You are right. It's perfectly true what you say. Taking you on your own valuation, though, there's yet another possibility—one that it seems to me you've either ignored or overlooked." Sir Austin raised his eyebrows. "And that is?"

"You mention the possibility of the message having been sent by a confederate of the murderer. How about it having been sent by a friend of the victim? A more likely contingency, I should say, than the other."

"What became of him, then, Bathurst? Where is he?"

"He may have been overpowered and carried away, or, on the other hand, he may fit in with Dr. Forsyth's suggestion. You recollect what that was, don't you? That there's a second dead body to be found somewhere."

"Is that your theory, Bathurst? Do you believe it?" Mr. Bathurst smiled as he removed a tasty morsel of sole from the bone.

"I didn't say so, Sir Austin. Upon mature consideration, I'm inclined to think that, after all, one of your hypotheses may eventually be found to fit the proposition. But I'm not sure which one of them."

"Despite the unusual nature of—"

"Despite the fact of it seeming to be so very extraordinary. By the way, perhaps you can give me some information on another point? Julius Maitland was by way of being a friend of yours, you said. That fact should assist us considerably. It should give us certain 'knowledges' of the man that in nineteen similar cases out of twenty would be permanently withheld from us. We start with a bias in our favour as distinct from the usual handicap. What sort of a voice did he possess? How would you describe it? Was it very personal—very distinctive? The sort of voice that would be recognizable anywhere?"

Sir Austin thought hard for a moment or two.

"I should describe it as a rather heavy voice. Strong on the lower register. If he sang at all, I should say he would be either a heavy baritone or a bass."

"Good! That places him to a certain extent. I always think that the voice is the most definitely personal quality that each one of us carries about in our physical make-up. I am certain that it's by far the most difficult physical feature, for example, to hide or to disguise even. Strive how we may, and skilfully at that, to achieve the latter, there's a timbre about it that will out sooner or later. Has Julius Maitland ever telephoned to you—spoke to you personally on the phone, I mean?"

"Several times, Bathurst, especially fairly recently."

"Did his voice retain its personal characteristics over the telephone? Some voices, you know, do much more than others. You will recognize the voice of one man at once, whereas another man's voice seems to change considerably when used under telephone conditions."

Sir Austin nodded: "I know what you mean. I should say that Maitland's voice did retain its distinctiveness on the phone, some of it certainly. I usually could tell it was he directly he rang me up."

"Better still, Sir Austin. That gives me a definite foundation upon which to build. When we've finished breakfast we'll do a little touring round."

Inquiry of the head waiter elicited the information that the Friningham Central Exchange was situated opposite the public offices in High Street, next to the municipal library and fire station. Fortunately, the young lady who had been on duty on the previous Wednesday afternoon was in attendance that morning. The supervisor would make arrangements at once for her to be interviewed. The name of Sir Austin Kemble worked wonders! The girl in question, who gave the name of Gladys Loftus, was a rosy-cheeked, intelligent person who answered the questions put to her very readily. Mr. Bathurst found that she remembered the particular call very well.

"I put a call through to Friningham 088 on Wednesday afternoon. I remember it perfectly."

"Was that what you were asked for?" inquired Anthony.

"What do you mean, sir?"

"Were you asked for the police station by a number?"

"Yes, sir. The police station here still retains a number. It's new premises, you see, sir. It used to be a private house and hasn't long been used as the police station. Of course most people just ask for 'Police' when they want to put a call through, but there is a number still used sometimes."

"I see. Now think very carefully, Miss Loftus. Can you describe the voice that put the call through? Did you happen to hear the message that passed?"

Gladys wrinkled her brows and shook her head.

"I didn't listen in, sir. I simply plugged the call through. I was a bit excited that afternoon. I'd won a prize in a sweep—fifteen shillings and sixpence. I drew Sacred Beetle. But I'm trying to remember what kind of a voice it was that called me up. It was a man—I'm sure of that. A rather high-pitched voice, I think. It had a kind of sing-song tone about it. I know," she concluded hopefully, "the sort of voice you hear in the Brightlingseat district. My father was concerned with the yacht-building work down there and I've often heard similar voices in those parts."

"You would assert, then, quite definitely, that the man who called you up was not a man with a heavy, low-pitched voice? You would be prepared to say that without a doubt, eh?"

Gladys Loftus nodded her head with decision.

"Oh, yes, sir! I am quite certain of that. It was not a heavy voice I heard by any means. I would swear to that."

"There's one other point, Bathurst," put in Sir Austin. "There's one other question that it seems to me we might ask Miss—er—Loftus. Did you hear anything else, young lady—beyond the telephone call itself? Any other voice or noise, for instance?"

This time the girl shook her head emphatically. "Nothing, sir, nothing at all. Only the exchange and the number."

"Humph! Anything else about which you desire to inquire, Bathurst? Any other point worth attention? No? We'll get along then. Good morning, Miss Loftus." He pushed something into the girl's hand. "Buy yourself some chocolates, my dear. I expect you like 'em. All the girls seem to like chocolates nowadays. Personally, I prefer bullseyes—always did, from the time when I was a boy at school and used to buy 'em in the tuck. Come along, Bathurst."

Clear of the telephone exchange, Anthony turned to his distinguished companion, who appeared to be still chuckling over the gastronomic reminiscences of his schooldays.

"Our next place of call, sir, with your acquiescence, of course, will be the Majestic Hotel. I am somewhat interested in the Mr. Ponsonby whose name we heard mentioned in connection with the bungalow that was the scene of the crime. I have an idea that we shall discover something illuminating."

Sir Austin's name and reputation caused the almost immediate appearance of Mr. Southcott, the manager. It was a most unusual state of affairs for the Majestic to be without two or three guests whose names were what may be termed household words, and Mr. Southcott, when he first had been informed of the murder, experienced considerable difficulty in repressing a feeling that had Julius Maitland only decided to stay there—well, the terrible tragedy of the bungalow in Pin Hole Way would never have taken place. He felt that to a certain extent the dead man had contributed to his own murder by this piece of almost unpardonable negligence.

Just before Southcott's arrival to give audience to the two men who had called upon him, Mr. Bathurst thought it policy to have a few words with the commissioner. The latter listened attentively and then signified his agreement.

Sydney Southcott was not at all impressive in appearance. Inclined to corpulency, largely due to over-indulgence in more than one appetite, he had a mincing manner that seemed a strange incongruity. Allied to this he was able to deliver platitudes in stained-glass attitudes in a manner worthy of a Member of Parliament or even an eminent divine. As he descended to the apartment into which he had ordered that the two gentlemen should be conducted he found himself wondering what could be the exact purpose and the real significance of their visit. He could not see that the fact of the Majestic temporarily housing the two young Maitlands could altogether account for the presence there that morning of Scotland Yard in the person of Sir Austin Kemble himself. He entered the room, therefore, in a condition of even more mental wonderment and uncertainty than was usual.

"Good morning, gentlemen! Pardon me having kept you waiting for even a few minutes. You will, I am sure, understand that I am a busy man, a very busy man, especially at this particular time of the year. What can I do for you, gentlemen?"

Sir Austin waved his hand with a lordly gesture that would have graced even the magnanimity of manumission.

"You have been informed who I am. I will not waste any of your time. Mr. Bathurst and I have called in reference to the murder of Mr. Julius Maitland. But doubtless you have guessed as much."

Mr. Southcott put his lips together both primly and precisely.

"I am not—er—backward in putting two and two together, Sir Austin. And I—er—usually total them to four. But I can't see any connection whatever that I can possibly have with the crime you have just mentioned." He lifted his fair, indeterminate eyebrows half-questioningly and yet half in protestation.

"Be easy, Mr. Southcott, on that point. Mr. Bathurst and I are merely seeking a little information, information that I may describe as extraneous to the actual murder, but nevertheless of some importance. Mr. Bathurst wishes to ask you one or two questions. Please answer him to the best of your ability."

Sir Austin gestured invitation in Anthony's direction and the latter accepted it. He had been watching Southcott with a certain degree of interest. He was quick to read character, and so far the manager of the Majestic had failed to impress him very favourably. He determined to waste little time, but to get to the main point at once.

"There are only two questions I wish to ask you, Mr. Southcott. I've come to you for just two reasons, the more important of which is that you no doubt know everybody in Friningham worth knowing."

Mr. Southcott inclined his head with the gravity of an alderman distributing prizes at an elementary school. It was evident that he considered that Mr. Bathurst had paid him a very high compliment.

"Undoubtedly. You could not have come to a better man in that respect. There is nobody in Friningham better equipped with that knowledge than I—than me, I should have said." He deserted the frying pan of the English grammar for the fire. "That is between you and I, of course."

Mr. Bathurst smiled at the nominative.

"I felt sure of it. I said to Sir Austin Kemble here, 'Southcott will be our man.' Now, what I want to know is this. Have you ever seen or heard of Mr. Julius Maitland in Friningham or even in the district adjoining?"

"Never! I have never seen him down here, or even heard of him having been down here. I am sure that had he paid the town a visit in the ordinary way—that is to say, openly, and not—er—*sub rosa*—he would have stayed at the Majestic. But he has never stayed here in his life."

"My own idea precisely," murmured Mr. Bathurst. "Thank you, Mr. Southcott. You have confirmed my opinion. Now for my second question. Who is Mr. Ponsonby, the owner of Ravenswood?"

"I couldn't tell you at all. Not a local man, certainly."

"I am sorry to hear that. I imagined you might have been able to assist us with regard to that matter. You know nothing about him, then, beyond the fact that he owns that particular bungalow."

"Nothing whatever. I didn't even know that he did own the bungalow. In fact, I have never heard the name before."

Sir Austin manifested signs of extreme excitement. He was about to translate this into interrogative speech when a pregnant glance from Bathurst silenced him. The latter spoke quite coolly:

"You've never heard the name of Ponsonby, then, Mr. Southcott?"

"Never. I know nothing about the bungalow where the murder took place, Mr. Bathurst, beyond, of course, its geographical position in Friningham, and most certainly I know nothing concerning its owner."

Five minutes later, as Mr. Bathurst and the commissioner strolled along the beautifully kept promenade of Friningham, the former put the question that had been violently agitating the mind of each.

"Well, Sir Austin, what do you make of that piece of information? Who is telling the truth now? Southcott or Mr. Vivian Maitland?"

"Neither, very likely," came Sir Austin's answer curtly. "What do you think yourself, Bathurst?"

For a moment or two the latter made no reply. He was thinking of a look he had intercepted between Vivian Maitland and his elder brother. What exactly had that look been intended to convey?

CHAPTER XI

WHEN IDA GREATOREX had been swept into her marriage with Julius Maitland, partly by the impetuosity of the latter's passion and partly by the rebound of a previous love affair of her own, she had not been received too graciously into the Maitland family circle by two of its most important members, as has been stated before. The two to whom reference is made were Sylvia and Vivian Maitland, the dead man's daughter and younger son.

Second marriages are invariably and notoriously unpopular, and to none more so than to the family of the previous alliance. Ida Greatorex had found hers no exception and, although the atmosphere between her and the two had improved somewhat since they came to England, she could never entirely rid herself of the idea that Sylvia, in particular, regarded her as an interloper whose intrusion could never be absolutely forgiven. Sylvia's dislike of her stepmother (most unpleasant title of an equally unpleasant relationship!) was based, of course, upon one of the strongest human passions. Jealousy is the pernicious anemia in the life of character. Before Ida came into her existence so triumphantly, Sylvia had worshipped her father after the manner of some only daughters and had accepted without the slightest demur or criticism all that he did or said. But his marriage to Ida had completely changed the position. She suffered the indignity of relegation and, what was more galling still to her, the special place that she had hitherto occupied both in her father's heart and career was now in the occupation of another woman—a woman—young, pretty and vivacious—in every way charming, and very little older than she; a woman whom even the cleverest effort of cattiness found difficult to fault. So Sylvia sulked, for now all the swains did not commend her, and Ida Greatorex reigned in her place.

With Vivian Maitland, of course, the position was definitely different. In his case there was no condition of actual rivalry, for instance, with which to contend. But he had a distinct touch of the less agreeable qualities of femininity in his make-up and, like his sister, bitterly resented the place and its degree of intimacy that Ida took and held so artlessly and effortlessly. Valentine Maitland, the elder boy, had loved his dead mother much more than he did his living father. As a consequence, his stepmother's entry into the Maitland home affected him very differently and very much less directly, and the contemplation of Ida's close companionship with his father aroused within him very dissimilar feelings to those of his brother and sister. His mother had mattered more to him and, as far as he was concerned, she always would.

It had been the ardent and devout wish of Julius Maitland that Sylvia should marry into the peerage. He had determined that she should contract no other alliance. With that end very clearly in view, he had certainly not contemplated the attentions of Captain Lumsden with any tangible degree of satisfaction or appreciation. This fact had not eluded the observation of his keen-eyed and quick-witted wife, although he had said nothing whatever to her upon the matter.

The morning after the commissioner of police and Anthony Bathurst were at Friningham, Ida Maitland, after much consideration, determined upon a definite course of action. Certain things were troubling her and she came to the firm resolve that she would tackle them courageously before Sir Austin Kemble and this friend of his visited her. She returned again to the letter that Sir Austin had written to her and which she had received by the morning post:

My dear Mrs. Maitland:

As I arranged with you, I shall be calling upon you again to-morrow and bringing my friend Anthony Bathurst with me. Have courage and bear up! Remember what follows the darkest hour.

Your sincere friend,

AUSTIN KEMBLE.

She walked across to the cheval glass in her bedroom and surveyed her reflected image with a measure of apprehension. The trouble which she had been so suddenly called upon to face had taken toll of her—toll that was unmistakably portrayed in her appearance. With an almost wistful movement of the shoulders, she turned away from the mirror and descended the heavily carpeted stairs. Inside the lounge she pressed the bell.

"Copeland," she said a moment later to the butler, "please tell Miss Sylvia that I want to speak to her in here at once, will you? I think you will find her in the morning room."

The butler bowed and withdrew.

When Sylvia entered, Ida noticed that the pallor of her face was even greater than that of her own.

"What is it, Ida?" said the younger girl with an ill-concealed petulance. "I should be eternally grateful if you would leave me alone these days. I just want to be by myself and have nobody to worry me about anything. I just don't feel up to it. I'm fed to the teeth with everything—and everybody."

"I am sorry, Sylvia," said Ida, with gentle sympathy. "I feel intensely sorry for you, if you only knew it. But I want to ask you something, and I want you also to credit me with the best possible intentions for asking. Promise me you will, for the sake of all of us. Remember that I am suffering with you."

Sylvia looked up half-angrily.

"Really, I haven't the least idea what you mean, Ida, or even what you're talking about. Please be more explicit."

Ida shut her lips, and when she spoke her tone was distinctly harder and much less sympathetic.

"I will be explicit, since you have demanded so plainly that I should be. In a very short time I shall have a visit by the commissioner of police and a detective he is bringing with him, the kind of man, I am given to understand, who would worm secrets from the Sphinx. He will ask me questions, Sylvia. That is bound to happen—you know that well enough. I want to answer those questions frankly and truthfully. To be able to do that I want you to help me. I think you must know what I mean by now."

Ida's glance held the other girl questioningly. This time Sylvia's reply held a strong note of indignation.

"I'm sure I don't, Ida. I asked you to be explicit. I don't think you have been yet. Please explain more fully."

"Very well, I will. When I asked you to lead Red Ringan in on that dreadful Wednesday afternoon, I formed the opinion that you were very worried about something. There was nothing wonderful in my thinking so, because it must have been obvious to others besides myself. You not only looked ill, but you behaved and acted as though you were. Tell me what was troubling you, dear, and please believe that I have no desire to hurt you when I ask. In fact, all I wish to do is to help you."

Sylvia's eyes still flashed with a strong suggestion of defiance.

"You're making a mountain out of a molehill, Ida. If I did happen to be a little upset that day, what's it got to do with daddy's murder? Please don't be absurd. It's too absolutely—"

"We don't know what had to do with daddy's murder, but Sir Austin Kemble and his friend will be bound to want to know most things. They'll ask us all sorts of questions. What had happened to upset you?"

Sylvia tossed her head and frowned.

"*Must* you know? Is it so frightfully vital?"

Ida Maitland rose and, going across to her, placed a sympathetic hand on the girl's white arm.

"Do trust me, Sylvia, darling. Tell me all and let me judge of its importance or otherwise. Then I can take the responsibility of it all."

Sylvia squared her shoulders and made up her mind. "Look here, Ida, since you're so desperately persistent, I will tell you.

I can see that nothing else will satisfy you and you won't let me alone until I do. But first of all, play the game with me and I'll play it with you." She looked her stepmother straight in the eyes and the look held a strangely searching quality. "Why did daddy say he had gone to South Africa? Tell me, Ida, tell me truthfully! Have you any idea why he should have said that? Personally I can't—"

Ida's eyes showed wonderment as she gestured a denial.

"No, Sylvia, none. I can only tell you what he told me. I can't do any more than that, can I? All he said was that urgent business summoned him back there. He said he had not a minute to waste. There was a boat sailing at once and that he simply must catch it. He didn't even mention the boat's name. I can't tell you any more than that. I shan't be able to tell Sir Austin Kemble or his friend any more than that. I wish I could," she concluded simply. "I realize how bare and hopeless it sounds to tell anybody that."

Sylvia nodded in agreement.

"You've been frank with me, Ida. Now I'll be frank with you. I was worried over Nigel. Daddy had been on his hind legs about him the night before the day he was supposed to have gone away. He insisted that I should absolutely finish with him and never see him any more. It was awful. He said terrible things and kicked up an awful fuss. I think he wanted me to marry some old aristocrat and become the Countess of Somewhere or Something."

"That's just what I thought had been happening, although your father said nothing to me about it. I wasn't approached on the matter at all. Tell me, Sylvia, what was your answer?"

"I refused point-blank of course. I wasn't going to stand for that or take it lying down either. I stood up to daddy. I think he realized that he was the father of his daughter for about the first time in his life. It seems dreadful to think of, now that he's been taken from us. But what could I do, Ida? I couldn't possibly let Nigel down. It would have been too caddish for anything. Ask yourself. What could I do?"

"I don't see that you could have done anything beyond what you did do." Ida's assent came slowly, as though she were giving the matter the full weight of her consideration. "How did the matter end?" she asked.

"As most such things did when daddy couldn't get his own way. He just raved and carried on hideously and stormed out of the room. You ought to know that, Ida, better than any of us, without asking me. All great men do it, I believe."

Ida winced at the subtle thrust in her stepdaughter's words.

"He was hot-tempered, I know, Sylvia, and very, very impulsive. But his hot temper soon passed and he quickly cooled down. 'Small showers last long, but sudden storms are short,'" she quoted. "It was very true in your father's case. His 'violent fires' soon 'burned out themselves.' You never saw him again, Sylvia, after that?"

Sylvia bowed her head.

"I never saw him again. Now perhaps you are able to guess how dreadful I feel over it all." She burst into uncontrollable tears. "I wish I could go miles and miles away and get out and away from everything. I think that's the only way in which I could gain any comfort."

Ida Maitland, stronger and better-disciplined, let her tears have their way unchecked. She knew that they would bring some measure of consolation. Then she put another question to the white-faced girl.

"Tell me something else, Sylvia. I feel that I must ask you the question: Did you tell Captain Lumsden about what your father had said to you?"

Sylvia showed signs of hesitation before she answered the question.

"Yes," she conceded at length. "I will be perfectly frank, Ida. I told Nigel nearly everything daddy had said to me. But I don't think he was at all worried about it, if that's what you mean. Nigel isn't the one to crumple up at the first sign of opposition. Actually he was very bucked at the attitude I had taken against daddy. It wasn't everybody who had the pluck to stand up to daddy when he was on the ramp. You hadn't—for one." A spice of spitefulness garnished her last sentence.

"My position was different from yours, Sylvia. Surely you can see that? It shouldn't be very difficult for you at all events. It is easier to be a successful daughter than a successful wife. The atmosphere is not so electric, for one thing." A spot of colour burned in her cheek.

"I don't see how you can describe me as successful, after what I've just told you. I should have thought I was pretty unsuccessful."

"When did you tell Nigel about the matter?"

"On the same evening. He called round here about half-past nine."

There was a tap at the door and Copeland entered at Ida's behest.

"Sir Austin Kemble and a Mr. Anthony Bathurst to see you, madam. I am to ask if it is convenient."

"Show them in here, Copeland, will you? Sylvia, you stay in here with me. Don't worry, darling, and keep as cool as you can. I'm sure everything will come right in the end. Leave most of the talking to me."

As she spoke, they heard Copeland's voice outside the room.

CHAPTER XII

SIR AUSTEN bent over Mrs. Maitland's hand in his best stage manner and gently patted Sylvia's. Mr. Bathurst remained an interested spectator of the two attitudes, prior to Sir Austin's introduction. That effected, he took quiet and unobtrusive stock of the two ladies before him. "Young and pretty, the pair of 'em," he decided. The commissioner was quick to smooth over the preliminaries and as tactfully and as delicately as he could told Mrs. Maitland all that Mr. Bathurst had previously indicated as expedient for her and Sylvia to know.

"Now, Bathurst," he concluded, "I believe you want to ask Mrs. Maitland one or two questions. I am sure that she will do her best to tell you all that she knows and that you won't worry her unnecessarily."

Ida murmured her acquiescence. Mr. Bathurst bowed his appreciation.

"Mrs. Maitland, I understand from Sir Austin that your husband received an urgent message from somewhere or somebody summoning him to South Africa. Can you tell me when and how that message was delivered and how it reached him?"

"It must have come some time on the Monday before the Derby was run. But I don't know how he got it."

"Can you be certain as to its coming on Monday?"

"To this extent I can, Mr. Bathurst. On the morning in question, my husband was discussing the Derby with me—you know, stable intentions and so on. I am certain that there was no idea of going away in his mind then. I received a message from him very late on the Monday night."

"How? By letter?"

"No, by telephone."

"To here?"

"To this house."

"Anything more than the fact that he was called away so urgently?"

"Yes, instructions to tell his guests about it and to apologize to them for his absence. We were holding an eve of the Derby party on the following night. He remembered it and told me to tell them of his sudden departure."

"Nothing else?"

She thought hard for a moment.

"I don't think so." Then she corrected herself. "Yes, there was. He said that he hadn't a moment to lose if he wanted to catch the boat."

"Did he mention the name of the boat?"

"No, Mr. Bathurst."

"What time was this telephone call, Mrs. Maitland?"

"I should think about half-past eleven. Copeland could tell you better than I perhaps."

"Copeland?"

"The butler. I had sent him in here for something when the call came through. He came to tell me about it. He probably heard some of my conversation at the beginning."

"I see. So that Copeland could confirm the time. That should prove very useful to us. But at any rate there is no doubt that it was getting late. Now, Mrs. Maitland, have you any idea—any shadowy glimmering of an idea—as to what it was that could have called your husband away with such unexpectedness—with such tragic unexpectedness?"

"Only what I have said already. Only what he told me, that he was called away on a most urgent matter of business. South Africa, of course, was his home."

"Didn't you press him at all? I mean this. The whole thing was so totally unexpected, wasn't it? You, I take it, were overwhelmed with surprise and astonishment. You knew also your husband's tremendous desire to win the Derby and the wonderful chance he had of doing it. Didn't you demand to know more? It seems to me—"

"I had no opportunity to do so, Mr. Bathurst. That is just the impression that I had in my mind all the time he was telephoning. I was eager to know, but I had no chance. My husband rang off almost immediately." She gave her answer very simply and very directly and Sir Austin felt certain that it was true.

"H'm I see." Mr. Bathurst considered the reply for a brief period and then: "What was the last occasion, Mrs. Maitland, upon which you actually saw your husband alive?"

"On Monday morning."

"Was he in his usual frame of mind—in his usual spirits? Quite cheerful and so on?"

"Yes. I should say so."

"If I asked you what was uppermost in his mind on that Monday morning—business or the coming big race—which would you say?"

Ida frowned at what she considered a strange question.

"The Derby, Mr, Bathurst. The Derby, undoubtedly."

"Did your husband discuss it with you?"

"Partly. As I said, he was much more inclined to talk about that those days than anything else."

"Was it just a general discussion, Mrs. Maitland, or did it have any particular significance?"

"Just talk about our two horses and the campaign we intended to pursue with them at Epsom."

"Anything else?"

"I don't think so," she replied very slowly. "Oh, I know, he mentioned one or two of the big sweeps, I fancy."

Anthony watched her carefully, and decided to examine the question.

"Anything particular in regard to any of them?"

"Oh, yes, he intended to attempt to buy a half-share of the Red Ringan ticket in the Calcutta—at least, I think he said a half-share."

"That's very interesting, Mrs. Maitland, but, of course, a very natural inclination on his part. No doubt he fancied his horse's chance very considerably. Did he know who held the ticket? Can you answer that?"

"Yes, I can, as it happens. The Red Ringan ticket was held by Alec Pollock, the Baverstock trainer."

"Baverstock?" queried Anthony. "Isn't that the training stable adjoining your own stable at Queensleigh?"

"That is so, Mr. Bathurst."

"And what about your own horse, Mrs. Maitland? Was he going to purchase a share in that ticket? Did he know who had drawn it?"

"No. I asked him your question myself. We didn't expect her to beat Red Ringan, you see."

"I see. You thought your horse had no chance. Well, Mrs. Maitland, you will forgive me being so meticulously explicit, but I keep fairly well informed concerning most things. Wasn't it the intention of your people to reserve Princess Alicia for the Oaks? I seem to remember that the sporting papers foreshadowed it."

"You are quite right, Mr. Bathurst. That was so. But the Princess belonged to me, you see. I decided to run her in the Derby eventually."

"When did you come to that decision?"

"Is that frightfully important, Mr. Bathurst?"

"You must admit, Mrs. Maitland, in the light of after events, that it was a fortunate decision?"

"I'll be perfectly frank with you, Mr. Bathurst. I can see that it will be no good being anything else. It was when I knew my husband had gone away. I took the responsibility then myself. You see, it was like this. I loved my horse and I wanted her to take her chance. I knew that with Julius away nobody could dispute my decision. So I ran her. That's all there was in it. I was on my own, as it were, you see."

"So that the original decision not to run Princess Alicia in the Derby was against your judgment? Would it be true to say that?"

There was a slight hesitation on the part of Mrs. Maitland before she brought herself to reply.

"Hardly against my judgment, Mr. Bathurst. I don't know that I could agree with that statement. I would alter the word to obtain a truer version. I would say against my desire rather— against my inclination."

"You had discussed it with your husband, of course?"

"Naturally. At least two or three times."

"And you had agreed? You had come—?"

Mrs. Maitland bowed.

"We had agreed. There was no—"

"Thank you, Mrs. Maitland." Anthony turned to the younger girl. "I presume that you are unable to help us in any way, Miss Maitland? You can add nothing to what we have been told?"

Sylvia shook her head.

"I am afraid that I can add nothing at all, Mr. Bathurst. The news that my father had been summoned to South Africa came as a complete surprise and shock to me. At the time when it came, I wouldn't have dreamed of such a thing. I have no idea whatever what it was that took him there so unexpectedly. My father had not confided in me with regard to matters affecting his business for some time."

"I am sorry to be compelled to ask you what necessarily in the circumstances must be a very painful question. When did you last see your father alive?"

Sylvia pressed a handkerchief to her eyes. When she spoke, her voice seemed curiously dry and husky.

"At breakfast time on Monday morning."

"You noticed nothing unusual about him—either in mood or in appearance?"

"No, Mr. Bathurst, I can't say that I did. I think he appeared to me to be just as usual. But I noticed that one of the letters that he received by that morning's post interested him a great deal. I don't know whether—"

"How do you know that, Miss Maitland?"

"Because of this, Mr. Bathurst. I observed that my father read it and reread it several times. That was unusual with him. He usually read a letter and then pushed it to one side."

Mrs. Maitland intervened with a suggestion of assistance.

"That was the letter he had about the ticket holders in the sweeps. What I mentioned to you, Mr. Bathurst. I can help you there. My husband told me so. The letter was from a Mr. Dawson, a friend of my husband's at Talehurst. But I think my husband's interest in the letter was only natural and very genuine."

Mr. Bathurst nodded his head in complete agreement with her.

"No doubt you are right, Mrs. Maitland. Doubtless that was the information to which you say he referred afterward. At any rate, I think we should be quite justified, at this stage of the case, in thinking so. Would you mind me having a few words with the butler?"

"I was about to suggest exactly the same thing, Bathurst," interposed Sir Austin. "It struck me when he admitted us that it was just possible he would be able to assist us. He was probably pretty close to his master. Send for him, Mrs. Maitland, will you, please?"

"As you wish, Sir Austin. But"—she shook her head very doubtfully—"I don't see where Copeland can help us over anything here."

When he came Copeland presented a dignified figure.

He explained that his master's death had been a very great blow to him. His master had always treated him splendidly. There were very few better masters. He was able to confirm the fact that he heard Mrs. Maitland talking to Mr. Maitland on the phone late on the Monday evening. Then, in reply to one of Mr. Bathurst's usual questions, he was able to answer in such a way that the latter sat up immediately and took notice.

"Yes, sir. I can definitely state, sir, without any fear of contradiction whatever, sir, that on the Monday morning in question my master received a letter that gave him a severe shock. I am certain of my ground, sir."

Mr. Bathurst regarded him critically.

"I should be very pleased to hear more, and why you are so sure of what you say."

"I shall be very pleased to supply the whole of the facts, sir. About eleven thirty on Monday morning, a letter was handed in for Mr. Maitland. It did not come through the usual channels of the postal authorities, sir. It was delivered by hand, sir."

"Handed in by whom, Copeland?"

"By a lady, sir."

"Go on, Copeland."

"Mrs. Maitland was with the master, sir, when I gave it to him. She will, I am sure, be able to confirm what I am saying in respect of this."

Mr. Bathurst looked across at the lady for the corroboration.

"That is quite true, Copeland. But my husband did not open the letter in my presence, so I can't say anything beyond that."

"No, ma'am. That is obvious, ma'am."

"One minute, Copeland," put in Anthony. "If neither of you saw Mr. Maitland open this letter, which I understand was the case, how do you, Copeland, come to say that it upset him so?"

"I will tell you, sir." Copeland was unruffled and imperturbable. "If I may say so, sir, I anticipated your question. After all, these matters are a question of intelligence. I will tell you why I made the statement that I did. I happened to come into Mr. Maitland about half an hour afterward, sir. That is to say, half an hour after the letter was delivered. He was in an extreme state of agitation and a letter was in his hand. On the table close by where he was sitting was the identical envelope which I had conveyed to him previously. I deduced, sir, that it contained bad news—or, at least, unpleasant news."

Sir Austin caught Mr. Bathurst's eye and had great difficulty in repressing a chuckle. But he remembered the nature of the inquiry and the personnel of those present and pulled himself up just in time. He blew his nose to cover his emotions.

"Excellent, Copeland, excellent! You didn't see the letter, of course?"

"I imagine Mr. Maitland took it with him, sir. It wasn't here when I returned. But at the same time that I saw my master reading it—agitated-like—I noticed something else. Another document. It was as though he kept looking from one to the other."

"Referring to them, do you mean? Do you suggest that they had some connection?"

Copeland looked puzzled.

"I wouldn't go as far as to say that, sir. I would suggest, sir, very respectfully, of course, because it's not my place to make suggestions, that the two things were on his mind—the letter I took in to him and the other document. But that isn't to say that they had any connection of themselves. To say that would be going too far."

Mr. Bathurst remained silent for a moment or two as he turned over in his mind this new phase of the investigation. But Sir Austin Kemble, who had—for him—been very silent, came to the point immediately.

"What was—er—the precise nature of this other document, Copeland? Did you happen to set eyes on it by any chance? Or was it impossible for you to do so?"

Copeland coughed. It is just on the cards that the cough contained a fugitive hint at apology.

"Now that you have obtained the information that I have given you, sir, I will admit that I did catch a glance of this other communication. Just the merest glimpse—quite by accident. It was the draw for the Calcutta sweep. On it were the names of the horses, the numbers of the tickets that had been successful in drawing horses, and a list of people's names with their nom de plumes. I presume that they were the names of the ticket holders."

"I see. Quite an ordinary and natural communication to Mr. Maitland, taking into consideration the time and the attendant circumstances. Certainly nothing of a sinister or fear-provoking nature."

Mr. Bathurst awoke from his seeming reverie and became alert once again: "Can you remember, Copeland, if all the horses' names figured in this list of which you speak—or only some? Did it appear to be a complete list, estimating it roughly from the size of it? There are always a good many horses drawn, you know."

"I can not say, sir. I should say not, sir. The only names that I could positively assert were there, sir, insomuch as I saw them, were those of our own two horses—the two trained at Queensleigh. I certainly did glance at those, sir, as I stood by the table awaiting Mr. Maitland's instructions. Red Ringan had been drawn by a person named Pollock. I can not remember the name of the holder of the Princess Alicia ticket. The name was unfamiliar to me and the memory of it has escaped me."

"I suppose there would be no chance of your memory returning, Copeland?"

"I am afraid not, sir. My memory for names is not of the best, sir, I regret to say. If I may say so, sir, without appearing to be vainglorious, I have a really excellent memory for faces, but not for names or dates. Gifts are varied, sir."

"Taking you at your own assessment then, Copeland, please describe the lady that brought the letter to Mr. Maitland about which you have told us. That is, of course, if you saw her yourself. Did you take the letter in yourself?"

"I did see her, sir. The lady was tall, handsome, with very dark hair—almost black, in fact. Aged about—"

He pulled himself up, then continued:

"Very difficult to say, sir. The question of a lady's age is very awkward. But it was in the morning and I have had considerable experience of the best society, and allowing for the judicious use of cosmetics, I should say about the fifties, but I would not make the statement with too much confidence. I would be prepared to hear anything."

"Thank you, Copeland. I don't think I want to ask you anything else at the moment. Do you, Sir Austin? Or you, Mrs. Maitland?"

Neither did and Copeland withdrew. The door shut and with the sound of the man's footsteps retreating, Anthony spoke across to the woman who had been so suddenly widowed.

"You have observed, of course, Mrs. Maitland, what Copeland said about the Calcutta draw. Did your husband happen to tell you by any chance who was the lucky holder of the Princess Alicia ticket? I am not sure whether you answered that question just now. According to yesterday's press, there is no certainty even now as to the actual possessor of the ticket. Is there, Sir Austin?"

"I believe not, Bathurst. According to my information, the ticket was bought as one of a batch of five hundred by a Johannesburg firm of brokers. Most of the tickets were resold, I believe, anywhere, and everywhere. They are trying to trace the Princess Alicia one, but up to the moment I understand they are still uncertain as to the owner."

Mrs. Maitland waited for the commissioner to finish before she replied to the question that Mr. Bathurst had put to her.

"I am able to answer you quite clearly, Mr. Bathurst. But I'm very much afraid that my answer isn't going to help you very much. Because I was curious to know who had drawn my horse, I asked my husband if he knew—if his letter from Mr. Dawson had told him. He told me no quite emphatically. He told me he only knew the holders of what he described as the important tickets. It's a strange thing, but I asked him particularly, so I am very certain of the point."

For the second time since he entered the present arena as a combatant, Mr. Bathurst rubbed his hands momentarily mastered by the excitement of the exigencies of the case.

"Is that so, Mrs. Maitland? Is that so?" he permitted himself to remark. "Now that's distinctly interesting. Don't you think so, Sir Austin?"

The commissioner nodded with an air of solemnity, but he was careful to add nothing as his own contribution. He sought refuge in the safety of silence.

Ten minutes afterward, as Mr. Bathhurst very carefully guided the primrose-wheeled Crossley through the traffic congestion round Hyde Park Corner, he jerked a question over his shoulder to Sir Austin Kemble sitting behind.

"What strikes you as the most remarkable feature of this case, sir? Have you given it much thought?"

The commissioner pondered for a moment before he replied. Bathhurst had a deuced unpleasant knack of asking awkward questions. Eventually he burnt his boats:

"Finding Maitland's body at Friningham, I think, Bathhurst. I can't account for its presence there at all. Don't you agree with me?"

"I'm afraid I don't sir. I'll tell you what strikes me as being a most extraordinary occurrence. When Sergeant Mansfield gets the S.O.S. call from Ravenswood presumably Maitland was alive. Events were certainly pointing to the assumption. At any rate, the sergeant was quite justified in thinking so. Now, mark you, when he gets to the place from where the call came and finds the dead man, the doctor chap—Forsyth, I think that was his name—is prepared to swear on oath that the man there has been dead two whole days. And the man is Maitland, mind you. Forsyth has assured me on the time point, and he won't hear of contradiction. In fact, he told me he was willing to stake his whole medical reputation on the question. And what is more, to my own personal satisfaction I haven't the shred of a doubt myself. Now, Sir Austin, do you see at what I'm driving?"

Sir Austin knitted his brows.

"I think I do, Bathhurst. You are alluding to Mrs. Maitland's statement that—"

"Exactly, sir. That her husband telephoned her at half-past eleven on the Monday night. According to Doctor Forsyth and all that medical science has taught him, he should have been dead seven or eight hours by then. We are confronted therefore by a most extraordinarily peculiar set of circumstances. The man is dead (according to the doctor), then alive (according to the widow), alive two days afterward (according to the sergeant), and then dead again (according to both doctor and sergeant). An exceedingly interesting little problem, Sir Austin, and one that I find—" Mr. Bathurst stopped the car dexterously for his distinguished passenger to alight. "I think I'll sleep on it, Sir Austin. I think that will be the best treatment to give it. But before that come in and have a spot."

Sir Austin rose from his seat with enthusiasm.

CHAPTER XIII

"I HAVE two fields to explore, Sir Austin. Say when, will you? That do? Have a splash with it?" Mr. Bathurst passed the siphon. "The two fields are these. You remember that the dead man had an appointment on Monday afternoon, don't you?"

"Yes. According to the terms of a letter that Sergeant Mansfield found on him, wasn't it?"

"Yes. That letter was from a firm of solicitors—Barraclough, Laurence and Tolworthy, a London firm, of Basinghall Street. They're going to be my field number one."

"Sounds as though I'm back in the service," grinned the commissioner. "But I certainly agree with your idea, Bathurst. It might lead to something, especially if Maitland kept the appointment."

"I think so. I'll have a word or two on the phone with a man I know who's in much the same line—in Cornhill. Peter Daventry—I've mentioned him to you probably more than once. He's a good boy and he'd do anything for me."

"Good. And what's your second line of country?"

"Queensleigh!" returned Mr. Bathurst with very definite emphasis. "Queensleigh and the Queensleigh district, the home of Maitland's horses, his trainer, perhaps his jockey." He rose to his feet and paced the room excitedly. "I cannot rid myself of the conviction, Sir Austin, that the key to the problem will be found down there somewhere. The idea is fast becoming a certainty to me. There's been some dark intrigue going on that had a turf significance which for the moment I can't fathom. I can only grasp and grope at it. My data are insufficient. But I shall lay my hand on the crux of the question eventually and then we shall see, sir."

"Which field are you exploring first, Bathurst? Do you intend to—"

"I incline to the three legal gentlemen, I think, sir. They're nearer to hand for one thing."

"Very well. Go to see them by all means as early as possible. When you run down to Wiltshire, I'll come with you. Don't forget to keep me posted."

That night Anthony Bathurst did as he had indicated to Sir Austin Kemble—he slept on the problem of Julius Maitland's murder—but he turned it over very thoroughly in his mind before sleep would come to him. He slept on them that night and all day Sunday.

Basinghall Street, the following morning, was quickly reached in the Crossley and shortly after his arrival there Mr. Bathurst was in the uninspiring presence of the founder of the firm, Mr. Tobias Barraclough. Peter Daventry's information over the telephone had been to the effect that Barraclough, Laurence & Tolworthy was a pretty sound firm, a trifle old-fashioned, perhaps, but nevertheless possessing a reputation in legal circles that was unblemished as far as he himself knew. No breath of suspicion had ever been wafted over them as far as he was aware. Certainly nothing of the kind had ever reached him. But beyond these general impressions of the firm's standing, he knew nothing. Mr. Barraclough appeared to Anthony to be a typical old-time solicitor, almost Victorian both in method and appearance. Slow, unimaginative, prosaic, but beyond doubt a "safe" man and eminently reliable, a man who could be trusted to handle the most delicate of matters with profound discretion.

He handled Sir Austin Kemble's card on this occasion in a similar manner, obviously impressed but at the same time reluctant to admit anything of the kind. Anthony had made use of the card (containing his own name as well) designedly.

"Mr. Bathurst, I think you said?" Barraclough queried. His was the manner of a precisian and he came to no sudden decision.

"That is so, Mr. Barraclough, and I will not waste your time. As you will have inferred by now, I have called to see you in reference to the unfortunate death of Mr. Julius Maitland."

Mr. Barraclough sat back in his very comfortable chair, took a pair of old-fashioned spectacles from the breast pocket of his coat and carefully adjusted them upon his nose. Then he essayed a slight cough.

"Ah, yes. Um! I did wonder if that were the *raison d'être* of your visit. The fact of the commissioner of—er—police being concerned—" He paused and tapped the card with the rim of a finger nail.

Mr. Bathurst lost no time:

"I believe I am correct in stating that the deceased gentleman was a client of yours?"

"You are, Mr. Bathurst."

"And that he either had an interview with you on Monday afternoon or that he should have had such an interview? That one had been arranged?"

Mr. Barraclough was silent for a while, a silence which Mr. Bathurst respected and possibly understood. At length the solicitor answered the question.

"He had the interview you state, but not quite at the time."

"May I ask you upon what subject was the interview? You will remember, Mr. Barraclough, that, as far as can be seen at the moment, it is a case of murder that is being investigated. Therefore I am forced to ask."

Mr. Barraclough pursed his lips very properly.

"I think I am in a position to appreciate that. I quite see that there is a certain urgency. But you must let me think things over for a minute."

The minute passed.

"I must ask you to allow me to consult one of my partners. It is only right that I should."

He pressed a bell. To the tall handsome young man with the somewhat dissipated features who answered the summons he spoke very quietly.

"Mr. Cruden, be good enough to ask Mr. Tolworthy to come to me in here, will you? Tell him that I am not alone and that I wish to see him on a matter of grave importance."

"Cruden?" said Mr. Bathurst upon the young man's departure. "You will pardon me, I feel sure, Mr. Barraclough, but was I right in catching the name of your clerk as Cruden? Any relation to the late Mr. Maitland's trainer by chance?"

"Son," was the laconic reply. "But here's my partner, Mr. Tolworthy."

Mr. Tolworthy was tall and thin, with a dried-up appearance suggestive of many years spent in a country like India. But he looked, despite his liver, just as safe and as reliable as his senior.

"This is Mr. Anthony Bathurst, Tolworthy," said Mr. Barraclough. "His business is in connection with the late Mr. Julius Maitland. He has applied to me for certain information and represents the commissioner of police at Scotland Yard. Upon consideration—and very, very careful consideration at that—I have decided to answer the question that he has asked me. If he asks me any more, I may answer him—or, on the other hand, I may not. I must be discreet. We have always been that. But I have sent for you, as a member of the firm, because I wish you to be present to hear my answers. I have no liking for taking risks."

Mr. Tolworthy blinked, showed definite signs of surprise, but intimated by a quick jerk of the head that he had thoroughly assimilated what Mr. Barraclough had said and was in agreement with his ideas.

"In reply then to your first question, Mr. Bathurst," the latter went on, "Mr. Maitland called here on Monday morning in reference to the purchase of a bungalow at Friningham. The name of the bungalow was Ravenswood and its address was Pin Hole Way. You realize the importance of my statement."

This time it was Anthony Bathurst's turn to express surprise. He immediately translated his amazement into words.

"Where he was eventually found murdered?"

Mr. Barraclough inclined his head in grave assent.

"Exactly. That was my meaning. Perhaps I had better explain the position a little more fully. It would, I think, help matters considerably. Some four or five months ago, Mr. Maitland called upon me here—I forget what about for the moment. But the call was ordinary and quite in the nature of everyday business. When he was here, he met another client of mine. In the course of conversation—quite a commonplace, everyday sort of conversation, just as I said—this other gentleman happened to mention that he had a very charming bungalow for sale down at Friningham. Just as it stood—with furniture complete. He told Mr. Maitland so. I remember the incident quite well. On Monday morning, Mr. Maitland phoned me to know if the bungalow that had been mentioned before were still on the market. I told him I would inquire as to the fact and would acquaint him as soon as I possibly could. I did so. The offer was still open. I made an appointment with him for the afternoon, sending the letter round to him by hand. But he came round to the office here almost at once. The afternoon, he said, was inconvenient to him, as he had another important engagement. He bought the bungalow—Mr. Ponsonby was quite agreeable to immediate possession—took the keys which I had procured for him and—well, that was the last I saw of him. Or ever shall see, I very much regret to say."

Mr. Bathurst caressed his cheek with his long, supple fingers. Here was evidently a great deal of food for thought. But his intervention was rapid.

"Who delivered your letter?"

"One of our junior clerks."

"Did Maitland say why he wanted to buy it? Any particular reason?"

"None at all."

"He seems to have been summoned to South Africa according to all my other information."

"From whom, may I ask, Mr. Bathurst, does that information come?"

"From his widow. He telephoned to her late on Monday evening. It is confirmed by the butler. He overheard some of the conversation that took place. So there is no doubt on the point. Why do you ask?"

"I merely wondered, that was all."

Anthony looked at him very shrewdly. His next question to the solicitor indicated what was passing through his mind.

"Did Mr. Maitland say anything to you which would make you regard the South African project as surprising?"

Mr. Barraclough removed his spectacles, wiped the glass very carefully and then equally carefully replaced them. As was usual with him following upon this operation, he coughed.

"I would rather not answer that question. I have not sufficient knowledge. To do so might savor of an injustice to his memory. To build edifices of opinion upon the foundation of a chance word spoken here and there, or upon a stray sentence spoken perhaps at random, would be egregiously unfair. You appreciate my point of view, Mr. Bathurst, I am sure."

Anthony felt that the time had come to let loose his heavy ammunition.

"When Mr. Maitland reopened the question of the sale of this bungalow, I take it that you got into communication with your other client, Mr. Ponsonby, at once?"

"We did. But I was not aware that you knew Mr. Ponsonby by name."

"I heard it mentioned down in Friningham. He was quite willing to sell, of course?"

"Quite. Mr. Maitland gave him the price for which he was asking. It was a pretty stiff price, too."

"You imply that Mr. Maitland wanted above all to get hold of the bungalow? He was determined to get it?"

"No, not altogether. Mr. Maitland was a very rich man. And he was not a parsimonious man, as many rich men are. From my knowledge of him as his solicitor, I should say he rarely, if ever, haggled over a price. It was customary for him to ask a price and pay it." Mr. Barraclough coughed again—a little nervously perhaps—and proceeded. "It is now my turn, Mr. Bathurst, to ask you a question. I am going to assume, with your permission, the role of inquisitor. You said something just now that Ravenswood belonged to Mr. Ponsonby?"

Anthony's eyes met his steadily and unwaveringly.

"From Mr. Vivian Maitland, Mr. Barraclough."

The latter gentleman's eyes narrowed perceptibly as he considered this last piece of information.

"Mr. Vivian Maitland? I had no idea—"

He broke off abruptly and looked at Tolworthy questioningly. But apparently his partner was unable to help him. Suddenly Mr. Barraclough's face cleared.

"Of course. I can see what happened. Mr. Maitland, no doubt, informed his son that he had purchased the bungalow from Mr. Ponsonby. That is the explanation. For the moment I was a little—"

"I think not, Mr. Barraclough." Mr. Bathurst's tone was both cold and decided.

"You think not? I don't quite—"

"I don't think the son was informed by the father, as you suggest. If he were, it places him in a rather awkward position. Don't you agree with me?"

Mr. Barraclough raised his eyebrows a little superciliously.

"You mean—"

"I mean this. To know that Ponsonby owned Ravenswood is a perfectly innocent piece of knowledge—*per se*. But to know of it in connection with his father and remembering that his father's dead body was found there might conceivably be proved to be guilty knowledge. You see what I mean, don't you? Mind you, I merely use the word 'might.' Like you, Mr. Barraclough, I must be careful what I say. But the knowledge, coming from the source that you suggest, definitely places Vivian Maitland in a certain circle. I won't say within a circle of suspicion, because that at this stage of the case would be going too far. For instance, that same circle—we will call it a circle of tangibility—would include you, Mr. Barraclough, you, Mr. Tolworthy, your Mr. Laurence, if there be a Mr. Laurence, your clerk, perhaps, Mr. Cruden—" Mr. Bathurst paused for a moment to let his words sink in and then continued: "And of course any friends or acquaintances of yours or theirs to whom the information might have been imparted."

Mr. Barraclough showed no signs of disturbance and accepted the situation as Anthony had described it with complete imperturbability.

"I cannot contradict you, Mr. Bathurst, because to do so would be not only absurd but illogical. I hope that I am never either."

Anthony smiled and rose from his chair.

"You must allow me to thank you, Mr. Barraclough, for your kindness and consideration. I have only one other favour to ask you. Can you give me Mr. Ponsonby's address? You will understand that it is now imperative for me to see him."

"Mr. Ponsonby's address is the Copper Beeches, Wokingham, Berkshire. It is a few miles from Reading, I believe. You will find him a very charming man, Mr. Bathurst."

The forty miles or so to Wokingham were quickly disposed of by the Crossley, and Mr. Bathurst eventually pulled up before a very comfortable-looking hotel for lunch. It bore the somewhat unusual sign of "Ye Olde Wilde Honeysuckle," but its cuisine was of the very best. A Clover Club as a preliminary put him on good terms with himself, and a very appetizing portion of cold roast duckling, garnished with a most uncommonly delectable stuffing, put him on even better. In fact, the stuffing was so strikingly excellent that Mr. Bathurst prosecuted inquiries as to its composition and made a note for future reference—chopped chicken liver with breadcrumbs, butter, the yolks of two eggs, eschalots, parsley, thyme, salt, pepper and nutmeg. A cigarette over a black coffee completed a miniature meal that in its way was commendably good, and shortly afterward Anthony was ushered into Mr. Ponsonby's library, feeling at peace with the entire world.

Mr. Ponsonby expressed his most sincere grief at the tragic circumstances surrounding the death of Mr. Maitland. Of course he felt implicated. That is, to a certain extent, having sold his bungalow to the dead man so shortly before his death. It was extremely difficult for him to picture his bungalow in such a terrible setting.

Mr. Bathurst then put the question concerning which he had felt it so imperative to undertake the journey: "Could you, Mr. Ponsonby, tell me if you have ever negotiated with either of the late Mr. Maitland's sons concerning the purchase of the bungalow?"

"Answering your question, Mr. Bathurst, in the form in which you have put it, no."

Anthony smiled at him.

"Please enlighten me. I am sure you mean to—"

"I have never negotiated with either of the sons about purchasing Ravenswood. That was exactly, I think, what you asked me, wasn't it? But I let Ravenswood to young Mr. Vivian Maitland some short time ago. That, you will admit, is a slightly different matter."

"When? Could you say?"

Mr. Ponsonby's brows furrowed in thought. He appeared to be making a calculation.

"At the latter end of March or the beginning of April, not long after Lady Day."

"Did he apply to you or did you approach him?"

"He applied to me. I let it to him for a fortnight. Furnished just as it was—and is now, I suppose."

"Why did he want it? Do you know?"

Ponsonby shrugged a pair of irresponsible shoulders.

"I didn't inquire. The bungalow was standing empty, and when he asked if I would let it to him for a fortnight, I couldn't see any good reason why I shouldn't. He paid me very handsomely for the use of it."

Mr. Bathurst thought that remark over very many times on his journey back to London. But why had Vivian Maitland stayed in Friningham for a fortnight? In the very residence where subsequently his father was found murdered? Was it a coincidence or was it—?

CHAPTER XIV

THE ELEVEN o'clock restaurant-car train out of Waterloo was comfortably empty, so that it was a comparatively easy matter for Sir Austin Kemble and Mr. Bathurst to obtain corner seats in a first-class compartment.

"I was rather surprised to get your message, Bathurst," said Sir Austin, as he settled down at his ease. "As a matter of fact, I rather expected that you would have gone down by car. I should have enjoyed the run down and we could have lunched in Salisbury. Why didn't you go by road?"

"I have come by train on purpose, sir, deliberately and with malice aforethought. You will remember that I told you the day before yesterday that I fancied the germ of the Maitland mystery might be found in the Queensleigh district. That is why I am running down there. I have an idea at the back of my brain that we shall discover something very important that will have an immense bearing upon the crime. You will see more of what I mean when we get down there." He accepted Sir Austin's Henry Clay with a becoming gratitude. "Next to Queensleigh is Baverstock, on what I will call the Templecombe side of it. Queensleigh is about four miles or so from Tisbury. Ever had to change at Templecombe?"

"No. Why? What's its peculiar attraction?"

"None that I've ever been able to find, and I've had ample opportunities of discovery. It's one of the Southern Railway's gardens of sleep. It's a proper haven of rest, I can tell you. Ask any Shirburnian, old or present. There's one I know rather well. He was there about Arthur Carr's time, just before the war—Roger Moffat."

Sir Austin nodded his head.

"Now you mention it, I fancy I was hung up there once myself, Bathurst. I was on my way one afternoon in late October to Sidmouth. I was called in to investigate a very strange case of murder. The press called it the 'Jacob's ladder mystery.' The body of a murdered woman was found on the beach and bore peculiar abrasions on the neck and wrists. Remember it?"

Anthony shook his head disclaimingly.

"Before my real time, sir. I was at Uppingham, I think, when it happened, sir. But I believe I have a cutting of it in my news book. Wasn't the murderer a local ironmonger and a prominent bigwig?"

"Quite right, my boy. The case created a big stir at the time. He retained what d'ye call him for the defense, if you remember. But the case for the Crown was overwhelmingly clear and most admirably presented, from the point of view of the accused man, relentlessly presented. And the judge's summing up was masterly, too. The prisoner never stood an earthly. He tried to prove an alibi. To tell you what the jury thought of it, they were away exactly thirteen minutes."

"I'm always a bit worried over a murder case, Sir Austin, when the defendant puts up a defence based upon an alibi. I think that to every right-thinking man a verdict of guilty in these circumstances must be just a little disquieting, unless, of course, the alibi has been thoroughly shaken. Makes you wonder how many innocent men have gone to the scaffold. When you think of cases like those of Adolf Beck and Oscar Slater, you wonder still more."

Sir Austin cut in with some aggression.

"You needn't worry about this particular case, Bathurst. The alibi was extremely flimsy and entirely lacking in support. Even the eminent counsel who defended was afraid to push it too far. Had he done so, it would have proved double-edged. He was a master, you know, at that sort of thing. He always knew just how far to go and where to stop, which is a secret that all advocates don't appreciate. It's an art in itself. I remember when I was a subaltern in India—" and Sir Austin launched upon a lengthy vindication of his point.

Mr. Bathurst, from courtesy, listened with attention. Sir Austin warmed to his subject until he grew hot.

When they ran into Queensleigh, Mr. Bathurst was still listening. He pointed across to a siding as they entered the station.

"Horse boxes, Sir Austin. They're still preferred, you see, by most trainers to the more modern motor vans. Even, I believe, for transport over short distances."

They alighted on the gravelled platform.

"I'm not hurrying away from the station, Sir Austin. I've a mind to ask one or two questions before we leave. Do any of them know you down here?"

"I've never been here in my life, Bathurst. But don't let that worry you. I'll soon make myself known, don't you fear. These country stations can do with a bit of waking up."

He approached an official who was evidently the station master and introduced himself. The station master seemed immediately impressed. He put himself, upon the commissioner's instructions, at Mr. Bathurst's service.

"Just a few questions, station master, if you don't mind," said Anthony. "It's just a mere possibility that you may be able to help us. Were you on duty on Monday afternoon of last week?"

"What time, sir?"

"I couldn't place it with very much exactitude," returned Anthony. "But let me think for a moment. Let us say somewhere between two and six. That will give us a fairly wide margin—it should be sufficiently wide, I think." He repeated the time: "Between two o'clock and six o'clock, then."

The station master shook his head emphatically. One might have thought that he derived satisfaction from the fact that he would be unable to answer the questions that were coming.

"No, sir. I was off duty from midday that afternoon. It was my rest time. You mean Monday afternoon of Derby week, don't you, sir?"

"That's right, I do. Who, then, would have been on duty here on that particular afternoon?"

"One of the porters, sir—Underwood's his name. He's here now, if you want to see him."

"Thanks, I will. Bring him along, will you?"

The station master did as he was directed.

Underwood was a young man, strong and healthy-looking. His face matched the colour of his Southern Railway tie.

"Yesterday afternoon, sir?"

"No, my man. The afternoon of the previous Monday. I am referring to the week before this. You were on duty, so I'm informed. I want to ask you a question. Did you know the late Mr. Julius Maitland by sight?"

Underwood's face gleamed with a certain look of satisfaction.

"Very well indeed, sir. You see, he was a pretty frequent visitor down here. And very unlucky for most of us down in this quarter, sir. There's hardly a man, woman or child down here in Queensleigh that didn't 'ave a little bit on Red Ringan."

"I've no doubt about that," rejoined Mr. Bathurst.

"I expected something of the kind. Now tell me this, if you are able. Can you tell me if Mr. Maitland came to this station on the Monday afternoon in question?"

Underwood pushed his cap to the back of his head and ran his fingers through his hair. Mr. Bathurst waited for a few seconds and then continued.

"Have you read any accounts of the murder, Underwood?"

"Not what you'd call details of it, sir. I just read that he had been found dead in a bungalow at some seaside place—Friningham, wasn't it?" He again appeared to consider Anthony's first question. Eventually his face showed signs of clearing. "Now you mention it, sir, Mr. Maitland was down here that Monday afternoon. He traveled down on the one thirty-three. It's a fast train that stops here only specially if wanted. By request, that is. It was a favourite train of his, when he came down about that time of the day. I was on duty taking tickets. I remember it quite well now, sir. I'll tell you why. I've got two things that help me to recollect it. Mr. Maitland was the only first-class passenger that got out at this station the whole of that day. That's the first thing! The second thing is this. It was that afternoon—pretty late, too, at that—that young Mr. Cruden went back to town. He went up on the five twenty-eight. I put his case on the rack of his compartment for him. He had been down for a long week-end. I'm certain it was the same afternoon, because each time my thoughts went to the Derby that was to be run on the Wednesday following."

Mr. Bathurst slipped a Treasury note into the porter's willing hand.

"Thank you, Underwood. I feel sure you are right about the day. Now tell me something else. Do you happen to remember the direction Mr. Maitland took when he left this station?"

The porter pointed up the hill.

"He went straight up the hill, sir. I can tell you that for certain. There wasn't a conveyance of any sort waiting here at the station, so he had to walk."

"Is that the road that leads to the Queensleigh stable?"

"Yes, sir. At the top of the hill the road divides in a kind of fork. You go straight on for about a mile for Queensleigh. The other way—where it branches off to the right—will take you to Baverstock."

"We will take the road to the top of the hill, Sir Austin," said Mr. Bathurst, "the road that Julius Maitland took. When we get there, we will take our bearings. Thank you, Underwood, and thank you, station master. We shall probably see you again later."

"I hope to blazes you aren't going to walk me off my feet, Bathurst. I didn't come down here prepared for that. I'm not so young as I was, you know. Can't we rake up a car or something from somewhere?"

But Mr. Bathurst for once in a while was adamant. "I'm afraid a car wouldn't suit our purpose, Sir Austin," he returned. "Remember that the dead man was here just over a week ago. I want to go over the ground rather carefully and you can do that very much better walking than breezing along in a car. Unless I'm very much mistaken, Julius Maitland was not bound for his own stable at Queensleigh but on his way to see Mr. Pollock of Baverstock when he came down here that last time."

The top of the hill reached, the two men stopped and surveyed the situation. A weather-beaten and time-ravaged signpost pointed the two ways. "To Queensleigh 1 mile." "To Baverstock 2 miles."

"Now, Sir Austin," declared Anthony, "we have this to go on. We are not travelling entirely in the dark. We know that Maitland expressed to his wife on the Monday morning his desire to negotiate with Pollock, the trainer at Baverstock, for a share in the Red Ringan ticket. I think that was one of the reasons at least for bringing him down here. There may have been another—I am not quite sure yet. My ground is not so certain in that respect. But we will proceed, Sir Austin, with your permission, of course, in the direction of Baverstock."

Sir Austin grunted what may have been a remark of assent or, on the other hand, may not. It was very evident that he did not regard this Wiltshire walking tour at all favourably. How far was this confounded Baverstock, anyway? Two miles? And not a pub on the road in all probability. That would be in the nature of the last straw. His mind went disgustedly back to an experience he had known in the neighbouring county of Hampshire. On that occasion he had covered eight miles—eight, weary, slogging, dusty, monotonous miles—damned dry the whole time. He had formed the opinion then—

They had done about half a mile when an unfriendly and decidedly unwelcome milestone peeped from the recess of a ditch—"Baverstock 2 miles."

Sir Austin snorted.

"There you are," chimed Anthony, with a laugh, "we're at least holding our own! But you'll find the milestone accurate. The distances on the signposts are not. Not so bad, sir, strolling gently along as we are, taking our time. You'll hardly notice the distance at all."

Sir Austin groaned. It seemed to him that he had been cheated of half a mile.

"Oh, no. If I shut my eyes, perhaps I'll think I'm flying."

The road turned suddenly here and, with an exclamation, Mr. Bathurst stopped dead in his tracks. A big tree stood on the corner and at its side ran a hedge with a sheltered strip of grass that skirted the white road.

"Sir Austin!" he called. "Look here!"

Round about the rough stretch of grass adjoining the hedge and under the lee of the tree there were scattered seven cigarette stubs and eleven dead match ends. Anthony picked them up and counted them carefully to make sure of the exact number. He examined each one minutely.

"All the same brand of cigarette, sir."

The commissioner grunted again. "What about it?"

Mr. Bathurst whipped out a magnifying glass and extended his long body along the grass strip. After a period he rose and walked back to the road.

"It may have nothing to do, of course, with our case, Sir Austin—I realize that it's over a week since it happened—but we can't afford to neglect anything reasonable that comes within our scope. Remember, too, that a small village in an unfrequented part of the country is very different from the towns to which you and I are accustomed. A car has stopped here fairly recently and the occupant—a man, I should say—waited there for something. During his wait he smoked at least seven cigarettes."

"Nothing extraordinary in that, Bathurst, that I can see. Quite an ordinary happening for any motorist. Besides, our man Maitland wasn't in a car. Remember what the porter Underwood said. Maitland was walking."

"I wasn't thinking of Maitland, sir. It certainly wasn't he. I'm well aware of that. It might more probably be the man that killed him." Anthony smiled at Sir Austin's puzzled face.

"My dear Bathurst," said the commissioner incredulously, "I've worked with you so often that I'm fairly used to your stage-craft by now, but I'm dashed if I'm able to follow you over this. What on earth do you mean? Julius Maitland was killed at Friningham in Essex."

"He may have been, sir. It is possible, I grant you. But I wouldn't go further than that, as I read the case. For there is also the chance that he may not have been. Personally, I incline to the opinion that he was killed somewhere else and his body conveyed to the bungalow at Friningham. It seems to me that the evidence points that way. If I were forced to name a district where I think the murder was committed, I should plump for somewhere round this district where we are now. Say either in Queensleigh or in Baverstock. Or of course somewhere in between the two, but that's inclusive."

Sir Austin looked more puzzled than ever.

"And that's your real opinion, Bathurst? Well, well, I had no idea you were after such a solution as that. Such an idea, I will frankly admit, had never struck me. As to the car that you state stopped alongside here—"

A childish voice broke in upon what the commissioner was saying.

"A motor car did stop along by that hedge, sir, surely. A very nice motor car, too. One day last week it was, too, sir, in the afternoon."

Sir Austin and Mr. Bathurst swung round with a certain amount of astonishment to survey the speaker who had caused the interruption. When their sight was rewarded, their astonishment grew. They saw a little girl in a pink cotton frock under a white pinafore. She held by the hand a small chubby-faced boy, in all probability, judging by the physical likeness, her brother. In her disengaged hand she carried a blue mass of harebells.

"This is a Heaven-sent intervention, Sir Austin," murmured Anthony, as he stepped across to her. "We couldn't have hoped for anything better. Providence is ranging itself on our side. Well, little girl, what else can you tell us about the car that stopped here? Anything that you can remember."

"A gentleman was standing by it, sir. He stood just by the hedge there, smoking. My brother was with me. We had been playing in the meadows over away near Baverstock and were coming home. Just before we got here, there was a heavy shower of rain and me and Dicky had to stand up under a tree up there for shelter." She pointed up the road. "But it soon passed over and then we came along here. That was when we saw the gentleman."

"What sort of a gentleman was he? Young or old? Dark or fair? Tall or short? Was he anything like me or like this gentleman that's with me? Tell me as much as you can about him." Anthony smiled down at her as he put the questions.

"A young gentleman, sir, and a stranger. Nobody that lives down here. And very nice-looking—much better-looking than the gentleman what's with you now. It was a dark gentleman and he spoke ever so nice. Not very tall he was."

Anthony repressed another smile at the unfortunate reference to Sir Austin.

"Did he speak to you, then? Is that what you mean? What made him speak to you?"

"If you please, it was me that spoke to him first. Seeing that he was standing there smoking, I asked him if he's got any cigarette cards. I've got five complete sets, sir, of cigarette cards. I'm collecting for Dicky now. He's got three complete and twenty-nine of another set." She jerked the silent Richard—neither yea nor nay—up to her side with a gesture that she probably intended as corroboration of her statement.

"Did he give you any cigarette cards?"

"No, sir. He said he hadn't got any. But he laughed and gave me half a crown instead. He said it was to be between me and Dicky. I've bought a fountain pen that writes with my half and Dicky's bought a big Noah's Ark, with every animal in it, including the kangaroo."

Mr. Bathurst turned to Sir Austin with signs of amusement.

"What do you say to augmenting with me the finances of the partnership, sir? Even though you don't appeal to the lady's style of beauty. Be generous, sir."

Sir Austin glared at the little girl somewhat fiercely but nevertheless produced half a crown from the recesses of his pocket.

"Thank you, sir," said the pink-frocked little girl. "I shall call this my fairy corner, because it brings me good fortune every time I pass it. Not that the gentleman with you to-day, sir, looks anything like a fairy. I didn't mean it like that, although, of course, there are wicked fairies as well as good ones. Come along, Dicky!" She twisted the small boy round, adroitly adjusted her grip on the harebells, and was just about to make her departure when she turned and took Mr. Bathurst's breath away. "Would you like to know the number of the gentleman's motor car, sir? I saw it and I can remember it, too. If you like, I'll tell you why."

"Proceed, Sherlockina!" cried Anthony. "For your two humble and unworthy slaves are all attention."

"It was KN 0013, sir. My name's Nellie King and I'm thirteen next Shrove Tuesday. I'm going to have pancakes on my birthday. Mother's promised us them without fail. You see how I remembered the number, don't you, sir?"

She curtsied and tripped away deftly, Richard King two or three laborious paces in her wake, but reminded of that fact very regularly by a peremptory tug of the hand from his astounding sister.

Anthony wiped his forehead with his handkerchief. "On the whole, Sir Austin," he said, "a very cheap five bobs' worth."

CHAPTER XV

"REGISTRATION number KN 0013," echoed Anthony, as he watched the figure of the young person in pink growing smaller in the distance. "What a stupendous piece of luck! KN, I fancy, are the registration letters of the Maidstone district, or at any rate of somewhere in Kent. I must look it up when I get back to town."

He walked to the hedge and looked over into green meadows that rolled away into the blue beyond. The only building in sight looked like a disused cowshed.

"Sir Austin," he called over his shoulder to the commissioner, "come and have a look over here, will you?"

Sir Austin frowned, but obeyed and presented himself at the hedge by Mr. Bathurst's side.

"See that footpath, Sir Austin?" Anthony pointed to a worn brown track that wended its way across the emerald expanse of meadow.

"What about it, my boy?"

This, Mr. Bathurst had long discovered, was the commissioner's usual question when confronted with the unusual or the unexpected.

"I wouldn't mind laying you a wager, Sir Austin," said Anthony, "that that track which you can see across the fields there is a footpath that's a short cut between Queensleigh and Baverstock. You often find them crossing fields between two country villages. They're the rule rather than the exception."

"Very possible, Bathurst, very possible. You may be right. I've seen a good many like that one, to be sure. What's your particular point in the present relationship?"

"Only this, sir. Anybody making his or her way along this footpath between Queensleigh and Baverstock would be visible from where we are standing now. There's a pronounced dip to the meadow down there. But, on the other hand, the person walking along down there would be unable to see a car or even a person standing behind this hedge. Do you get me?"

"Assuredly, my boy. Just what I was thinking myself."

"I'm going down into that meadow, Sir Austin. I've got an idea. Coming? Something tells me we're on the heels of a discovery."

Anthony found a break in the hedge a few yards lower down the road and pushed his way through, Sir Austin following him.

"Where are you going, Bathurst?"

"Don't quite know, sir, at the moment. But I can't forget that stationary car up there and something tells me that we're warm, as I told you just now."

As he spoke, he made a dive into the longish grass of the meadow just to the right of where they were walking. He tossed his find to the commissioner. It was yet another cigarette end, similar to all the others that had lain beside the hedge.

"Our friend of the motor car came this way, sir, that's a certainty. What made him leave the road and come across here? To intercept somebody? To speak to somebody? Or to—?"

Mr. Bathurst paused to consider, his brows knitted in thought. They were approaching at almost a right angle the brown track that found its way across the meadow. Suddenly Mr. Bathurst stopped, gazed round and came to a decision.

"I'm going to have a look at that cowshed over there, Sir Austin. Come with me, will you? My idea's developing. I have an idea that a visit to it will prove interesting. It's a bow at a venture, perhaps, but not altogether. I've sound reasons for thinking so."

The partly dilapidated shed that they approached evidently belonged to one of the farms that could be seen dotted around in the distance.

"I don't suppose, Sir Austin," said Anthony, "that more than half a dozen people come this way in the course of an ordinary day. On Sundays, perhaps, but on a week-day, no. Bear that fact in mind, sir. It's open, but almost private."

The shed had an entrance about seven feet in height on its left facing them as they walked toward it and, of course, on their right. It was obviously in disuse, but perhaps it had not been in this condition for very long. On its other side as they entered, and behind the row of cow stalls, was a square opening. The aperture may best be described perhaps as a window minus the glass. It was about five and a half feet from the ground. On the stone floor of the shed was a carpet of straw, litter and dried grass, soft and yielding to the feet. Old sacks on straw heaps, rotting and mildewed, lay in each corner of the shed, where they had been tossed probably months before. Gardening implements long past efficient utility, worn-out brooms, an old broken milking stool completed its equipment. Rusty nails and hooks peeped from its dusty and cobwebbed lime-washed sides.

"Well, Bathurst, now you're here, what's the bright idea? The only use I can imagine this shed being put to would be as a shelter from the rain."

Anthony chuckled and flung a quizzical glance in the commissioner's direction.

"Remember what Sleuth Nellie said, Sir Austin? There was a heavy shower of rain on that Monday afternoon." He walked round to the darker places of the shed very thoughtfully. Suddenly he gave an exclamation and approached the lime-washed side, his eyes gleaming with excitement. "Come over here, Sir Austin, will you?" He pointed to the dauby white of the lime-wash. "Look!" he cried in triumph. "Look, Sir Austin! There's a story for all the world to read."

Red against the white was the imprint of a hand, a left hand, the marks of five red fingers.

"Four fingers and a thumb, Sir Austin!" cried Anthony, his face flushed with triumph. "Whose? Never mind for the moment. Let me introduce you to the spot where Julius Maitland was murdered."

CHAPTER XVI

"DAMN IT, boy," conceded the commissioner, "but you've done great work! I think I can see now the way your mind's been travelling. Get busy—there may be valuable clues in here."

Mr. Bathurst needed no invitation. He had cast a quick glance round the shed, one of those completely sweeping glances of his that always seemed to absorb everything immediately, and then started to pull at a heap of rotting straw stacked in the far corner.

For a moment there was a tense silence. Then Sir Austin gave a startled gasp as Anthony pointed to the straw that had lain toward the bottom the heap, but was now exposed to the light of day. It was covered with blood.

"See what little straw there is on the floor down there, sir?" Mr. Bathurst pointed to the floor of the shed underneath the mark of the five red fingers. "This blood-stained straw in the corner is the straw upon which the dead body of Julius Maitland lay. It was dangerous to leave it as it was. The murderer hid it here afterward."

Sir Austin nodded, too interested to put his thoughts into speech.

"It might have lain in this corner here for goodness knows how long. He's a cool customer, this killer of Maitland. Hullo, what's this?" As he moved, something tinkled on to the part of the stone floor that was uncovered by straw. Mr. Bathurst bent to pick it up. "A scalpel, Sir Austin. An instrument used by surgeons for minor cutting operations. I expect you have seen something of the sort before. I am not surprised to find it figuring in the case."

"How so, Bathurst?"

"The cuts on the knuckles of the dead man's hand. Remember them as we stood in the bungalow? They were slashes, if you remember, of a rather peculiar kind. I imagine that there was a struggle, that one of the contestants had this knife affair in his hand and that in the struggle that ensued Maitland's knuckles got cut." He looked up at the impression of the hand again. "Funny thing, sir, but that mark isn't noticeable as you enter. Otherwise, I should have seen it at once. Come over here and have a look. It's not till you get this side of it that it strikes your vision. A question of light and shade, I suppose. There are five things without which I never travel, sir," Anthony continued. "A fountain pen, a box of matches, a piece of string, my magnifying-glass and a tape measure. We now have an occasion demanding the immediate use of the last."

Taking the tape measure from his pocket he measured the height of the red-hand mark—sinister in two senses—from the floor of the cowshed. It measured five feet five inches.

"There were two ways, I take it, sir, that that mark might have been made. It might have been made with intention, with an idea to mislead an investigator, for instance. Or—what I think is the more likely—the person that made it leaned against the side of the shed, seeking support of some kind. We will assume the second of these suggestions of mine to be the truth—temporarily. What height would you say the dead man was?"

Sir Austin considered the question carefully.

"I should say anything between five feet nine and five feet eleven. He was stout and well-built. That tends to take a man's height off, Bathurst—in appearance, that is."

Anthony nodded.

"Well, say five feet then, Sir Austin. I don't think that will be very far out. Now my point is this. When a person supports himself or herself by placing a hand on such a thing as a wall, for instance—and the side of this shed in this case answers to the position of a wall—his or her hand reaches a spot approximating very closely to the person's height. This mark here that we are examining is five inches lower than I should have expected Maitland's hand mark to have been, judging from his height. But now the question arises—what about our unknown motorist who we know almost certainly was in that meadow over there? Nellie King, the Queensleigh crook hunter, described him as not very tall, didn't she?"

"She did, Bathurst. But I don't see—"

"There are many things I don't see, sir. I realize that only too well. When we go back to-night, I'll run over the main features of the case with you during the train journey. It will help me considerably as well as helping you. But there is still one more point in connection with this shed—the scene of the murder, don't forget."

Sir Austin's brows went up in interrogation.

"Yes?"

Anthony rubbed his hands and warmed to his work. "You will remember that Maitland's death was caused by a bullet that severed the carotid artery and passed out. Doctor Forsyth couldn't find it, could he? It wasn't in the bungalow at Friningham for the simple reason that the shot hadn't been fired there. All the evidence was against that. Sergeant Mansfield, as he listened to the phone call, heard no revolver shot. Maitland had been dead for two days. But that bullet ought to be here somewhere." He looked anxiously all round the four sides of the shed. "The only place inside here where the struggle could possibly have taken place is here," he muttered to himself musingly. "The cowstalls make the other side impossible. Now assuming—" He stopped and addressed Sir Austin. "I'm puzzled, Sir Austin. There ought to be the mark of the passage of a bullet somewhere. It should be fairly high up, too. It can't be anywhere low down. Julius Maitland was five feet ten, remember. The height puts the cow stalls out of the reckoning. It should be here, or there, or behind you, sir. Damn it all, sir, it must be somewhere here!"

Sir Austin shook his head with distinct emphasis.

"No sign of any bullet anywhere round here, Bathurst. No sign at all. You're wrong this time."

Anthony paced the length of the shed two or three times, his eyes everywhere, then he turned smiling.

"Never mind, sir. After all, there may be a very good explanation—in fact, there must be. I'm going outside again—round to the other side of the shed for a moment."

"Hold hard a minute, Bathurst. It's all very well your making sure about the unknown motorist, as you call him, being in this affair and taking part in the struggle you've pictured so realistically. It seems to me you may be jumping very easily to false conclusions. I've been thinking of something else. What about the woman's hair between the fingers of the dead man's hand? Where does that fit in?"

Anthony smiled at him again.

"I haven't forgotten that, Sir Austin, for a moment. Don't you worry with regard to that. I've rather a fantastic explanation that will cover that when the time comes."

The commissioner stared at him somewhat wonderingly, but, receiving no encouragement from Mr. Bathurst to prosecute the question any further, began poking idly with his stick at the tangled litter of straw still upon the floor of the shed. Suddenly his stick seemed to feel something harder than the straw itself, some object concealed within the straw. He pushed away the top-lying straw with the point of his stick and disclosed a small light-brown cardboard box. It was about four inches square.

"Look here, Bathurst," he said. "What's this box doing here? Looks too clean to have been in here very long. Come and have a look at it."

Anthony's face appeared on the other side of the aperture behind the stalls. He had gone out for a tour of inspection in accordance with his expressed intention.

"What's that, sir? I didn't properly catch what you said. But there's a most interesting little matter out here. I'll come in, though. Hold on a moment."

Sir Austin bent to the floor and picked up the object his stick had found for him. As he touched it, something loose rattled within it. The commissioner removed the lid very curiously, with Mr. Bathurst peering over his shoulder. The box held nothing beyond three lumps of sugar. Ordinary white lumps of sugar, such as are used by thousands of misguided people to ruin the taste of their tea. Mr. Bathurst removed one of the lumps from the box and turned it over in the palm of his hand with much curiosity. Then he held it to his nose and sniffed at it. He fancied he could detect a slight odour. Upon being interrogated, Sir Austin fancied that he could do likewise.

"Most extraordinary business, don't you think, Bathurst?"

"Extraordinary that these should have been left behind. But the leaving behind can't, I think, have been deliberate. Purely accidental, I should say. Sir Austin, I am gradually completing my case." He walked to the entrance again. "Come out here, Sir Austin. Come and look at the back of this shed."

Weeds of all kinds and in thick profusion were climbing the side of the building where the two men now were. Anthony pointed to the aperture behind the stalls. The black wood at its edges was weather-stained and liable to break off and splinter at the slightest pressure. Three of its corners held a cobweb, but in the lower right-hand corner the filmy strands of the web that had been there had gone and only a few dusty, stunted web threads remained to proclaim its previous existence.

"There you are, Sir Austin. That's what I found interesting. The clue of the broken cobweb. I'm open to bet you level—all in, run or not—that that cobweb was broken on the Monday afternoon that Maitland was murdered, and broken by somebody standing outside. All the same, I won't deny that my views of the case are changing. I have had to modify my opinion on several points. But I know how Julius Maitland was killed and I think I know why. And one of three people killed him. But I'm—"

"Who are the three people, Bathurst?"

"Unhappily I can only definitely put a name to one of them. The other two—no, I'm not at all decided about the other two, Sir Austin. You must give me more time and just a little more data." He looked at his watch. "What do you say to a cup of tea, Sir Austin? Without sugar! Do you know, I have an idea that Pollock, the Baverstock trainer, might turn out to be an excellent host. What do you say to putting my theory to the test?"

CHAPTER XVII

ALEC POLLOCK, big, burly and brusque, came from the stables to receive Sir Austin and Bathurst. He had been superintending the boxing of a green two-year-old colt and it had taken him much longer than he had anticipated. He frowned as he came near to them. He detested strangers hanging round his stables and he prided himself upon the fact that he had the shortest of short ways with touts. The air of Baverstock was unhealthy for them.

"I didn't catch your name," he said churlishly to the commissioner of police. "The lad you sent down either couldn't remember it properly or you didn't give it to him. But please let me know your business as soon as possible, so that you can clear off the premises. I'm very busy at the moment, and it doesn't suit me to have strangers messing round my stables."

"And it doesn't suit me, sir, to be told that, not by a long chalk, sir." Sir Austin Kemble thrust out an aggressive and pugnacious jaw. "There is my card, sir. So now it won't be a question of your stable lad's memory. You will see who I am."

Pollock looked at the card quite unconcernedly, although his tone changed for the better.

"Then why didn't you give your card to the lad you sent down for me? You can't expect me to recognize you in a moment. What do you want here?"

"A little chat with you, Pollock, a chat which I don't think you will refuse. At all events, I shouldn't advise you to. It won't be good policy on your part."

Pollock looked at the two visitors as though he were turning the matter over in his mind. Evidently a man of very strong opinions, thought Anthony, a man whose own mind meant much to him. Eventually the trainer reached a decision.

"If you will come inside, Sir Austin Kemble, I will give you five minutes. I hope that will be sufficient. I am a busy man, as I said, and my time is valuable."

"You are not alone in that respect, Mr. Pollock."

Sir Austin Kemble, still bellicose, followed the trainer inside and motioned to Mr. Bathurst to accompany him.

"If you will excuse me for a moment or two," said Pollock, "I will prepare one of the rooms. We don't expect visitors in these parts, especially of a week-day afternoon, so you can guess we're not exactly in apple-pie order."

"But surely," put in Mr. Bathurst, "you had a visit from a very distinguished visitor indeed one afternoon last week?"

"One afternoon last week?" queried Pollock. "I don't quite gather what you—"

"On the Monday afternoon of last week," added Mr. Bathurst, "to be precise."

Pollock furrowed his brows as though deep in thought.

"On the Monday afternoon of last—?" He almost echoed his visitor's question.

"Yes," proceeded Anthony, airily. "I refer, of course, to the late Mr. Julius Maitland. I am convinced that you must have seen him very shortly before he was murdered."

Pollock's face went ashen grey, but he possessed quick powers of recovery.

"Not knowing when he was murdered, I can't answer that question very well, can I? But if you'll just wait a few moments, as I said, I'll take you to a room where we can talk properly. No doubt you two gentlemen could do with a cup of tea."

"He's coming round, Bathurst," whispered Sir Austin, as Pollock left their sight. "He fairly wilted under your broadside. I was most amused at it. Splendid, my boy, splendid!"

They could hear the trainer's voice in the distance, and Anthony fancied that he could hear the tones of a woman's voice in a kind of murmured reply. Pollock was soon back to them.

"If you come this way, gentlemen, I shall be better able to talk to you."

As they followed the trainer Mr. Bathurst saw from the corner of an eye a woman cross the passage and pass from one room to another. The impression that she made upon him was that she was tall and dark, but she crossed his vision very quickly and in that part of the passage where he had seen her the light was none too good.

The three men passed into a comfortably furnished living room. Nothing particularly handsome about it, nothing particularly artistic, but everything in it good, and, above all, comfortable.

Pollock motioned his companions to two spacious chairs.

"Now, Sir Austin, I am ready. Please be as brief as possible. I have much to do before bedtime tonight, as I think I told you. A trainer's life is far from being a bed of roses."

The commissioner accepted the challenge with alacrity.

"I will do as you desire. My friend here gave you the key to the purpose of our visit just now. Julius Maitland called here to see you on the afternoon of the day that he was murdered. I will go even further than that: On the very afternoon that he was murdered. We know that beyond any power of contradiction. Will you please tell us the reason of his visit?"

Pollock's face showed certain signs of unmistakable anxiety. But he did not answer the commissioner's question, so Sir Austin followed up his query with a direct statement.

"In fact, Mr. Pollock, we have every reason to believe that you must have been the last person to see Mr. Maitland alive— with the exception, that is, of the person that murdered him."

This time Pollock's jaw set rigidly and determinedly.

"Somebody must always be in that position, Sir Austin, if you will allow me to say so, in any case of murder. The fact that I am in that particular position on this occasion doesn't—"

The commissioner intervened.

"I will not dispute that. I am not here to discuss that even. I am not accusing you at all. I merely mentioned the fact to you because I considered it was important. Surely you can realize that? All I desire is an answer to my question. I will repeat it. What was the reason of Mr. Maitland's call upon you that afternoon?"

"Well, Sir Austin, I do not see why I should mind giving you that information. My conscience is perfectly clear in the matter. Mr. Maitland came here to make me an offer in respect of the ticket I held in the Calcutta sweep. As you are probably aware, I had drawn his horse, Red Ringan. When he heard that, he came to see me. Quite a natural sort of visit, you will admit, in the circumstances."

"Did he make you the offer?" Mr. Bathurst put his first question.

"He did. And I accepted it."

"May I inquire the terms?"

Pollock paused for a moment, but his hesitation soon passed and he then answered:

"Twelve thousand pounds for half a share. Needless to say, it proved a very good investment for me as things eventually turned out. For I take it that his widow will not repudiate the transaction." His lips twisted into a grim smile. "Mr. Maitland's death cost me a cool sixty thousand pounds, gentlemen, although, as you suggest, I was the last man to see him alive. Believe me, I would much rather that he had remained alive."

Taking his pipe from his pocket, he filled it with studied deliberation and put his hand round the bowl after he struck the match to light the tobacco. Mr. Bathurst found himself watching him with a strange fascination. This case was becoming more interesting than ever. Pollock got his tobacco well burning and tossed the match away. When he looked up again, his eyes met the eyes of Mr. Bathurst, who was still regarding him fixedly. The trainer met the glance fairly and squarely. But the question which immediately emerged from Mr. Bathurst's lips was in the nature of a surprise for him and certainly disturbed his equanimity.

"Mr. Pollock, was the question of the Red Ringan ticket in the Calcutta the only matter that brought Mr. Maitland to Baverstock that afternoon?"

But Pollock mastered himself again and, when he answered, was as cool as ever.

"The only matter that brought him, as far as I know, of course."

Mr. Bathurst seemed dissatisfied with the answer. After a moment's consideration, he spoke again.

"Let me then put my question in a different form. I appreciate the exact terms in which you have answered it. Was the sale of the Red Ringan ticket—or the half share of it—the only matter that was discussed during Mr. Maitland's stay here?"

The trainer's peculiarly coloured eyes narrowed perceptibly.

"What else do you imagine was discussed? Mr. Maitland was a—"

"That is not answering my question, Mr. Pollock," interposed Anthony quietly. "That is asking me one, isn't it? An old method of—"

"I am afraid that is all I have to say. I warned you that I wanted you to be as brief as possible. I do not wish to appear discourteous, but—"

Pollock rose from his chair with every indication that he desired the interview to terminate. But Mr. Bathurst was of an entirely different opinion.

"I will be brief, Mr. Pollock. I will ask you a very direct and pertinent question, all in the cause of brevity and to expedite matters as much as possible. What relation were you to the murdered man?"

Anthony's eyes blazed with excitement, while the commissioner felt a wave of amazement surge within him. What the devil was Bathurst after now? Pollock caught at the heavy walnut sideboard for support. No sound issued from his lips. Then he gave a slight gesture of surrender, of weakness, as though he realized at last that the ammunition of the attacking party was too much for the quality of his own arms. For a minute or so there was silence.

"Sit down, gentlemen," he said at length. "I will tell you the whole truth. I wish now that I had from the start. You will pardon me a moment. I will not keep you waiting very long."

He walked to the door and Sir Austin half rose in his heat, doubtful and undecided, as though about to prevent him. But at a shake of the head from Anthony, he desisted. Pollock made a slow exit and they heard him calling to somebody, presumably in another room. "Whom has he gone for, Bathurst? His wife?" Anthony put his finger to his lips, and again shook his head.

"He'll be back here in a moment, sir."

He had scarcely made the remark when the door opened and a lady entered, escorted by the trainer. A tall, handsome, dark woman whom Mr. Bathurst judged to be somewhere in the late fifties. When Pollock spoke to her, Sir Austin gave a gasp of surprise.

"Sit down, mother," said the trainer. "I have told you who these gentlemen are. As far as I can see, they know nearly all there is to be known."

The lady's lips half-parted incredulously as she flung a quick and inquiring glance in their direction. Then she tossed her head back with a mixture of pride and defiance.

"If they know all, Alec, what is it that you want me to tell them?"

Pollock looked helplessly at her, but Mr. Bathurst came to his rescue.

"Ask your mother to tell us all she can about the late Mr. Maitland—shall we say, rather, about your father, Mr. Pollock?"

CHAPTER XVIII

POLLOCK GAVE yet another gesture of helplessness and resignation.

"Tell them everything, mother. It will come from you better than from me. Even now I'm at a loss to put two and two together properly."

The lady seemed as mystified as her son as he yielded the position to her, but she got to grips with the inevitable:

"Although I haven't the least idea how this news has got to the ears of Scotland Yard, I will be perfectly frank and tell you all my unhappy history. My son tells me that it will be better if I do so."

Her voice had a certain harshness and roughness of tone. Mr. Bathurst was unable to decide at the moment if the harshness were natural or inspired by emotion. It did not seem to him that she was quite all that she looked. But, nevertheless, her voice, harsh and rough though it was, rang with sincerity and truth.

"Julius Maitland, as you knew and called him, was, in reality, Julius Warwick, of Kimberley, South Africa. I met him there forty years ago. I was eighteen at the time we met. He was twenty-seven. I was a girl—foolishly headstrong, I suppose, and, like most girls of that age, very romantic and easily swayed. He was a man—and just becoming a successful man. I fell very badly for him and married him. Yes," she went on, apparently in answer to a look from Sir Austin, "you needn't worry about that. We were married all right, in a little church on the outskirts of Kimberley, and I hold my marriage lines to this day. In the following year my son Alec was born. There he is over there. About this time my husband was engaged extensively in I.D.B. He was laying the foundations of his fortune that way. And I was told afterward that Kimberley and the district adjoining eventually became too hot to hold him. At any rate, whether this was true or not, he disappeared. He walked out of the house one morning and I never saw him again for over thirty-eight years.

"He deserted me with a baby boy a few months old—swine that he was. I was terribly distressed. I made frantic efforts to trace him—all of no avail. Eventually I did a thing of which ever since I have been thoroughly ashamed. I pinned a note to my baby's clothes—he was about fifteen months old at the time—and I left him in a street car in Jo'burg, but, before God, the real fault was not mine—it was the fault of the cur who was murdered last week. Anyhow Providence was merciful and the boy fell into good hands and you see what he has made of himself, despite the start his precious father gave him." She paused and looked at Pollock, standing silent in the corner of the room, her eyes shining with maternal pride. "They called him Pollock—that was his baby way of lisping Warwick—and the name stuck. Well, gentlemen, news reached me after a time that my husband had been killed in a railway smash out Port Elizabeth way. It seemed authentic and, to cut a long story short, things improved after many years and I got on the track of my boy. I worked at this clue and that, and at last I heard on good authority that he was a successful race-horse trainer over in England. I sailed at once and sought him out. I held out conclusive proof to him that I was his mother. And then, gentlemen, going back to London with him from here one afternoon last summer, when I had been down for a visit, I saw my husband in the train. Julius Warwick.

In a first-class carriage. And he saw me and knew me, for his face changed colour.

"His conscience smote him. It took me a long time to get over the shock and surprise, and I didn't want to make a scene in the train. I determined to wait and speak to him privately. When the train reached Waterloo, he managed to evade me, and for a long time, try as I would, searching and inquiring almost everywhere, I couldn't set eyes on him again. Then a month ago his photograph leaped to my eyes from one of the society illustrateds. Lo and behold! he was Julius Maitland now, the famous South African millionaire and owner of the Derby favourite, Red Ringan. Oh, he'd risen in the world, had Julius Warwick! Married, if you please, to a third wife and with two sons and a daughter by a second. Bastards, the three of 'em!" she cried bitterly and vindictively.

"Come over here, Alec. Sit down here by me." A spot of high colour was now blazing fiercely on each of Mrs. Warwick's cheeks. "I will now come to the events of the Monday before the Derby. That was the morning, under the strange hand of fate, that I chose to disclose my identity. Alec here and I talked it over and we determined that Mr. Julius Maitland was not going to be allowed to get away with it altogether. He should at least pay for the wrongs and injustices he had done me. I delivered a note to him at his town house. The butler took it in. For months he must have lived under my sword of Damocles and feared in his guilty heart that I should find him. He knew now that I had and that the day of reckoning had come. I asked for certain terms in exchange for my silence. Now, gentlemen, I come to the most remarkable part of my story." She paused again as though seeking the right words with which to proceed with her narrative. "After I had delivered the letter to the straight-faced lackey that took it, I went straight to Waterloo and travelled down here to Alec.

"We were both in the throes of excitement—he over the Red Ringan ticket that he had drawn in the Calcutta, I over the fact that I had struck a blow at my husband, a blow for which I had waited a lifetime. We had lunched and talked matters over pretty generally, and I leave you to judge of our consternation and astonishment when we saw Julius Maitland walking up the approach to this house. We arranged it that Alec was busy, of course, getting horses off to the Epsom meeting that was commencing on the following day. When I walked in on them, and he saw who I was, he showed the yellow streak that he'd always had in him. I suppose I was the last person in the world he expected to see down here. Anyhow, we quarrelled—that was natural, I suppose. I had a thousand bitter things to say to him that had been on the simmer for nearly forty years. You can guess what I felt like when they all boiled over together. When he realized that I had no desire to claim my rights and live with him or to go back to him at all, he changed a bit. But, of course, I wanted my price, as I had told him in my letter, and was determined to have it. I introduced him to his son—my Alec here. You should have seen his face! I think he thought for a minute that there was a sound thrashing in front of him, so he was ready to promise anything. He changed his tune, I can tell you. He offered me a posh bungalow at Friningham to live in and ten thousand pounds a year on the condition that I kept silent and that Alec kept silent as well. As a matter of fact, he told me that he had already made arrangements with regard to the purchase of the bungalow almost directly after he had received my letter in the morning. Well, to come to the point and not waste any more time, I accepted the conditions and I left him to settle the Red Ringan ticket question with my son—and his son. I never saw him again. At the last gasp he cheated me." She cupped her face in her hands and rocked herself to and fro in her chair. "On the Thursday morning I heard about the murder. No bungalow and no ten thousand pounds a year for me! I am not one of fortune's darlings—never have been. To run him down after just on forty years for that!"

Pollock broke in here.

"What my mother has told you about Maitland's visit here is absolutely true. I can vouch for every word of it. I arranged the sale of the half-share of the ticket with Maitland and he left here about half-past three. I saw him off the premises, and, from the way he went, I should say he took the short cut to Queensleigh across the meadows. As a matter of fact, I pointed it out to him."

"He took the short cut to hell," cried Mrs. Warwick, "and he found it forty years too late! But if any man should know the way, he did."

Mr. Bathurst raised his hand. To listen to more recriminations from this ill-used lady would result in sheer waste of time and that was the last contingency that he desired.

"A remarkable story, Mrs.—er—Warwick. I presume that must still be your name. Now will you please tell me something else?" He looked at her intently. "Did Maitland—or Warwick, if you prefer to call him so—give you the actual address of the Friningham bungalow with which he intended to present you—in which he intended to install you?"

"Yes, he had it all pat. He had laid his plans all right that morning. It was the one in which he was found, if that's what you're thinking of. You can rest assured on that point. I remember the name and address well—Ravenswood, Pin Hole Way, Friningham."

"Thank you, Mrs. Warwick. Did he by any chance take the keys of the bungalow from his pocket and show them to you?"

Mrs. Warwick stared at Mr. Bathurst with an amazement that she made no attempt to conceal.

"I don't know your name, young man, but it seems to me that you know more than is good for you. That was exactly what he did do."

Anthony smiled at the somewhat doubtful nature of the compliment and turned to Sir Austin Kemble.

"That explains one or two things that up to the moment have been rather obscure to me. The possession of that definite piece of information is going to help me very considerably."

But Mrs. Warwick was not finished with yet. She had something more still to say.

"Another thing I'd like to know—very much like to know. I've told you a lot, and now I want you to tell me something. How on earth did you know that Julius Maitland was my Alec's father?"

"I didn't know, madam. Believe me it is the truth! I merely guessed."

Her eyes rounded in astonishment.

"You guessed? How could you—"

"But I had reasons for my guessing. When I hazard I always have. In this instance, three reasons, to be exact."

"Three reasons? I am sorry, but I don't—"

"I will attempt to enlighten you. In fact, I feel that I owe you the explanation, for I suppose I must have startled you. When I examined the body of your late husband in the bungalow at Friningham, I noticed—among other things of course—that in life he had been distinguished by three rather unusual physical peculiarities, unusual in the sense of all the three of them coming together in one person. He had in the first place very uncommonly coloured eyes, green with a curious fleck of lightish brown running across them. Secondly, he had an excessively spatulate thumb—perhaps the most extreme one of its kind that it has ever been my lot to encounter. Thirdly, his ears were almost lobeless. His ear seemed to merge into his cheek. The lobe that should have been at the base of the ear was almost entirely missing. Each ear was the same. Now, Mrs. Warwick, the value of circumstantial evidence is increased relentlessly by its accumulative power. Sitting here a short time back I noticed the eyes of your son. They were the eyes of Maitland. Suddenly I saw a strong suggestion of the dead man's face in his. When I looked at his thumb and saw that it was similarly spatulate, my suspicion increased. There remained his ears. The fact that they were lobeless, like the man's with whom I was comparing him, made my suspicion into almost a certainty. Only the question of the actual relationship was left to be determined. I considered it very carefully. There were three great probabilities. Brother? Son? Nephew? I put a general question to Mr. Pollock. He answered it by bringing you in to see us, and his age seemed to be against his being Maitland's brother. That decided me. You were his mother. He addressed you as such. I banked on the fact that he was Maitland's son. The coincidences were far too overwhelming to be disregarded. Quite a simple matter, you see, Mrs. Warwick, when it is explained to you."

"You are right," was her reply. "My husband had the three peculiarities you mention, and Alec here took all three from him. They were his only legacies, thank God. In everything else he takes after me."

Pollock put his hand upon her shoulder to placate her. As he did so, Mr. Bathurst rose for Sir Austin to follow his example.

"I don't think that it will be necessary for us to stay down here any longer. The mystery of Julius Maitland's murder is not yet solved, but your story will dispel many of the clouds that threatened to overhang it. I have high hopes that before the week is out the sky will be comparatively clear. Good afternoon, madam, and good afternoon to you, sir. That is the short cut to Queensleigh, I take it, that Maitland took when he left here on that Monday afternoon?" He pointed to the distant path, brown and arid, that wended its way across the green meadows.

"That's it, sir," said Pollock. "Keep straight along the same path and you can't miss the road leading down to Cruden's stables at Queensleigh. A matter of about an hour's walk from here, although I've done it many a time in less than that."

"Thank you, Mr. Pollock. Sir Austin and I will certainly take it. But not for an hour or two, I am afraid. By the way, I haven't mentioned it to you before, but I have a strong belief that Maitland was murdered in that disused old cowshed standing about two miles from here. Do you know where I mean? Just past where the road from Queensleigh railway station takes a sudden bend." Mr. Bathurst spoke with an almost detached air.

Pollock whitened under his outdoor tan.

"What? You don't say so, sir?" He caught at Mr. Bathurst's sleeve convulsively. "Don't let my mother hear you say that! It will—"

"Why not?" questioned Mr. Bathurst. "What will it do?"

The trainer shook his head.

"I am sure it will upset her badly to know that. She's been sorely shaken these last few days, although she tried hard not to show it. Who could have done it, sir? Who could have done it?"

Mr. Bathurst, lingering for a moment by the hall stand, gave his shoulders a gentle shrug.

"That is still to be found out. To-day we don't know. But to-morrow, perhaps—it is always as well to remember, Mr. Pollock, that to-morrow is also a day. What charming colours they put into mackintoshes nowadays! Good day!"

"I didn't notice the cup of tea, Bathurst," said Sir Austin a moment or two later, "either with sugar or without, although he suggested such a thing when we first went in. Did you forget to remind him?"

Anthony laughed.

"A thousand pardons, sir, I clean forgot it. But if you possess your soul in patience for a few minutes, a cup of tea shall be yours. Do you remember the last cottage we passed after leaving the field path on our way down here?"

"I can't say that I gave it particular attention. Why?"

"It bore a sign that teas and mineral waters could be obtained therein, I presume, for proper and adequate mercantile exchange of the currency, Victorian, Edwardian or Georgian, although it didn't actually say so. What do you say, Sir Austin? Shall we spend an hour or so in there?"

"I should find a cup of tea extremely consoling, Bathurst. But I don't know about spending an hour in there. These cottages where they serve tea are invariably frightfully stuffy and usually by no means clean. I could make out what you meant by telling Pollock we should be an hour or two before we went back again. By Jove, what damnably low ceilings these doorways have!"

A stout and comely woman, who wiped her hands upon a coarse apron, appeared before them and took their order.

"A pot of tea for two," said Mr. Bathurst, "bread and butter and any cake you happen to have lying about."

The lady of the apron ushered them into what was evidently the front parlour. The commissioner was surprised to see Anthony go to the window, take his bearings and look at his wrist watch. He returned to the unsteady round table upon which the hand-wiping lady was busily laying a cloth that had never been white and was now in half mourning. When she had departed for the purpose of bringing in the more important things, Anthony spoke gravely to his companion.

"I don't want you to sit in view of the window, sir. I don't want either of us to be seen if anybody happens to go by."

Sir Austin favoured him with an uncomprehending stare. Anthony embarked upon a further explanation.

"I interested Mr. Alexander Pollock just now in a certain disused shed. Do you remember? I passed on to him certain information that previously only you and I knew, excepting, of course, those who possessed guilty knowledge concerning it. I passed the information on to him deliberately. I am anxious to see if either he or his mother is particularly moved by it—if they evince any interest in cowsheds. We command the path from here and also the village street of Baverstock. I propose to give them an hour and a half. That, I think, should be ample. That is why I hinted that our return would be delayed. Ah, here's your tea, Sir Austin. Pour mine out, please, and let it cool. I cringe in craven fear before boiling tea."

But neither Alec Pollock nor Barbara Warwick made any movement that afternoon that Mr. Bathurst was able to detect.

CHAPTER XIX

"WE MUST certainly call at Queensleigh on our way back, Sir Austin. To neglect an opportunity of speaking to Maitland's trainer would be incredibly foolish. He was undoubtedly in close touch with Maitland during those last few days. Something happened during that time that was unexpected. I am not alluding to the ultimatum that Mrs. Warwick presented to her husband. There must have been something else besides that."

Anthony stopped as though inviting the commissioner's opinion on the matter, but Sir Austin, who was nearing the completion of six miles' walking, which was approximately six miles more than he cared about, ventured none. Thereupon Anthony continued.

"What's the name of this Queensleigh trainer, Sir Austin—Cruden? I seem to have a fairly vivid recollection of a Cruden who gave the world a *Concordance*. Told you where to find Abana and Pharpar and all the rivers of Damascus, besides references to such people as the Ammonites, Amalekites and Jebusites. Ever have to refer to 'em, sir?"

"Never unnecessarily, Bathurst. I'm stronger, I think, on the New Testament than on the Old. But nothing to wave flags about even there. Still, I'm pretty sound on those apostle chaps—Matthew, Mark, Luke and Co."

Anthony repressed a smile at the evangelical promotion.

"How's the weather been the last ten days or so, Sir Austin? Can you remember with any degree of certainty?"

"Dry all the time, I should say, without the book. No rain at all. We had a couple of hours' rain in town on the afternoon of the now famous Monday, but since then there hasn't been a cloud in the sky that I can remember."

"Just my opinion, sir. I can remember no rain since Monday. But I wanted your assurance on the point to feel positive." He pointed away in the distance, "There's the Queensleigh stable." They had reached the mendacious signpost at the parting of the ways. "We turn to the right and go down the hill. The other way leads to the station."

From the reception given to them, Mr. Bathurst and Sir Austin Kemble were quick to see that Humphrey Cruden of Queensleigh was a different man from Pollock of Baverstock. He received them very courteously and Mrs. Cruden equally graciously. With his sensitive mouth and clean-cut features and her sweet face surrounded by silvery hair, they were a delightful couple.

"Sit down, Sir Austin," Cruden said after the introductory formalities were over, "and you, too, Mr. Bathurst. I shall be pleased to give you any information that lies in my power. Have you two gentlemen had tea?"

Before Sir Austin could lie, Mr. Bathurst, with his supreme passion for the sparkling jewels of truth-telling, shattered ruthlessly the roseate hues of the commissioner's anticipations.

"If you hadn't, Mrs. Cruden would have been only too pleased to get you some. But as you have, it doesn't matter."

Sir Austin realized that it was no good saying it did, but he made up his mind what to say at Waterloo when Bathurst suggested a filet steak with chips. It would be his turn then to practise abstinence. But Cruden was talking and he must listen to what he was saying.

"I know of nothing that can throw any light upon Mr. Maitland's death. It was a great shock to us all. As far as I could see during the few days prior to the big race, he was in the best possible spirits. Don't you think so, Monica?" He turned to his wife for confirmation of his statement.

"Most certainly. He was so keen, you see, to win the Derby. I don't think I've ever seen a man that was keener."

Cruden took up her words and amplified them. His wife had started a train of thought in his mind.

"So keen, gentlemen, that he got a proper bee in his bonnet over his wife's mare, Princess Alicia. For some reason or the other, he determined up to the last moment that the mare shouldn't run in the Derby for any consideration. I think Remington was the real cause of it all."

"Michael Remington?" questioned Mr. Bathurst instantly. "The jockey?"

"Yes. Remington had taken a great fancy to the Princess, as we called her—and still do for that matter—when she was a two-year-old. And she made such abnormal improvement from two to three years that Michael swears now that, give him the mount on Princess Alicia, she'll always beat Red Ringan. He wanted to ride her in the Derby, but Mr. Maitland refused point-blank to have anything of the kind happen, so he had orders to ride Red Ringan."

"That's rather interesting," put in Anthony. "So Remington was a bit disgruntled over it, eh?"

Cruden appeared to realize where Mr. Bathurst's question was leading him, so he attempted to withdraw somewhat.

"H'm! I wouldn't use the word 'disgruntled.' He was a little sore, perhaps, but I wouldn't put it at anything more than that.

And, of course, gentlemen, the result of the race didn't make him feel any better—you may be convinced of that. Please don't think that I intended to convey the suggestion that Remington harboured anything like malice or resentment against Mr. Maitland. That would be absurd and also unfair to him."

"How did Remington take his disqualification? Badly?"

Cruden made an eloquent gesture with his hands.

"How could he take it? He simply had to put up with it. I have always found Michael Remington a sportsman. But it was a great disappointment to him. The sequel must have been bitter indeed. He rode a wonderful race to win that Derby."

"To beat his favorite Princess Alicia?"

"Hardly so, Mr. Bathurst, although it actually happened like it. But the real facts were these: Remington was engaged in an intensely exciting duel with Steve Donoghue on Sacred Beetle. He thought the Princess was in the ruck—well beaten—and didn't know that she had managed to make ground so fast and get up. He thought that he and Donoghue had the race to themselves. He was amazed when he saw her colours flash by, only beaten a head, and realized that Sacred Beetle was third. That explains your question, I think, Mr. Bathurst?"

"I see. Now tell me this, Mr. Cruden. I'm a most curious beggar, am I not? What made Mrs. Maitland change her mind and run Princess Alicia in the Derby? Have you any idea? It seems such a sudden change of plan."

"I shouldn't say that Mrs. Maitland changed her mind altogether. In fact, that would be very far from the truth. It was always her desire that Princess Alicia should run, right from the commencement of the present season."

"When you got orders from Mrs. Maitland that her horse was to run after all, were you surprised?"

"Yes, very—coming as late as they did. I will admit that. It was quite an eleventh-hour decision. I thought everything was settled."

"Did you ask her the reason for the change of plan?"

"Yes, of course. But you will understand my position. To a certain extent I must be guided by my patron's wishes. When

I questioned her, she stated that her husband had been called away on business, that she was left in full responsibility, and that she had reached a definite resolve to run her horse. I straight-away wired the change of plans re Princess Alicia to my head lad at Epsom. She was already at the meeting, you see. I had sent her for the Oaks on the following Friday and several others of my string."

"How did Mrs. Maitland communicate with you? Phone?"

"Yes, early on the Wednesday morning."

"On the Wednesday!" Mr. Bathurst reflected for a moment. "And she had heard from her husband on the Monday night." He rubbed his cheek with his fingers. Sir Austin watched him interestedly.

"You didn't attend the Epsom meeting yourself, then, on the Tuesday?"

Cruden shook his head.

"No, I had nothing of any account engaged. Only an old horse in a Selling Plate. Randall, that's my head lad, went. I was to follow on Derby Day."

"It was very early on the Wednesday morning that Mrs. Maitland phoned, if it's any help to you to know that. Because I took the message to my husband that he was wanted." Mrs. Cruden contributed this piece of information.

Mr. Bathurst thanked her in his best manner. As he was doing so, Humphrey Cruden turned in the direction of Sir Austin.

"I feel that there is one more thing that I should tell you, sir, although it goes against the grain somewhat for me to have to do it. But I feel that it is my duty." Sir Austin raised his eyebrows.

"Certainly, Cruden, what is it you wish to tell us? Something that you think has a direct bearing on the case?"

Cruden made a gesture that was almost in the nature of a remonstrance.

"As to that, Sir Austin, I really couldn't answer. That will have to be for you to decide. But in all these murder cases information of the highest importance is very often obtained by going back and recalling incidents that may have happened perhaps a long time ago. That is so, isn't it? It is evident that somebody killed

Mr. Maitland. Granted that, there then comes the question of motive. People look round and try to find one. Now I'll tell you something, gentlemen. Goodness knows, it may have nothing to do with the case whatever—on the other hand, it may. At any rate, since I heard of Mr. Maitland's murder, the incident has become fresh in my mind." He turned to his wife. "You know to what I allude, don't you, Monica?"

Mrs. Cruden nodded her head in an emphatic and vigorous affirmative.

"I do, Humphrey, and I think you're doing the right thing in mentioning it to the commissioner of police. I'm inclined to think that if you hadn't, I should. For I haven't been able to get it out of my mind since I heard Mr. Maitland was dead. Tell Sir Austin Kemble all about it."

Cruden cleared his throat nervously.

"One day last summer, gentlemen, very nearly a year ago, Mr. Maitland came down here, as of course you may guess he often did. He wanted to discuss certain plans with me with regard to his horses and their future engagements. We travelled back to town together, as I had some fairly important business in town to see to later on the same day. On the journey to town an incident occurred, and I thought my companion was going to drop dead from shock. He saw something on the train that frightened him badly. In my opinion it was a woman. But Mr. Maitland denied it when I taxed him with it. Told me a pretty transparent story about his heart being dicky, which I pretended to believe but didn't. But I'm certain that there was a woman on that train who gave him a nasty startler."

Sir Austen began to nod, but Cruden continued.

"I haven't finished yet. I've seen that woman three times since then and on each occasion she has been accompanied by Pollock, my neighbouring trainer here at Baverstock. Also—and here's the curious part about it—Pollock was on the train that very day about which I've just told you. I can't help thinking that it may be more than a mere coincidence."

Cruden sat back in his seat with the air of one who had discharged an extremely unpleasant duty, but Mrs. Cruden seemed eager to supplement her husband's story.

"And I, too, have seen a woman such as my husband describes with Pollock—twice. Out on the downs near here. From my husband's description of the woman he saw on the train, I have very little doubt that it is the same one. Extraordinary, don't you think it, gentlemen? She isn't a woman of these parts—I'll swear to that."

Sir Austin's eyes traveled in the direction of Anthony's and from what he saw therein he deemed it politic to leave the question of the next remark to that gentleman himself.

"It is, Mrs. Cruden, and when one remembers that Pollock, the Baverstock trainer, was also mixed up with the murdered man over the big prize in the Calcutta sweep—or what was thought to be the big prize rather—it tends to become more extraordinary still. However, we shall have to look into the matter, and, as in everything else, time will tell. We must be patient, that is all." He brushed an imaginary speck of dust from his sleeve. "By the way, Mr. Cruden, there's a question I must ask you before I go. Had Mr. Maitland ever mentioned the fact to you that he had purchased, or intended to purchase, a bungalow at Friningham?"

Cruden and Mrs. Cruden shook their heads.

"I called on his solicitors," proceeded Mr. Bathurst, "Messrs. Barraclough, Laurence and Tolworthy—before Sir Austin and I came down here. Whilst there, we had the pleasure of meeting your son incidentally. It appears that Mr. Maitland's connection with the bungalow where he was found dead came about through another client of the same firm. I thought perhaps your son might have—"

Mr. Bathurst gave the information nonchalantly, but he was prepared to watch the trainer's face very carefully. Was it his fancy or did Humphrey Cruden grip the arm of his chair a trifle more tightly?

"Indeed? My son holds the position of managing clerk to the firm that you mentioned. But he never discusses their business with any of us down here."

Cruden smiled as he furnished the information, but again Mr. Bathurst fancied that the smile was a little forced.

"Really! So he won't follow in your footsteps down here at Queensleigh, Mr. Cruden?"

"I'm afraid not." The trainer was terse now and the curtness in his tone was most marked.

"Didn't care for the life, I suppose?"

"Not very much, I'm afraid. It often happens like it, you know—father and son temperamentally opposite. I'm afraid, perhaps, that parents have a tendency to dominate their children too much, especially with their ideas and beliefs. I'm sorry about Dick myself, but it wouldn't do for all of us to be alike, you know, gentlemen."

Anthony smiled in warm agreement.

"Of course not. It takes all sorts to make a world, and, after all, the boy's not very far away from you. I expect you see quite a lot of him down here, don't you?"

"Not a lot, Mr. Bathurst. He runs down occasionally, but not as often as you might think, seeing that we are not a very great distance from London. He was here on the Monday prior to the Derby—the day I understand that Mr. Maitland was murdered at Friningham."

"Now I come to think of it, Mr. Cruden, I already knew that. The porter at Queensleigh station happened to mention it casually to Sir Austin and me in the course of some conversation we had with him. Told us your son was down here for a long week-end or something and went up on the Monday afternoon. Caught a train somewhere after three o'clock or thereabouts. Anyhow it doesn't matter much."

"I didn't actually see him go that afternoon, so I can't say definitely. I was busy." Cruden smiled gravely. "That's a job that's usually reserved for his mother, isn't it, mother?"

Mrs. Cruden smiled back in her turn.

"I expect Mr. Bathurst understands it is. He either has or has had a mother himself. Probably most of us mothers spoil our sons, more or less."

Anthony held his hand out and Sir Austin followed his example. Mr. Bathurst said good-bye to his hosts and had reached the hall some little time before Sir Austin had completed the formalities of his leave-taking. Anthony could hear his gallantries to Mrs. Cruden as he waited. But eventually the commissioner joined him.

"We have nice time for our train, sir," he said on the way to the station. "We can take matters easily. I know how thoroughly you dislike hurrying."

"I'm glad to know you know it, Bathurst. Once or twice to-day I might have been forgiven if I had doubted your knowledge, for it was not apparent on the surface."

"I propose to run over the case in the train with you going home. It has been a very interesting one and also very instruct-ive. Perhaps on the whole, the most—"

"Don't speak of it in the past tense, my boy. We haven't reached the solution yet, not by any manner of means. You may have ideas—I may have ideas. But there's more to come yet—though say what you like."

"I won't contradict you for a moment, sir. Your judgment is as sound as ever. But one more link will, I fancy, make my chain complete. And that missing link, if I may say so, is as good as forged already. That is why I spoke as I—"

Sir Austin broke into his statement.

"The hair in the dead man's hand, Bathurst! Hair from a dark woman, who's got to be found. Mrs. Warwick is dark—I couldn't help thinking of that all the time she was talking to us. Or have we to find another dark woman to satisfy the equation?"

Mr. Bathurst put a cigarette in his mouth, lit it and felt for the railway tickets.

"On the contrary, Sir Austin, a dark woman is the last person for whom I propose to look."

Sir Austin stared at him critically.

CHAPTER XX

Anthony opened the door of the first-class compartment and motioned to Sir Austin Kemble.

"Take the corner seat, Sir Austin, facing the engine. Make yourself thoroughly comfortable and I'll talk to you. That is, of course, if you feel disposed to listen."

The commissioner needed no extended invitation to do as Mr. Bathurst suggested, for, besides being mentally fatigued, he was physically tired. Anthony refused the offer of a cigar and proceeded carefully and with extreme deliberation to fill his pipe.

"I propose for the next hour or so, Sir Austin, with your permission, to run over the case with you generally. When I said a short while back that our journey to-day had made my case pretty nearly complete, it is just possible that I allowed myself to be a little too optimistic. We shall see. Certainly, I don't wish you to take me too literally. I should like to have an interview with our mysterious motorist and I also should like a few moments with Michael Remington. I think each interview should prove distinctly profitable." He paused and thought for a moment. "Then there is a third person—that fascinating third person that so often turns up in cases of this kind and complicates matters. But apart from these things—none of which should give us any trouble to speak of—I am content for the moment to bask in the sunshine of my optimism and look backward upon the case rather than forward toward what I am sure eventually will prove to be only imaginary difficulties."

Sir Austin luxuriously inhaled the aroma of his cigar.

"I'm pleased to hear it, Bathurst. Get on with it, then, my boy. Let me hear your conclusions."

"I'm hardly in a position to do that. That stage of the case is not yet reached. The conclusions must wait—for a time at least. But I'll let you into the light of a lot that I am thinking."

Anthony regarded the commissioner half-humorously and his thoughts went back to the day of his first introduction to him. He remembered the incidents of that morning at the Yard and how worried Sir Austin had been at the vehement attack made upon him by the *Daily Bugle* in relation to the Seabourne murder, that strange affair of the Peacock's eye. When he ultimately spoke, the commissioner felt surprised. He always did when faced with the unexpected.

"I expect, sir," said Mr. Bathurst, "that you know the best place in which to eat a mango?"

Mastering his first emotions of astonishment, Sir Austin Kemble chuckled knowingly.

"I know what an Anglo-Indian will tell you. You mean—in a bath. That's the right answer. That's what you mean, isn't it?" He chuckled again.

Anthony smiled.

"Exactly, sir. And, of course, you know why an Anglo-Indian says so. The fruit is so excessively juicy and the output of the juice when the fruit is bitten is so difficult to control and to keep within decent limits—physically and sartorially—that the European, when he is mango-masticating, accomplishes the feat most successfully in his bath. The only place where he feels at perfect liberty to indulge in a decently healthy bite and at the same time remain clean and comfortable. Now this case, Sir Austin—this affair of the five red fingers, as I will temporarily describe it—reminds me of a mango. If I bite into it too hard and too vigorously, I am apt to be overwhelmed with too many facts of undoubted importance. Too many threads of evidence. I won't say too many clues. To do so would savour of ingratitude. The clueless crime is the investigator's nightmare. But, anyhow, to come to the point and justify my allusion to the mango. When we come to consider carefully all the features of this most extraordinary case, it would be as well, I think, if we, as it were, divested ourselves of all other thoughts and, let me say, mentally undressed ourselves, ready for the bath. Do you catch my meaning, sir?"

The commissioner emitted a sound intended no doubt for approval. Anyhow Mr. Bathurst accepted it as such. He continued where he had left off.

"In the first case that it was ever my lot to investigate, my difficulty—that is to say, my chief difficulty—lay in the separation of the clues. The job of determining which were true and which were false."

"Are you alluding to that affair in Sussex—at Sir Charles Considine's? There was a body on a billiard table, wasn't there?"

"That's the case, Sir Austin. It was my baptism of crime. This present case of ours reminds me of it in some ways. Which are the clues from which we shall glean our solution? Which are the clues which, if followed, will lead us nowhere? Therein lies the crux of the whole matter.

"Now, sir, I will tell you what I think. I want you to consider, for the time being at least, the following points, because they seem to me not only relevant but also authentic, that is to say, true factors in the case. Affecting very definitely the main outline. They are seven in number and I will enumerate them seriatim." He proceeded to tick them off on the tips of his fingers with the stem of his pipe. "Number one—that although Sergeant Mansfield heard so many sounds of the struggle when the telephone call came through to him, he never heard what should have been the loudest sound of all—the revolver shot! Acting upon that, therefore, and making that somewhat strange occurrence our starting point, we have definitely established this afternoon that Julius Maitland was murdered many miles from Friningham, in a disused shed between Queensleigh and Baverstock, with which former place he has a connection.

"But, of course, as I told you, I suspected something of the kind. Having got our start, therefore, we will proceed." His pipe went to his next finger. "Number two—Maitland's death was actually announced to the police by telephone. Why? And by whom? We discussed that point before, you and I, down at Friningham, and suggested, if you remember, more than one solution. I imagine I have found the true solution. We shall see. Point number three—and I find this most intriguing, Sir Austin—Mrs. Maitland states that her husband did not know the name of the person who had drawn Princess Alicia in the Calcutta. Yet Copeland, the butler, very definitely informs me that his master did have this information. He saw, so he says, the names of the two Queensleigh horses on the list that Julius Maitland had. Question, who is lying—Maitland, Mrs. Maitland or the admirable Copeland? It is impossible for each to have been truthful. I think I know the answer to the question that I have just asked. It will not be difficult to test my opinion, because we know the man from whom the letter containing the list came. The fourth point is the car that stopped near the shed on the way to Baverstock, the car of which we have the number, thanks to the inimitable and irrepressible Miss King."

"May be a false number plate, my boy. Don't be too sure! Don't overlook that possibility." Sir Austin straightened himself in his seat. It was all very well for Bathurst to—

Anthony cocked his head to one side.

"Perhaps! Don't think so—that is to say, if I read the case aright. Where were we? I remember. Point number five. Maitland was not all he seemed and his real wife and son, the two main limbs of the skeleton within his cupboard, are with him a short time before he is murdered, at a short distance from the spot where his murder took place. We have heard their explanation. We have possibly attempted to test it. Are they telling the truth? Points number six and seven are small to describe, but nevertheless overwhelmingly important. Because they belong so intimately to the murder itself. The scalpel and the three lumps of sugar! I flatter myself that I have fitted them into their respective pigeonholes. They are by no means incongruous. But I want to make absolutely sure before I commit myself—even to you! That is the main case as I see it, Sir Austin, and as I present it to you."

Sir Austin frowned, for he felt that he had a considerable amount to say himself.

"I have the greatest respect for your ability, Bathurst, as you know full well. I have known you now long enough to make that statement unreservedly. But it seems to me that you have not traveled far enough. For instance, there are so many points upon which you have not touched at all. Take the fact of the hair in Maitland's hand. It was the hair—"

Anthony smiled again, good-humouredly, however. "Quite true, sir. I'm well aware of it. I could give you at least a dozen other points. There was the hair, as you say, there were the curious twigs on the way to the bungalow, there was the strange knowledge of Vivian Maitland, the violin on the Chesterfield, the person who was heard laughing, the presence in two parts of the case of Cruden junior, but why go on? There is no point in doing so at this juncture."

Sir Austin's face was set, grimly contemplative.

"Most remarkable, that, Bathurst! About young Cruden. I noticed that you attached a great deal of importance to it. To say the least it was—"

Anthony knocked the bowl of his pipe on the heel of one of his shoes.

"Yes, I certainly haven't let the fact escape me." He smiled at the look on the commissioner's face. "After all, sir," he continued, "to use a hackneyed phrase in connection with affairs of this nature, it comes back to a question of motive. Who benefited by Maitland's death? If two people fit that category, who benefited the more by the death? Mrs. Warwick—the dark lady of the Maitland sonnet—she didn't benefit, did she, sir? I can't forget she's dark, you see. A most important matter, that."

The commissioner knitted his brows. He was puzzled at what seemed a change of position on Bathurst's part.

"But I thought you said that a dark woman was the last person for whom you proposed to look? How do you reconcile—"

"That with what I have just said?" put in Anthony, completing his sentence for him. "Don't forget, Sir Austin, that dark is the antithesis of him."

Sir Austin gazed at him curiously. It was almost a gaze of commiseration.

"Waterloo, I fancy," said Mr. Bathurst.

CHAPTER XXI

THE REVEREND Curtin Wogan Dillon, M.A., vicar of Latch-ingford, in the county of Kent, and rural dean of Bradstock, adjusted his *pince-nez* as he propped the morning paper against the cruet in front of him.

"Dear, dear!" he ejaculated. "What an appallingly poor show, to be sure! Even allowing for the state of the wicket, and there wasn't a great deal of sun at that. Let me see, that leaves Kent with only one hundred and forty-one to win and all to-day to get them in. An hour of Frank Woolley will settle it." A heading from another column caught his eye and caused him to frown. "Rubbish—utter rubbish!" he murmured. "Change the l.b.w. rule, indeed! What on earth will they be up to next? Can't they let the greatest of all games alone? How many runs do they expect? Demuriel!"

Doris Muriel Dillon, only daughter of Latchingford's vicar and Bradstock's rural dean, came at her father's call. She always did. The name Demuriel had been bestowed upon her by her brother, Pat, in their earlier days. The bestowal was happy—she was demurely beautiful and beautifully demure. English with Irish blood, blue-eyed and fair.

"What is it, daddy?"

"Read that," he asserted, stabbing at the offending column, regardless of etiquette, with the business end of his egg spoon. "Did you ever read such drivel in all your young life?"

The June sun glinted on her golden hair as she read what her father had pointed out to her. The vicar was dark and Demur-iel had inherited the fair English beauty of her dead mother. It soon became obvious, from the expression on her face, that she shared her parent's opinion on the law of obstruction.

"It's tripey, daddy. All these would-be improvers of cricket forget the thousands that play on the village green. It's positively ridiculous!" She laughed merrily to give point to her words. "Think of the Latchingford batting averages if this proposed alteration of the law came into force! They'd all be decimal parts of one!"

"Of course, of course, my dear. Just what occurred to me," returned the Reverend Curtin, considerably mollified to find somebody who shared his opinion on this vital point. "They can never pass it. It's too utterly revolutionary. By the way, where's Pat?"

The girl tossed her head toward the ceiling.

"Shaving when I last saw him. Why? Do you want him particularly?"

The vicar frowned.

"I like him to be down to breakfast at the proper time. It's only the right and proper thing. I shall have to speak to him about it. He's getting exceedingly lax. I suppose life in the colonies is different from life in the motherland. Ah, well"—he broke off and applied a generous portion of butter to a square of crisp brown toast—*"tempora mutantur."*

Demuriel permitted herself the luxury of an unseen grimace.

"I suppose it's like everything else in life, daddy. Full of give and take. Advantages come from one direction for which the inevitable penalties have to be paid in another. You know, like they say when they first start to teach you bookkeeping—'every debit has a corresponding credit.' That's how it is with Pat. He's gained a tremendous amount of knowledge and experience, for which I suppose he and others have to pay in other ways. And of course other people have to share the payment with him."

Demuriel continued the subject, for the opportunity had come for which she had been waiting for some time. She determined to grasp it. But she knew she had to do so lightly and without appearing to be too deadly serious.

"By the way, daddy, it's just occurred to me. What do you make of Pat these days?"

The vicar looked up.

""What do you mean, Demuriel?"

"Well, I don't know quite myself, when it comes to putting it into words. How shall I put it?" She paused, thinking hard. "Don't you think, daddy, that he seems very temperamental lately? For about a fortnight now, I think. Possibly for even longer than that. Ever since he arrived, perhaps, but at first in the excitement and delight at getting home again and seeing us all, it wasn't so apparent and we didn't notice it anything like so much. But I'm certain there's something on his mind, and I can't think what."

"You're fanciful, sweetheart. It's only natural that Pat should be a bit above himself coming home again after all those years. What else would you expect or have? There's nothing on his mind, take it from me. Why, yesterday he was as chirpy as a cricket. There was no holding him—you could see that he hadn't a care in the world."

"That's just it, daddy dear. That's just what I've been trying to say. Sometimes he is like that, as lighthearted as the Guv'nor General himself on a fast wicket. But at other times he's as depressing as a Louis Hall playing against Lancashire on an August Bank Holiday. Properly down in the dumps."

At this Pat entered the breakfast room and grinned cheerfully and benevolently in the direction of his sister.

"You're late, Pat," she declared with an attempt at severity and a direction of her head toward their reverend father.

"Sorry, old girl, my razor wasn't too good this morning. I shall have to run into Bradstock for a supply of new blades. Hope I haven't kept you waiting too long. Well, dad, what's the best news this morning? Hat trick by Freeman?"

The vicar looked over the top of the newspaper. Patrick applied a jug of hot milk to his porridge and prepared to eat and to listen.

"No, nothing very startling. Notts batted disappointingly, though. Kent should win by seven or eight wickets. It will be hardly worth your while running over there to-day. There's a big and ludicrously absurd agitation to alter the l.b.w. rule and a hint that Hobbs may go to Australia again, after all."

"Good business!" replied Pat. "Pass the bacon, Demuriel, will you? And the kidneys. Thanks, old girl." He helped himself liberally.

"There are no further developments in the Maitland murder."
The vicar had turned to another part of the paper. "Did you ever
run across Julius Maitland in South Africa, Pat? He must have
been out there part of the time while you were there."

"Never met him in flesh once, guv'nor. Of course I heard a
good deal about the joker. He was a big noise, naturally. But
our ways lay apart." Pat paused. "I'm not altogether sorry, dad,
at that. I fancy from one or two things that I heard dropped in
pretty reliable quarters that his record out there was not too
burnished bright. Bit of an outsider, I fancy. I shouldn't describe
him as one of the angelic host."

The vicar frowned.

"I don't know that I appreciate your comparison, Pat. It is
hardly—"

"Sorry, guv'nor, but you know what I mean. I expect the
fellow that croaked him had a thundering good reason, if you
only knew."

The vicar shook his head with an air of hopeless resignation.

"I can't go as far as to admit that, Pat. Murder is a dreadful
thing, and the less we attempt to minimize its wickedness, the
better for us as a nation. I am afraid that the world is very evil—"

"And that the times are waxing late, eh?" sallied Pat.

"There is not enough industry in the country," went on the
vicar, ignoring the interruption. "Everybody is in a hurry to get rich
quickly. Something for nothing! I believe the present vernacular
has it 'money for jam.' We have competitions in the newspapers
offering almost fabulous sums of money to the winners, and I am
told that the amount of gambling among the women of the poorer
classes is positively astounding. We have these huge sweep-
stakes—just look at this paragraph that I have just been reading."
He pushed the paper across to his debonair son.

The latter read with evident interest.

"Calcutta Sweep! Owner of Winning Ticket Traced at Last!"—
"We are given to understand upon excellent authority that the
holder of the Princess Alicia ticket in the big Calcutta sweep is
now definitely known. For certain private reasons, however,
which for the time being are not to be disclosed, the lucky winner

of the immense sum involved desires that his identity should remain a secret from the general public, and we learn that the ruling authorities of the Calcutta Turf Club are not averse from respecting these wishes. It will be readily understood that, as these tickets sometimes change hands several times, it is no easy matter to trace the actual possessor of any particular ticket. We are informed that the prize will not be paid over until the winner's convenience. Moreover there will be an interesting sequel—wedding bells." Pat handed the newspaper back.

"Although I agree with every word you've said, guv'nor, on the evils of gambling—very nice, too. And very much more grateful and comforting than a kick in the tummy."

"Your expressions are coarse, Pat, especially so in your sister's hearing. Please try to modify them. Suppose one of the churchwardens were to hear you."

Demuriel grimaced gracelessly at her brother's grin.

"Anyhow," he went on, "I wish it were me. What a lot I could do with it! And each way at that. You should have that new altar cloth you've been wanting for years, dad, although I expect you'd say it was tainted money or something, eh?"

"No, I don't think so," returned the vicar. "Although the idea of the original gamble merits my strong disapprobation, I would never refuse to put money to good use, and I can think of no better use than—"

Demuriel executed a Charleston behind her parent's back.

"What date are you sailing, Pat?" asked the vicar.

"The last Tuesday in July, sir. Rotten luck, isn't it? But I can't see a way out. I shall miss Canterbury Week, but I suppose it can't be helped. The firm is pretty good to me in most ways, so it's up to me." He walked to the window that looked out on the sweet-smelling garden. "I think I'll pop up to town to-day, sir, if you don't mind; that is. I should want the car if convenient. Did you want it yourself for anything? Say no!" He surveyed his father somewhat anxiously as he put the question to him.

"I don't think so, Pat. Anyhow, whatever happens, if you want it particularly, I'll manage without it, my boy. Where are you going?"

"I've one or two matters to see to, sir. There's my passage for one thing, I want a stick of number five from Fox's or somewhere, and I simply must get some new clothes; in fact, I want a new rig-out altogether. My dinner jacket's in a disgusting condition. I shall be back to tea probably, unless I do a show somewhere. I hear Tallulah's last thing is extra. If I'm not back by five, don't expect me till last thing."

Demuriel broke in airily.

"Are you going alone, Pat?"

"I am that, my winsome child. Why do you ask?"

She shrugged her shoulders expressively. "For no particular reason, Pat. I thought that you might be taking Lee up—that was all."

"Good Lord, no! I haven't seen Joe for several days now. Expect he'll miss me again when I get back to the Cape. I've half a mind to take him with me, if he'd come. I'll go and get the car ready."

He strolled out whistling cheerfully, his hands thrust deep into the pockets of his plus-fours.

"What on earth did you mean? Why should Pat take Lee up to town? Whatever put the idea in your head?" The vicar surveyed his daughter with some signs of surprise. Demuriel smiled sympathetically.

"I don't know, daddy. The idea did just come into my head for the moment, that was all. You know how Joe worships the ground Pat walks on. He's never tired of singing his praises. And there's no reason why he shouldn't worship him, to be sure. Because I've a kind of a sort of an inkling that I do myself. And I'm not the only one in the vicarage that does that either. You silly old goose."

She kissed the vicar upon the tip of his nose to give point to her opinion. He made no attempt to resist the invasion. Then his eyes caught the clock.

"Goodness me! Eleven o'clock and the breakfast things not cleared away yet. Come into the breakfast room, Maud!"

She pressed the bell for the maid. For a moment there was no response. She pressed the bell again. Then she opened the door of the breakfast room a trifle wider. As she did so the sound of voices came to her ears. She saw the figure of the maid approaching the breakfast room. Maud carried a visiting card.

"A gentleman to see the master, Miss Doris. Here's his card. He wants to know if it's convenient for him to see the master now. I told him the vicar was in but—"

Miss Dillon regarded the card with interest. "Anthony L. Bathurst." She peeped out and saw Bathurst's tall, athletic and well-groomed figure at the vicarage door. Then she saw her brother come round from the garage to the front of the vicarage.

"Good Lord," she heard him say, "Bathurst—by all that's wonderful!"

Bathurst turned at the sound of Pat's voice.

"By Jove, Dillon," he cried, after a momentary hesitation of a second or two. "I had no idea when I came down here that I was coming to see you."

Demuriel watched intently and saw the two men shake hands with an unusual cordiality.

CHAPTER XXII

Miss Dillon had just enough time to put in some really finished and telling work in front of a mirror before she found herself being introduced to this tall and—upon her own secret admission—altogether pleasing stranger. "Looks as though he could hold his own with the best of 'em," she communed with herself. "My father and my sister, Bathurst," she heard her brother say. "Anthony Bathurst—at Uppington and Oxford with me. I expect you remember the name, though."

The tall stranger bowed to her and shook the vicar warmly by the hand.

"Delighted to meet you, sir, and you too, Miss Dillon. Very delighted, although I admit that to meet you here in this fashion is a very great surprise to me. I had no idea that it was you to whom I was coming."

Demuriel noticed that his face suddenly seemed to assume a look of gravity.

"Won't you sit down, Mr. Bathurst?" The vicar became the perfect host. "Please sit down. You have breakfasted, I presume?"

"Thank you, sir—yes. I had an early breakfast. Early, that is to say, for me. Nine o'clock is my usual time, but this morning was an exception."

The vicar nodded. "You have come by car—doubtless?"

"Yes. Quite a charming run down, isn't it. I couldn't help thinking on the journey that Kent has been well named the garden of England. Thank you—I will smoke."

He accepted a cigarette from Pat Dillon's case, gave it a casual glance and lit up. The vicar nodded again.

"Yes, yes, Kent is a delightful county. We are, of course, delighted to see you and to welcome you, Mr. Bathurst—any old schoolfellow of Pat's is naturally doubly welcome, but perhaps you will be good enough to—"

"Explain myself—and my visit," questioned Anthony, smilingly. He went on at once. "I must, of course."

He settled himself comfortably in the chair into which the vicar had waved him, and leaned over to an ash tray. For a moment or two there was silence. Then Mr. Bathurst embarked upon his explanation.

"First of all, sir, and you, Dillon, I want you to understand as I have already said that when I came down here I had no idea to whom I was coming. And frankly, finding you as I have done, hasn't made my task any easier, or I may say—any more comfortable. It has rendered it just the reverse."

He paused for a second and the vicar took advantage of the pause to frown somewhat. Finding Mr. Bathurst serenely impervious to the quality and dimensions of the frown, he glanced in the direction of his son. He was surprised at what he thought he saw. Pat Dillon's face wore an unmistakable look of anxiety. There was no doubt about it. Before the vicar could translate this look into intelligible terms Mr. Bathurst was proceeding with his explanation.

"But I should like you to know, sir, that the questions I am about to put to you are not inspired by any sense of what I will call idle curiosity. Therefore, you will not regard them as impertinent. Briefly, I represent Sir Austin Kemble—the commissioner of police—and as you will see from that—Scotland Yard."

The vicar's frown deepened. What was coming next? Mr. Bathurst's next words came to him as though from a distance. He seemed to hear them vaguely.

"You are the owner I believe, sir, of a twelve horsepower blue Morris-Cowley? Am I right?"

The vicar was surprised to find that although everything seemed so far away, he still retained the powers of reply. It appeared to him that they came back to him out of the beyond— as it were miraculously.

"Yes, Mr. Bathurst," he heard himself answering.

"The registration number of the car is KN 0013?"

"Quite correct."

"Now," thought Anthony—"Sleuth Nellie's memory passes into the crucible. How will it stand the test?" He addressed himself once again to the vicar of Latchingford.

"Then perhaps you will be good enough to tell me this. Was your car by any chance anywhere in the county of Wiltshire on Monday afternoon of last week? To be more exact—in the Queensleigh or Baverstock district?"

The vicar looked at his questioner blankly—entirely without understanding. "I'm afraid I don't quite—at least, I don't—on Monday afternoon of last week, did you say? Let me—"

Demuriel broke in impulsively.

"You weren't out in the car that afternoon, daddy. So you can't answer. Pat had it out all the day. Don't you remember, Pat?" She swung round on her brother for corroboration of her statement. Pat Dillon contracted his brows in an effort of remembrance.

"Did I?" Anthony also turned in his direction.

"Were you in the Wiltshire district that afternoon, Dillon?"

After a moment's hesitation the man addressed replied: "Yes—I think I was. In fact, I'm sure of it now you mention it, and bring it to my mind. But I've been all over the country during the last week or two—and remembering's not easy—see."

"Good," said Bathurst. "That's excellent. We progress. I'm very glad that you have been able to confirm my theory. What you tell me tends to clear the air considerably. You will realize what I mean within a few moments. You were just touring round, I take it, Dillon?"

"Yes. Just having a tootle round. I lunched in Salisbury—I fancy, that particular afternoon and ran on for a few miles—Hurstbourne—Queensleigh—several other places—I can't bring any more of them to mind at the moment. What's the idea, Bathurst? I confess that I'm a little—"

Anthony looked grave again: "I told you that you would realize my meaning better later on. You will. Give me a little time. Did you know Julius Maitland—the murdered South African millionaire?" Anthony could have sworn that Dillon whitened a trifle under his colour as the significance of the question came home to him.

"I never met him, Bathurst. Why do you ask?"

There was a dogged determination in Dillon's tone. He gave the impression that he had become defensive.

"I have reason to believe that Julius Maitland must have been in the same district of Wiltshire as you were—at almost the same time—on the Monday afternoon in question. I wondered if you knew him."

"But why—Bathurst?" persisted Dillon, "why? Surely you must have some definite reason—"

"I think it only fair to my son Mr. Bathurst," intervened the vicar, "to tell you that he never met Julius Maitland during the whole time of his stay in South Africa. Strangely enough, I have asked him the same question quite casually—myself."

Anthony felt his pulses quicken. This was news, indeed.

"South Africa, sir?" He turned to Pat Dillon again. "Have you been in South Africa, then, Dillon?"

Pat nodded. "Of course, didn't you know that?"

"Candidly, I didn't. I can't remember any news of it ever reaching me after I came down from Oxford." Anthony paused as he turned over in his mind this new and, to him, surprising piece of information.

"I'm home on a holiday leave, Bathurst. Going back toward the end of next month. But returning to what I was asking you—what prompted your question with regard to my having seen Maitland? There must be some—"

"I will be quite frank with you, Dillon. There is no earthly reason why I should be otherwise. You stopped your car on a corner of the road about two miles from Baverstock. The road turns very sharply at the spot which I am describing and there is a very fine tree that stands there. In the distance—over the hedge to the left there stands an old shed. You did stop your car there, didn't you?" Anthony spoke very quietly.

There was no disguising now that Pat Dillon was distinctly rattled. A dull flush spread over his face.

"I did. What of it?"

"You had no special reason for so doing?"

Again there was just the suggestion of hesitation before Dillon answered.

"Special reason? None whatever! I was taken by the view and had a rest there. That was all. Smoked several cigarettes there and eventually drove away. What on earth gave you the idea that I had a special reason for stopping there?"

"I didn't say that I ever had the idea, Dillon. I asked you the question, that was all. You were alone in the car, of course? Please don't misunderstand me. I assure you that it gives me—"

Pat Dillon stuck his jaw out very resolutely. He had made up his mind.

"Of course I was alone. Very much alone."

"Thank you. Did you get out of your car at all?"

"Yes, I strolled round it—for a few yards, I suppose, either way. I certainly didn't go far. But what the—?"

"You didn't go farther away than a few yards?"

"I did not."

"You didn't go across the adjoining field by any chance?"

"Of course not."

"Thank you, then, very much, Dillon. There's nothing more, I think, that I wish to ask you. Thank you, too, sir, for your kindness. You must look on me as an intolerable nuisance." Mr. Bathurst bowed to the vicar. The vicar protested flutteringly and mendaciously that the whole affair had been a pleasure to him. Mr. Bathurst bowed to Miss Dillon. The lady supplemented the statement of her father.

"One minute, though," said Mr. Bathurst, "one minute— just before I go. Do you happen to have a gypsy encampment or settlement in the near neighbourhood?"

Demuriel was about to reply when a look in her brother's eyes checked her. She found herself wondering at what she did. For there was grave foreboding in her mind.

"No, can't recall anything of the kind, Bathurst, why? Did you want to—?" Pat's voice seemed affectedly nonchalant.

"It doesn't matter. I was merely attempting to follow up a theory of mine—that was the only thing. Now I'll say good-bye."

"Where's your car, Mr. Bathurst?" questioned the vicar. "Did you leave it in the village or—?"

"It's in the lane, sir, a few yards away, not more."

"Come through the garden, then, Mr. Bathurst. You can make the lane lower down. We of the vicarage are rather proud of our garden. Both the flower and the kitchen. To us they represent—"

"Don't mention 'the kindly fruits of the earth,' daddy," cut in Demuriel, "there's a dear. I'm sure Mr. Bathurst—"

Anthony smiled: "I'm sure I shall, Miss Dillon, whatever you were going to say!"

Demuriel flushed entrancingly. The company of four passed through the vicarage garden, Anthony murmuring his admiration and toying idly with two dried twigs that he had carelessly picked from a heap of garden refuse. He handed them to Pat Dillon with a smile playing round the corners of his mouth.

"Here you are, Dillon," he said. "Something to take you back to the old days. A couple of twigs from the old Uppingham birch! The birch of tradition! But we've only two of the six scholars here. Four are missing. Done any acting lately?"

"Played in a show for the church organ fund a week or two ago."

Anthony shook hands and walked to his Crossley. The Dillons watched him and it until the car had travelled out of sight.

"A charming man," said the vicar.

"I like him," said Demuriel. "He has a way with him."

These two opinions were passed.

"What perfectly poisonous luck," Pat Dillon muttered, "and old Bathurst of all people," and then, very forcibly: "Damn Bathurst! I wonder what he meant exactly by—"

CHAPTER XXIII

A MILE AWAY from the vicarage of Latchingford, in which village he had stopped to make one or two additional inquiries and to examine at least one double-crown poster advertising theatricals in the vicarage grounds, Anthony examined his map. As he thought, Talehurst lay under ten miles away—to the east of his present position. He decided to take the next good road travelling in that direction. He had not to wait very long, a winding lane, offering a very fair surface, exhibited a signpost that read "Talehurst—7 miles." Mr. Bathurst turned the Crossley down it with dexterity, and before long found himself approaching an old church bearing a grand old Norman tower ivy mantled and grey. He stopped the car and alighted. Its weather-beaten notice board told the world that the church was "St. Margaret's—the Parish Church of Talehurst, Kent. The vicar—the Reverend Lewis George Lumsden, M.A. (Oxon)." Other church notices followed in the usual order. Mr. Bathurst rubbed his hands at what he evidently considered was cheering news, and pushed open the gate. He strolled quietly toward the church porch. From a rail on the side thereof a register of electors swung suspended. Mr. Bathurst took it and opened it—turning the leaves over with the utmost care. The most diligent search resulted in the discovery of three Dawsons who were entitled to put crosses on ballot papers. They were Douglas Septimus Dawson, gentleman, Red

Roofs, Talehurst; William Charles Dawson, Farm labourer, 5 Anns Cottages, Talehurst, and Albert Jellicoe Dawson, postman, 37 Dagworthy Lane, Pinxbridge, Upper Talehurst.

In the circumstances choice between the three was a matter of supreme ease. The particular Dawson whom Mr. Bathurst was desirous of seeing must be the "gentleman" who resided at Red Roofs. There should not be so many big houses in the neighbourhood to make Red Roofs very difficult to locate. Enquiry of a vacant-looking youth who was propped up against the front of a dilapidated general store elicited the fact that if Mr. Bathurst kept to the lower road through the village it would be impossible for him to miss Red Roofs. It would be the first big house on his right. A matter of a few minutes established the truth of this statement and Anthony found himself ringing the bell of a fine old house that in no way belied its name. He scrawled a pencil note on the visiting card which he handed to the maid servant.

"Mr. Dawson will be pleased to see you, sir," she stated a few moments later. "Will you please come in."

Anthony, upon being shown into the library of Red Roofs, was surprised to find that he was confronted by one of the finest physical specimens of man that it had ever been his good fortune to encounter. Dawson was magnificent in every particular—suggestive more than anything of a viking of old. Piercing blue eyes and flaxen hair only called greater attention to his size and scope.

"I observe what you have written on your card, Mr. Bathurst. But I do not know that I can understand—I am rather at a loss. In what way can I assist your investigation?"

"I think you will understand very shortly, Mr. Dawson. Were you a friend of the late Mr. Julius Maitland?"

Dawson shook his head.

"Hardly—an acquaintance, let us say. I met him in racing circles—that was all. That was how we became acquainted."

"You wrote to him, I believe, over the week-end that preceded the Derby and his murder?"

"I did. I have important business interests in Calcutta, am a member of the turf club, and as a consequence I get inspired information sometimes. I do with regard to the draw for the Calcutta sweep—I did so this year. I sent the information to Maitland. I may say that it was sent at his own especial request. He had written to me on the matter."

"Thank you, Mr. Dawson—that was the impression that I had gathered. You are aware then of the identity of the holder of the winning ticket—the Princess Alicia ticket?"

Dawson looked disturbed. For a moment there was a silence, broken only by the ticking of the clock upon the mantelpiece. At last he replied to Mr. Bathurst's question.

"I don't know that I can truthfully answer that. Tracing the actual holder of a ticket in a big sweep like the Calcutta is far from easy. There is so much redistribution. So many firms, banks and so forth buy up such big blocks. I have also seen the recent announcements on the subject in the press. For some reason the name is being kept private for a time. But—to answer the question you put to me—I know the name of the person that was given to me on my cablegram from Calcutta as having drawn Princess Alicia. The name that I sent on to Julius Maitland with the others."

"You can remember it?" Anthony's question came curt and brisk.

Dawson smiled—a genial grunt. "I had a second look at my own list after the disqualification of Red Ringan. I wanted to know myself when Princess Alicia was officially declared the Derby winner. Ordinary and natural curiosity on my part, don't you think?"

Anthony willingly conceded the point that Dawson made. Then came swiftly to the issue. "Will you give me the name?"

Dawson caressed the line of his chin.

"Will you in your turn give me the assurance that my part in the affair will not be divulged?"

"Absolutely, Mr. Dawson. The information you give me will not necessarily be published even. I have a theory of my own with regard to the murder of Julius Maitland, but there is, of course, the possibility that I may be wrong. But I have a strong idea that you are in a position to give me information that will help me tremendously toward a solution."

"'Pon my soul—but you've a persuasive tongue, Mr. Bathurst." Dawson paused yet again irresolutely and evidently not quite sure of himself. But he almost immediately continued. "I'll tell you what you want to know as one gentleman to another. After all, it must be published sooner or later. The name was Patrick W. Dillon."

Mr. Bathurst let go a low whistle.

CHAPTER XXIV

INSPECTOR GARTH thrust his hands into his jacket pockets, looked across the room at Sir Austin Kemble, and stuck his jaw out somewhat aggressively.

"I understand you wish to see me, sir."

"Yes, inspector, I want to see you about the Maitland case. First of all—what have you to report?"

Garth wiped the palms of his hands with his handkerchief.

"Quite a lot, sir. First, the dead man's antecedents. I followed up the information you gave me relating to his earlier history in South Africa—just as you suggested. After his marriage with and desertion of the lady known as Miss Barbara Reindorp, he married again. His second wife's name was Ada Zulch. She died of diabetes about eight years afterward. The three children that we know as Sylvia, Valentine and Vivian were all hers. Then years after he married Miss Greatorex—the lady we know now as Mrs. Maitland. Your information identifying him as Warwick eased matters a great deal for us. One thing, however, emerges pretty clearly from the mass of facts that we have been able to ascertain. He was very active in the I.D.B. game, and he found more than one place too unhealthy for permanent residence. The South African police are pretty well agreed upon that point. That's that! Second, the three lumps of sugar that you found in the shed down at Queensleigh. I handed those lumps to Dr. Patterson for analysis. I had his report yesterday. Poisoned, sir! Every lump of the three. Just as you suspected, Sir Austin. What's perhaps even more to the point, Dr. Patterson hasn't yet been able to trace the poison—what it exactly is, I mean. He says it's something pretty obscure in the poison line that he hasn't met before. Anyhow, that disposes of my second point. Third, that letter you handed to me. The letter from Studdenham and Company."

Anthony Bathurst raised his eyebrows. He had been following Inspector Garth's recital very closely and with the keenest attention. But this last point that the inspector had mentioned was entirely new ground to him.

"Pardon me a moment, Sir Austin," he interposed. "But I'm in the dark here. To what letter does the inspector refer? I don't think I've heard of it."

"A letter that was sent to the Yard the day before yesterday, Bathurst. It was stated to have a bearing upon the Maitland case."

"From whom?"

"Studdenham and Company—the big turf people."

"Big commission agents, aren't they? What did they say? I'm very curious to know."

"I have the letter here, Mr. Bathurst," remarked Garth. He handed it across to Anthony, who read it with interest. It read:

STUDDENHAM HOUSE
SHAFTESBURY AVENUE

To the police authorities engaged upon the investigation of the murder of Julius Maitland. The Managing Director of Studdenham and Co. feels it his duty to inform those investigating the death of the late Julius Maitland, that the said gentleman made a statement to the firm of Studdenham and Co. on the morning of the day upon which he is supposed to have died that the authorities may or may not consider to be important. The Managing Director will be very pleased to place this information in the hands of the authorities concerned if those authorities will make the necessary arrangements for the transmission.

"H'm," remarked Anthony. "Have you been to Studdenham House, then, inspector?"

"I have, Mr. Bathurst. I went along there yesterday afternoon. And I have seen the writer of that letter—the managing director himself. His name is David Kidd. I will tell you what he told me. What I was going to tell the commissioner just now. It may be important—it may not. Personally I'm not sure." He jerked his head.

Mr. Bathurst took a cigarette from Sir Austin Kemble's proffered case and smiled encouragingly at Inspector Garth.

"Carry on, inspector. I am all attention."

The inspector coughed. "On the Monday morning before the Derby was run—the day that we are told that Mr. Maitland was killed—he telephoned to Studdenham concerning his horses. But perhaps I'm moving a bit too fast. For your information, gentlemen, I will tell you that Studdenham's do very big business on the turf in more ways than one. One of their special stunts is to offer large sums of money for the tickets in the very big sweeps that hold the favorites—the fancied horses—in other words, the horses that have been heavily backed with them. This plan enables them to lay off a lot of the money at much better odds than they would get if they hedged in the ordinary way and backed the particular horse with other big bookmakers. Also, they are sure of their money should the horse win. It is easier, you see, to buy a ticket holding the favourite for, say, fifteen thousand pounds than to invest fifteen thousand pounds on that same horse. The bet would probably have to be put on in parcels. You follow what I mean, don't you, gentlemen?"

"Quite, quite," ejaculated Sir Austin. "I've always understood that the offers of large sums of money for certain tickets in these big sweeps invariably emanated from concerns similar to Studdenham's. What was this phone message that came from Maitland? Was it just a general—?"

Here Garth broke in with some eagerness. "It was not what you would call a general message—in fact, it was just the opposite—it was very definite, and more than that, it was unusual. For some reason which Mr. Kidd is unable to fathom Julius Maitland deliberately went out of his way to inform Studdenham's that they need make no offer whatever for the Princess Alicia ticket, if they had considered the idea of so doing. He spoke to Mr. Kidd himself. He specially asked to do so. He told Mr. Kidd, when that gentleman tried to obtain more information from him, that they need entertain no fears whatever about Princess Alicia winning the race as on no account would she run. They could take his absolutely personal assurance to that effect. He refused to say any more than that. Anyhow, Mr. Kidd decided to stand by the information. Princess Alicia was not one of the more fancied horses, but being in the Queensleigh stable she had been backed by a good many people on the lookout for a decent price. Now he wishes he hadn't. He doesn't seem at all pleased with a wife who acts opposite to her husband's orders."

"One moment, Inspector Garth." Mr. Bathurst made the intervention. "Is Kidd absolutely certain that it was an authentic message from Maitland? That it was Maitland himself who was speaking on the telephone to him? It seems to me—"

"I raised that question myself, Mr. Bathurst, because I saw the apparent weakness, just as it has appealed to you. Mr. Kidd knew Maitland well, and knew his voice well—so he tells me— Maitland was very prominent in the racing world, as you know, and Kidd used to run across him fairly frequently. Mr. Kidd is certain that it was Maitland who spoke to him when I put it to him. He scouted the bare idea of it having been anybody else."

"Are you satisfied that it was Maitland, inspector, from what he told you?" Anthony put the question emphatically.

"I think so, Mr. Bathurst, I think I am. You see I've seen Kidd and talked with him. He should know, I suggest, sir."

"Very well. I agree that there's nothing like seeing a man and talking to him to assess his story correctly."

He rose and paced the room two or three times. Suddenly he swung round on to Sir Austin Kemble.

"Observe, sir, how those two horses of the Queensleigh stable keep cropping up! We get it on all sides. It's stupendous—the lengths to which a man's—" He broke off again just as suddenly—before the commissioner of police could reply. "By the way, Garth, what about Master Vivian? Did you follow up that line that I indicated?"

"Yes, Mr. Bathurst, I put several discreet inquiries round in the quarters that you suggested." The inspector put his hand in his pocket and withdrew his notebook. "I learn, on very good authority, that young Mr. Vivian Maitland at the present moment is paying a great deal of attention to no less a person than Pearlie Pilkington—Sir Charles Fenshaw's leading lady."

Mr. Bathurst nodded briskly at the receipt of the news. "Go on, Garth. You interest me. Any details?"

Garth looked at his notebook. "Yes, sir, that's why I'm referring to the book, sir. To the best of my information the acquaintanceship commenced about November last. In fact, one of my informants definitely placed it to have started on armistice night last year. Mr. Maitland and the lady met at a ball at Claridge's. During the month that followed—December—Mr. Vivian Maitland was present at the Diadem Theater for the performance of *A Dinner of Herbs* on no fewer than nine evenings in succession. Miss Pilkington's dresser mentioned it to several people—one presumes, therefore, that he was sufficiently encouraged to call upon Miss Pilkington in her dressing room. And they are still on the most friendly terms. There is no doubt about that. No later than three weeks ago Miss Pilkington was seen in Mr. Vivian Maitland's car in St. Margaret's Bay." Garth closed his notebook with a snap and an air of finality. "I'll tell you somewhere else, sir, in a minute or two. Not about Vivian—but concerning somebody else. It can wait a bit though—till we've finished this other matter."

"I saw Miss Pilkington in *A Dinner of Herbs*," remarked Sir Austin pensively. "I thought she gave a particularly finished performance. I should describe her as both charming and accomplished. I haven't seen better technique since Irene Vanburgh's—"

Mr. Bathurst cut him short. "You've done very well, Garth. What was the other matter you wished to tell Sir Austin?"

Garth looked a trifle uneasy for the moment, as though he were afraid of overstepping his duty to some extent. Eventually, however, he came to the point.

"Well, Sir Austin, it's like this. Very often in our line, as nobody knows better than yourself, when you're prosecuting a line of inquiry with regard to one particular man, you accidentally run across something important or interesting about somebody else. It has happened so on this occasion. Going after this information for Mr. Bathurst about Mr. Vivian Maitland I ran into something rather significant touching his brother."

"Valentine Maitland?" queried Sir Austin.

"Yes, sir, the late Mr. Maitland's eldest child. That is to say excluding the man we know as Alec Pollock."

Garth pursed his lips. "A month ago, gentlemen, Mr. Valentine Maitland was very seriously in debt. He's very addicted to a flutter not only on the turf but on the Stock Exchange as well. Also, he plays cards almost every evening. I am told that things have been going steadily against him for quite a long period now. So much so, that a week or two ago he owed money all round." Garth watched the effect of this announcement upon his two hearers. "It may be nothing, of course, gentlemen. I don't assert that it is. But I felt bound to mention it."

"To whom did he owe the money, Garth? Did you find that out?" Sir Austin asked the question with an upward jerk of the head.

"Not altogether, sir. But I know the names of some. I managed to obtain them. Miss Sylvia Maitland's fiancé—Captain Lumsden, was one of the gentlemen involved. Another was a Mr. Edgar Powell—the well-known actor."

"H'm," muttered Anthony. "I don't know that you ought to—" He stopped and pondered over something. Garth shook his head pessimistically.

"Its a nasty case altogether, Mr. Bathurst. I'm not denying that, Sir Austin, and you have cleared up a lot of points. To have established the scene of the murder means a lot. To have concentrated our inquiry in the Friningham district would only have wasted a lot of time. But all the same—" He shook his head again very doubtfully. Mr. Bathurst smiled.

"What you say is very true, Garth. It is an intricate case. I have not yet been able to identify the man that Sergeant Mansfield heard laughing. I am not yet absolutely sure as to what fact set the actual ball rolling at the first onset. So you see I share your difficulties to some extent. But as I said previously, your investigations with regard to Vivian Maitland have helped me no end. Are you coming, Sir Austin?"

Mr. Bathurst walked across the room for his hat. Inspector Garth accepted the situation philosophically.

"I appreciate what you say, Mr. Bathurst, but—! I don't know that I'm particularly worried about the man that Mansfield heard laughing. I'm very much more concerned about who killed Mr. Julius Maitland. That's the point that worries me."

"Don't let it, Inspector. As a matter of fact, I could have answered that question for you three days ago. At any rate—I'll tell you for certain in less than a week's time."

CHAPTER XXV

MR. BATHURST settled himself deeply in his own special armchair in an excess of comfort, thrust his long legs out to their limit, pushed his right hand into the appropriate trousers pocket and used his left for his pipe—at which he puffed steadily. His eyes were almost closed. He knew of no better way than this for the establishment of mental concentration which, in his case, was invariably assisted by a condition of physical relaxation. He desired if possible to bring back to his eyes the topography of the room at Ravenswood where the body of Julius Maitland had been discovered. Sergeant Mansfield's story of the telephone message that had brought the police to the bungalow had always intrigued him vastly, and had always held for him a most insistent interest. He constantly found his thoughts coming back to it. It had given him his first ideas regarding the crime, but at the same time had left him in a condition of semi-satisfaction only.

Was it possible for him to obtain from the Friningham theatre of operations a complete answer to the entire case? Or better than that—and truer than that—was it not correct for him to say now that the only link in the chain that remained for him to forge belonged to that part of it attached to and concerned with Friningham?

He turned over in his mind the sergeant's story—point by point—detail by detail. The voice had cried for help, had given directions as to where the help was needed and had actually mentioned the word "murder." Then had come the scuffling sounds of a struggle, followed by the voice of another man. After that the sergeant had heard strange laughter, laughter that he had described as—Mr. Bathurst could not remember with certainty the exact adjective that had been employed, but for the time being he decided to substitute "uncontrollable." He recalled that that was the impression of the laughter that Mansfield's story had given him when he had first listened to it. Following upon this laughter there had come the strains of a violin, and then the whole affair as heard by the sergeant had terminated in an abrupt silence, as though a string had snapped! Peculiar, that! He determined to attempt to visualize that room again as completely as possible. A spacious dining table—five chairs—an imposing sideboard—a gramophone—the Chesterfield with the violin bow and case lying thereon—the telephone with its receiver—

Mr. Bathurst suddenly stopped. Why had he not thought of that possibility before? His mind caught up this last train of thought as a tongue of hungering fire does paper. It unfolded manifold contingencies, but there was always the—After a matter of ten minutes' very careful meditation Mr. Bathurst rose. His grey eyes showed that strange gleam of excitement that told his friends when they saw it that he had accomplished something—the effecting of which particular something had afforded him a strong measure of satisfaction.

"I wonder," he murmured to himself. "I wonder." He rubbed the palms of his hands—satisfaction-sign number two to the initiated. "I should have a morning paper somewhere of Derby date. Wednesday it was."

Walking across the room to the low chair that stood in the corner by the fireplace and upon which it was his habit to toss his miscellaneous collection of daily and evening papers he went through the heap quickly and decisively until he found the paper that he required.

"Now for the programme—let's have a look at it," said he to himself. "If my theory be correct—the programme will tell the story."

He turned to the appropriate page and ran his eager eyes down it. Suddenly the gleam came into them again and the line of his jaw set more firmly. There it was—staring at him in the coldest of cold print. A smile played round the corners of his lips as he realized all that this latest discovery of his meant and signified. But what a doddering, purblind idiot he had been not to have understood the truth before! He decided there and then to see Vivian Maitland at once. Fortified by this last piece of information, and taking into consideration Inspector Garth's statement to which he had recently listened, he felt that there could be only one explanation of the former's first visit to Friningham. At any rate, he would immediately make sure and confirm his own opinion.

Copeland received him with some degree of condescension. Mr. Vivian Maitland was in. But he was not sure whether the gentleman would see Mr. Bathurst. As a matter of fact, Mr. Vivian Maitland did not care for—had Mr. Bathurst an appointment?

The latter smiled sweetly. Somehow he had the idea that Mr. Maitland would see him—after all, he had the honour of representing Sir Austin Kemble, commissioner of police. But he would send Mr. Vivian Maitland a message if Copeland would be good enough to deliver it.

Mr. Bathurst scribbled something on his visiting card, placed it inside an envelope which he took from his pocket, and handed it to the butler.

Within a moment or two Copeland was back, impassive as ever. "Mr. Maitland will see you, sir. Will you please step this way? Follow me, sir."

Mr. Bathurst entered the room indicated, and found Vivian Maitland hot upon his heels.

"Are you sure it is I whom you wish to see, Mr. Bathurst?" opened the latter. "Because my stepmother is in, and, frankly, I'm rather puzzled. I see that you say your business is of extreme importance. Surely, in the circumstances, you would prefer to see her? Have you any news?"

The innocent note in the tone of his inquiry would have reflected credit upon an *ingénue*. Mr. Bathurst's reply held something more than a tinge of gravity.

"If you have a moment to spare, Mr. Maitland, I should be exceedingly grateful for it. For it is you whom I desire to see. Many thanks." He took the chair that the young man offered. "I want to talk to you," he proceeded, "about that bungalow at Friningham in which your father's body was found—Ravens-wood—Pin Hole Way. That was the address. No doubt you remember the name quite well, Mr. Maitland." Anthony looked up quickly. Vivian changed colour. It was obvious that Mr. Bathurst's direct attack had disconcerted and surprised him. But he dissembled moderately successfully and answered the question that had been put to him with a fair amount of *sang-froid*.

"Yes, very well, indeed. It's rather a distinctive name, don't you think, and therefore more than usually likely to stick in one's memory. Why do you ask, though?"

Anthony eyed him coldly and challengingly: "I have been wondering for some time now, Mr. Maitland, why you chose at our first interview to tell me a deliberate lie in connection with certain facts about that bungalow?"

The man he had challenged had by now lost every vestige of colour from his face, but he still showed fight. Fight supported by something like bluster.

"What the devil do you mean, Mr. Bathurst? How dare you bring such an accusation against me? Who the hell are you to launch charges, anyway? I can assure you that I am not accustomed to having such things as that said to me. For two pins I'd—"

Anthony regarded him with a mixture of amusement and contempt, for had it come to a struggle between the two of them, Maitland would have cut a sorry figure. He waved Maitland away—unceremoniously.

"Sit down at once, and don't be a fool. Do you seriously think that I should bring a charge like that against you unless I were sure of my ground? What value do you presume to place upon my intelligence?" He paused and looked at Maitland sternly. "Once again, why did you lie to me?"

The man addressed seemed to sense that Mr. Bathurst was his master in everything that counted. "How do you mean?" he muttered sulkily.

"That's a little better," returned Anthony. "You're improving. I'll tell you what I mean in as few words as possible. You informed me upon the occasion of our first meeting that Ravenswood belonged to Mr. Ponsonby. When you made the statement I noticed that you spoke quickly and spontaneously and without giving yourself time to think of the significance of what you were saying. Immediately after that—without being questioned in any way—you supplemented your statement. You added something to it. You asserted that the information had been given to you by the manager of the Majestic Hotel. Thus did deception weave another tangled web. The net that you laid privily caught you and you fell into your own mischief. For Southcott, the manager of the Majestic, knows nothing about Ponsonby. I've seen him about it."

Vivian Maitland broke in—still aggressive and antagonistic: "How do you know that Southcott is speaking the truth? Why should you be so ready and willing to take his word against mine—?"

"Dear me, Mr. Maitland, how you do underrate my abilities, to be sure. I fear that in your circle of acquaintance intelligence must be conspicuous by its absence." Suddenly his tone changed, levity gave way to strength. He rose and stood towering over the other man. "I know more than Southcott's denial. I don't base my statements upon that only. I know almost all of this strange case that there is to know. Please understand that, Mr. Maitland. I know, for example, that you stayed in the Friningham bungalow some time during last April. I know why you stayed there, and with whom you stayed there. Certain publicities carry certain penalties you know. And I know who killed your father." Then just as suddenly again his voice softened. "Why didn't you tell me the truth at first? It would have helped me so much. Subterfuge and falsehood only spelled delay."

Vivian Maitland's face twisted from incredulity into a look of anxiety. "You know who killed—?" He paused, but quickly went on again: "I've committed no crime that I can see, Mr. Bathurst. I told you, I admit. But I had a reason—two reasons, if you stop to think, and if you know all, as you say you do. If I complicated matters for you, I'm sorry. But after all—a man's duty is to himself and to his—" He stopped again.

"Wife?" suggested Mr. Bathurst with a smile.

"Yes, Mr. Bathurst, you're right. It doesn't seem to make much difference—so I may as well admit it at once. I married Miss Pilkington of the Diadem Theatre on the fifth of April. We spent part of our honeymoon at Friningham—in Mr. Ponsonby's bungalow. It was imperative that I should keep it a secret from my father. If I hadn't—there would have been the very devil to pay—also Miss Pilkington was anxious that it should be kept quiet as well. We stayed at Ravenswood—that was her idea, too—it was great fun looking after ourselves for a fortnight. I had heard my father mention the bungalow and how Ponsonby wanted to sell it to him. So I got into touch with Ponsonby and he let me have it for the time I wanted. I went down beforehand to get the place ready. I can't say any more, because I don't think there's really any more for me to say. I'm sorry I didn't admit my association with the bungalow when I first met you. I can see now that it would have helped you."

"The coincidence frightened you, eh?" Vivian Maitland reddened.

"I won't say that altogether. Let me put it like this. It seemed to me that, inasmuch as I was the only person round my father who really knew anything about Ravenswood, I had better keep that knowledge to myself. It seemed to me to implicate me so thoroughly. But, of course, like a consummate fool, I made the slip about Ponsonby—and gave away the very thing I intended to repress. I hoped that it had passed unnoticed. But, Mr. Bathurst—tell me—who killed my father? What did you mean by your statement? I have been frank with you. Please be equally frank with me. To be free from worry and doubt—and vague suspicion—and fear—and growing anxiety—will mean much to me."

His voice held a pleading note that Mr. Bathurst detected and decided was genuinely sincere.

"Mr. Maitland," he replied, "to err is human. Perhaps I spoke a shade too certainly just now. Let me say rather—I think I know who killed your father. I know how he was killed—when he was killed—where he as killed—and why he was killed. As for the hand that shot him—well, as I said just now, I think I know that, too. But before I accuse—" He broke off and shrugged his shoulders. "I must be absolutely certain, mustn't I? I shall make certain very soon—and I shall call upon you to be present when I do. Good-bye, Mr. Maitland, and thank you for the interview. You will hear from Sir Austin Kemble in a very few days from now. He will make an appointment with you which you must promise to keep. I will leave matters for the moment at that. Good-bye."

Vivian Maitland bowed. "Very well, Mr. Bathurst. You rely upon me. But I am strongly afraid—" He shook his head ominously as Mr. Bathurst withdrew.

Bathurst drove straight to the Yard and was with Sir Austin almost immediately.

"I got your note, Bathurst," opened the commissioner. "You know that I'm quite prepared to fall in with your wishes. I understand that you want me to send for these people to come here. I notice also what you want said in the letters of summons. You desire me to question them, eh? Is that the idea?"

"Well, partly, sir, and partly not. Candidly, I'm not absolutely sure of one point—almost—but not quite. And as I've told you before, I never care about making the last move in a case of this kind until I haven't the shadow of a doubt. It's so easy to make a mistake. You remember the party we staged in the concluding stages of that grim little drama enacted near Mapleton—don't you?" Sir Austin nodded. "I've got an idea, sir, that something of the same kind in this affair should give me the feeling of certainty for which I'm seeking."

"Very well, Bathurst, I'll get it attended to for you. Into different rooms you say, eh?"

"Until the time is ready for you to see them, sir, if you don't mind." The commissioner looked again at the note to which he had previously referred.

"Is it absolutely necessary to have every one of these people? And who the devil's Joseph Lee?"

"I would rather, sir! As I see it, and as I know the circumstances—Julius Maitland might have been murdered by any one of six people. So you see that there is a big margin in which a mistake could occur. Lee's a man you and I haven't met yet. An interesting character, too."

Sir Austin frowned disapprovingly. "Are you as doubtful as all that, my boy? We mustn't take any risks, you know—hang it all—I can't."

Anthony smiled on him reassuringly. "As a matter of fact, Sir Austin—I'm not really doubtful at all. I'm prepared to prove that to you. Give me a piece of that foolscap."

Sir Austin obeyed. Mr. Bathurst took his fountain pen and scribbled a name across it. "There you are, sir. If things go as I anticipate they will—a most dramatic confession will be forthcoming. Surprised?"

Sir Austin stared at the name some time before he answered. "Well, I'm damned," he exclaimed.

CHAPTER XXVI

"Very good, Sanders. You say that everything is ready? Good then!" Sir Austin Kemble turned to Anthony. "Remington is here at last, Bathurst. He was the man for whom you were waiting, I believe? You are quite certain that there is nobody else?"

Anthony checked off a number of names. "Everybody's here, Sir Austin. We have sufficient chairs, I think. Good! You sit there, inspector, and have your man at the most convenient place."

"Are we likely to have trouble, Bathurst? Because, if you like, I'll—"

"I think not, sir. Each one of the people here imagines that he or she has been summoned in quite a friendly spirit regarding his or her depositions. No, sir, bank on me. I promise that I won't let you down. Besides, you know what I forecast." Sir Austin grunted—perhaps only partly satisfied.

"Very well! Bring them in that order, Sanders. You stay in here, Garth."

One by one they entered the room, each seeming to bear a different burden of responsibility. Mrs. Maitland, to call her still by the name by which she was known to the world, Sylvia and Captain Lumsden, were followed by Vivian and Valentine Maitland. They were conducted to a group of seats on Sir Austin's right. In their wake came Alec Pollock and his mother, Humphrey Cruden with his wife and son—with Michael Remington hard upon them. Then came the imperturbable Copeland. The last pair consisted of Patrick Wogan Dillon and his father, the Rev. Curtin Wogan Dillon, vicar of Latchingford and rural dean of Bradstock.

At a quick nod from Mr. Bathurst the doors of the room were closed by Sanders. Sir Austin Kemble rose and addressed the gathering.

"I have decided to conduct a semi-official inquiry this afternoon into the murder of the late Mr. Julius Maitland, for there are still one or two points upon which it is necessary for me to obtain further information. You have all been spoken to and interrogated before, or at all events, most of you have, and you have made various statements, so that you are aware of most of the points in connection with the case. Mr. Bathurst will make plain to you what more it is that we want. Mr. Bathurst?"

Anthony in his turn rose. "What I am going to say will prove a surprise, no doubt, to some of you. And there are certain features of the affair upon which I do not propose to dwell too long. For they are both private and painful and dangerously delicate. But it is vitally necessary for Sir Austin Kemble, in his official capacity, to get at the truth. It is equally necessary for everyone here to-day that the truth should be ascertained. I will first ask a question of Mr. Michael Remington."

The famous jockey stood up, ill at ease in the unfamiliar conditions in which he found himself. Mr. Bathurst got to work at once.

"You were first jockey to the late Mr. Maitland, were you not?"

"Yes, sir. I have been ever since he came over from South Africa."

"Was he keen on winning the Derby?"

"I should say so. None ever keener."

Remington's mouth twisted half-humorously.

"Would he have liked his wife to have beaten him?"

"Guess he'd have just hated it. He'd have liked it about as much as a cat likes cold water."

"Could Princess Alicia have beaten Red Ringan over a mile and a half on the Epsom course?"

"With Michael Remington up—every time!" His lips curled contemptuously.

"Did Mr. Maitland know this?"

"He did, sir."

"How do you know that he did?"

"Because I told him."

"Did Humphrey Cruden know it?"

"Aye, I told him, too."

"Did Mrs. Maitland know it?"

Remington hesitated. There was a stir over to his left, it seemed to concern both Cruden and Ida. But he answered without so much as giving a glance in that direction:

"Yes, Mrs. Maitland knew it. I told her before Red Ringan won the Craven Stakes at Newmarket in the early spring."

"Thank you, Remington, that's all I want to know. You may sit down."

Mr. Bathurst turned his attention to the company in general.

"What I am going to say now belongs to the more delicate stage of the inquiry at which I previously hinted. But if the case comes to trial, it must be remembered that it will all be made public—to-day it will be heard by a comparative few. And it has touched so many of you in various ways that it is only fair that all of you here to-day should know the truth. May I speak to you now, Mrs. Maitland?"

Ida Maitland turned her face toward him, but its loveliness was tinged with anxiety. "Remain seated, Mrs. Maitland, please. You are aware, of course, that I have no power at this stage of the proceedings to insist upon your answering my questions. But I sincerely hope that you will, because to do so will assist us greatly in our endeavours to arrive at a satisfactory conclusion." Anthony noticed the man at whom she looked before she answered. "It depends, I think, Mr. Bathurst." Her voice was low but clear.

"Very well. Let me try. Some time on the Monday morning before the Derby something happened that disturbed you profoundly. You had what may perhaps be termed a shock. I think I know what happened. You met a very old friend. That friend had some very amazing and surprising news for you. News that was destined to revolutionize your whole life. Will you confirm that fact?"

Ida Maitland looked scared beyond expression, but she did not deny the truth of Mr. Bathurst's statement. She bowed her head in assent. "Yes," she said, almost inaudibly.

Mr. Bathurst continued his recital: "As a result of this disturbance, you decided to follow your husband to Queensleigh. He had probably told you he was going there. Perhaps he may even have told you that he was going to see Mr. Pollock at Baverstock. Anyhow, you wanted to see your husband pretty badly. And so did the person who drove you down." There was a sudden gasp from Ida—it was the only sound that disturbed the almost uncanny stillness of the room. "I may even say," proceeded Anthony, "that you desired to see your husband for more than one reason. You were burning fiercely under the shock and agony of the almost irreparable injury he had done you—and you feared, I fancy, that in his heart he harboured yet another piece of wickedness and deviltry. As a matter of fact, he did. Between Queensleigh and Baverstock you saw your husband—almost unexpectedly. He was walking from the latter place to the former. You saw him from the car in which you were travelling. He was crossing a field when—suddenly—a heavy thundershower broke. Your husband ran for shelter. The place he chose for that was an old disused shed standing in the field about fifty yards from him and about three times that distance from the car in which you sat. You decided to seek him out then and there—and for the time being to leave your companion behind. He was the last man whom you wished your husband to see at the moment. You met your husband. You told him what you had that day heard. You may have discovered the further infamy that he was about to perpetrate, but upon that point I am hardly certain. But the talk lasted some little time. Anyhow, it doesn't matter—the next thing that you knew was that you were struggling with your husband—fighting for dear life. He was mad with a mixture of rage, jealousy and shame. You carried a small revolver; your husband was armed with a knife, which was of little use to him. In fact, his own fingers got slashed and his blood covered your left hand. Your husband was killed." Mr. Bathurst paused dramatically, and catching the eye of the assiduous Sanders, made a slight movement of the head. The latter flung open the door and there entered a dark-featured olive-skinned man who looked round with surprise at the surroundings in which he suddenly discovered himself. For a moment there was a dead silence, broken only by a sob from Sylvia. Ida Maitland sat on her left—white-faced and despairing, motionless—for the moment seemingly incapable of articulate speech. The others looked from her to the newcomer, their glances pregnant with wonderment.

"Mr. Joseph Lee?" asked Mr. Bathurst, with an almost exaggerated courtesy. "Would you mind stepping this way?"

Lee stopped—irresolute and wondering—then he caught sight of two familiar faces, and took a half step toward them. "I would like to ask you a few—"

Before Mr. Bathurst could complete his sentence another interruption came—tense and sharp as a shot from a gun.

"Stop!" cried a voice. "Stop! There is no need for this to go any longer. I killed Julius Maitland! Mrs. Maitland is innocent!"

A smothered cry left the lips of Lee, for it was the voice of Patrick Wogan Dillon.

CHAPTER XXVII

FLINGING ASIDE the restraining hand of the vicar of Latchingford, Pat Dillon rose to his feet and squared his shoulders to the emergency. Two exclamations came from the group of listeners almost simultaneously.

"Mr. Pat," cried Lee, "they told me to come—"

Then Ida Maitland's cut into his and silenced it.

"Pat," she called, appealingly, "it's not—"

"Sit down, Ida," he spoke quietly, almost softly. "Sit down—it will be better if you let me tell the story in my own way. Sit down—please."

His eyes mastered her, she yielded him the dominance and sank back again in her seat, her fingers gripping the sides of her chair tight and tensely.

"One moment, Dillon, before you start." Mr. Bathurst's voice was quietly insistent as his glance caught Sir Austin Kemble's. He was well aware what the commissioner of police was thinking. "How was it that you killed Julius Maitland if you didn't leave your car for a greater distance than a few yards?"

Dillon flushed.

"A few yards?"

"Yes, surely you remember what you told me. You said that you didn't leave your car expect to stroll round it for a few yards. How then could you have—?"

"I lied," cut in Dillon, with blunt directness. "I lied when I said that."

He tossed his hair from his forehead with a quick and impulsive gesture, and faced the ring of upturned faces unfalteringly.

"Put down what I say, Sir Austin Kemble. I killed Julius Maitland, but that isn't to say that I murdered him—not by a long chalk. The lady whom you know as Mrs. Maitland to me is Ida Greatorex. If I tell you that a few years ago we were on the point of becoming engaged, you will understand why. We met at the Albert Falls, twenty miles south of Maritzburg a matter of about four years ago. We loved each other—at first sight—and it didn't take either of us very long to discover the fact that it was mutual. But quite unexpectedly, and when everything was set, I got a change of job. I got sent up-country, miles away from Durban— where I was living at the time—suddenly and with little warning.

"Three months after I had been on the new work Ida's letters to me stopped coming abruptly. I wrote and wrote and wrote, but got no reply. I tried to get leave to go to Durban, but it was impossible. Then, my world stopped, shattered. I heard that she had married Julius Maitland. It was a bolt from the blue to me. You can imagine the bitter things I thought. But I am a proud man, and I determined to forget. I resolved to cut the memory of her out of my heart and life. I did, but three months ago the whole affair was brought back to me. There was a postal bribery case tried in Durban this March, and I knew one of the officials concerned. Certain facts leaked out which raised certain suspicions in my mind. To cut a long story short, I made some very pertinent inquiries and discovered that Maitland had bribed certain postal servants to intercept my letters to her and her letters to me. I saw through the whole thing." He paused and Barbara Warwick's voice rang through the room in support.

"Just the dirty trick that Julius would do. As I can vouch for to my cost. The swine!" Dillon disregarded the interruption and continued:

"I had a leave due in May, so I resolved to come to see Ida. I felt that I must, that I just had to—to tell her everything. He stole her from me—she should know how. And he should know that

she knew and that I knew. I had no idea what would happen—
that never entered my mind—but she was my woman, that was
all I could think about and all that mattered to me. Then something wonderful happened. I heard that I had drawn her horse
in the Calcutta sweep. But we'll talk of that later. I arrived home,
and on the Monday morning before the Derby was to be run I
came up to London from Latchingford by car, determined to see
Ida. I knew where she lived—I phoned to her and she met me.
When she saw me she looked as though she had come through
an earthquake. I told her the truth of what had happened. She
was still my woman. As Bathurst has said, we went after Maitland to have it out with him. Going down to Wiltshire, I told
her about my Princess Alicia ticket. When I told her, she had an
inspiration."

"'Pat,' she said, 'Julius knows. I'm certain of it. He's lied to me
again. That's why he won't let me run her. I'll run the Princess
now, whatever happens. And I believe she can win! Remington
says so—that fortune shall be yours. I'll repay some of the debt
I owe you.' You know how she met Maitland. I was going to see
him afterward. Bathurst's story is correct to a detail. He has told
you how the struggle started. But it went against her. She called
to me for help. I heard her cry out as I stood by the car. I rushed
to her assistance. Maitland was twisting her hand round so that
her little revolver was turned against her. My heart went to my
mouth, but thank God! I arrived just in time. I seized his hand—
the revolver went off, and Maitland fell dead on the straw of the
cowshed. We were both too stunned for a time to do anything or
to think coherently. Then we made our plans.

"If we told the truth, we realized—seeing who I was and what
had gone before—that things would look very awkward for us
and very black against us. So we resolved to give the police a run
for their money, and to make a proper mystery of it. We would
dump the body somewhere. There wasn't a soul about—we
tested that fact for a quarter of an hour. I watched from the door,
as a matter of fact, and Ida from the hedge, but didn't see a soul.
Then she felt in his pockets and discovered a bunch of keys with
an address label attached. She told me what it was—a bungalow

at Friningham that he had mentioned to her as being for sale. I ran the car forward along the road and then along the footpath. After putting the shed to rights and removing our traces, we got him into it and drove off to Friningham, planning and plotting our next moves. It was getting dark when we got there. We found the place quite empty and put him in the dining room where the police found him. But there was still the Derby question that we had discussed on our way down. Our plans were these. Julius Maitland had gone to South Africa. That would account for his disappearance. I would phone her to that effect when we got back to town. And Ida would run Princess Alicia, although she dared not take Remington off Red Ringan. With Maitland supposed to have been away, it would look too suspicious.

"If the Princess won, which was unlikely—with the stable lad riding—Maitland's body could be in the bungalow till it was discovered there, when—didn't matter! But if the Princess ran second to Red Ringan, as she should on form, and which was what actually happened—then Maitland's body should be found at once—Red Ringan would be disqualified and the Calcutta be ours. I say 'ours' purposely. But how on earth could we arrange for it to be discovered at the psychological moment without incriminating ourselves and giving ourselves away. That was the question for which we had to find an answer. This time it was my turn to have an inspiration. I have had a very faithful friend right from my boyhood. He's here with us to-day, though how the blazes they got on his tracks beats me. His name's Lee— he's a gypsy. Anything I ask him he'll do, and without asking questions, either. I noticed the wireless set in the bungalow at Friningham. Lee should come to the bungalow on the afternoon that the Derby was run and wait for the result to be announced.

"If Red Ringan won, with Princess Alicia second, it was arranged that he should phone the police at once and then get away. I laid the 'patteran' for him—that's a piece of gypsy lore he had taught me—between Friningham railway station and the gate of the bungalow on the Tuesday. I told him what I wanted done. I made sure that Maitland should be identified. I printed his name in capital letters on an envelope he carried. Lee went down there with the keys, picked up the 'patteran,' and every-thing after that went according to plan. That's about all, I think. When I came here to-day I wondered how much Bathurst knew—when I saw Joe Lee come in, I knew the time had come to talk. That's why you've been listening to me."

"My poor boy! My poor boy!" murmured the vicar.

Pat turned and faced Sir Austin. "But it was an accident, sir, a pure accident, and even if it hadn't been, it was justifiable. Any man would have done what I did—it was Ida's life against his."

The commissioner frowned. Before he could reply Mr. Bathurst took up the threads again.

"Thank you, Dillon. I know that your story is substantially correct, and I will vouch for it to Sir Austin Kemble here. But it is now my turn to say something more. Something that should reassure you tremendously. You will be glad to know that neither you nor Mrs. Maitland killed Julius Maitland. The bullet from your revolver was the one that splintered the clavicle and was subsequently extracted by Dr. Forsyth. Julius Maitland was killed by another person—who is here at this moment. And by the way, Lee, I must congratulate you on your last stroke before you decamped from the bungalow after sending the telephone message. I should describe it as a touch of genius on your part."

CHAPTER XXVIII

EVERY EYE was again turned upon Anthony. The gypsy to whom he had addressed his last remark grinned in appreciation and flashed a row of beautifully white and even teeth at the speaker.

"I guessed it would mystify more than a few, sir. The idea came to me all of a sudden though."

Mr. Bathurst permitted himself the suggestion of a smile. "I imagined so. But to resume. The struggle in the shed between Maitland and the two people whom he had wronged, that Mr. Dillon has just described so graphically, was witnessed by a fourth person. That fourth person happened to be on the spot by accident and actually passed at the back of the shed as the critical moment of the struggle was developing, at the time, I imagine, when Maitland himself appeared to be getting the upper hand. Two revolvers were fired simultaneously. The coincidence of their discharge was complete and the synchronization exact. This fourth person about whom I have told you fired through the square aperture at the back of the shed and the bullet went clean through Maitland's throat and out through the open door of the shed on the other side. I have no doubt that systematic and extensive search covering a wide area would unearth it. But I am altogether certain as to the identity of this fourth person.

"In circumstances of this nature it is very difficult to be absolutely sure, for there is so little evidence upon which an investigator can work and base his assurance. But I am almost sure! Will the person who saw Mrs. Maitland's revolver twisting slowly in her husband's grip until it menaced herself—before Mr. Dillon came to the rescue, who afterward fired at Maitland and killed him—confess that my reading of this strange case is correct?" And again Mr. Bathurst paused. He paused to see if his challenge were taken up. The seconds passed relentlessly, but no other sound broke the stillness. Everybody kept quiet. The faces of all present were white and strained—each, as it were, suspecting each—wondering—marvelling—save the one that knew the inevitable truth.

Lines of rare beauty began to dance in Dillon's brain as something seemed to tell him that Bathurst was at this moment very close to his quarry. They came to him half unconsciously—just segments of the whole—"unhurrying chase—unperturbed pace—deliberate speed—majestic instancy." He visualized the god of justice with the shining countenance of truth—and then he heard Anthony's voice again—coming as it were from a great distance—what was it Bathurst was saying—he was asking a question now. His words came to Pat Dillon as one word. "Perhaps I was too confident and asked too much. But all the same I do not retrace one step yet. Perhaps Mrs. Cruden will be able to assist me if I put one or two questions to her?"

All eyes turned to the woman addressed. Monica Cruden's left hand went to her face almost convulsively and for just the fraction of a moment Humphrey, her husband, and Dick, her son, were stung from their amazement and assailed by a yet dreader and more ghastly fear. But she shook her head and lifted her eyes toward Anthony.

"You need not ask me any questions, Mr. Bathurst. But I found it very hard to speak just now. If it happened as you say it did—I won't deny it. I fired my son's revolver at Julius Maitland, but, of course, I wasn't absolutely certain if my shot had killed him—because I felt sure the other revolver had gone off too. I did it for Mrs. Maitland's sake—I thought he was going to kill her. I saw her getting overpowered as I passed by—I saw the devilish look on his face. I had the revolver in my mackintosh pocket. I had taken it away from my son—I didn't think—I saw Mrs. Maitland's peril—I didn't think the other gentleman would be in time—to save her—I just fired—and I saw Mr. Maitland fall. I don't think that there is anything more for me to say, is there? If I must be punished for what I did—then, of course, I must be—" Her shoulders heaved, and her voice, curiously quiet and low, trailed away.

Mr. Bathurst's reply was gentle and sympathetic.

"Sir Austin Kemble will see you and your husband after the rest have gone, Mrs. Cruden. But we have the truth now, and these things are best cleared up, you know, otherwise the future may hold unmerited hardship and handicap not only for us, perhaps, but also maybe for others who are entirely innocent. Sir Austin, will you advise Mr. Cruden and his wife as to their best course?"

The commissioner tore up a piece of foolscap that he had taken from his breast pocket and came down the room. His mind was made up.

Mr. Bathurst looked at the commissioner questioningly. "There will have to be a trial, I am afraid, Bathurst, but I doubt if any jury would convict in the circumstances. A most remarkable case—right from the beginning. But you must dine with me to-night and explain one or two points about which I'm still in the dark. Ricardo's suit you?"

It did—admirably—and somewhere about eight thirty that evening Mr. Bathurst accepted a cigar from the commissioner and signified that he was prepared to furnish any information that was required.

"Start from the outset, Bathurst. What put you on the track first of all?"

"Well, sir, the feature of the case that first started me really thinking in essentials was the trouble taken to make sure that the police should discover Maitland's dead body. As far as I know it is unprecedented in the annals of crime. Why was it done? Why must the police be told on Wednesday afternoon what they had not been told on the Monday or the Tuesday? For the man had been dead two days remember. Presumably, too, the only people who knew that Maitland was dead were his murderers or their accomplices. Any innocent party would have informed the authorities in the proper way and through the proper channels. No, I felt certain that the message was a fake, engineered so that the police should go round to the bungalow and discover what they were intended to discover— the body. But again—why? Concerning the Derby, of course. I now felt certain that the affair had a racing significance. I said to myself: 'What happened when the news of Maitland's death was published and his horse, Red Ringan, disqualified?' The obvious answer was: The race was awarded to the second horse, Princess Alicia, which belonged to Mrs. Maitland, which ran—through a change of plan, mind you—at the very last moment. See my point, Sir Austin?"

The commissioner sampled his black coffee with the assurance of the connoisseur and nodded approvingly. Anthony went on:

"I decided, therefore, that Mrs. Maitland and her movements would bear close inspection unless something happened that thoroughly incriminated somebody else. For there was another point in connection with her that was interesting—her story that Julius Maitland had gone abroad was to all intents and purposes uncorroborated. Copeland the butler could confirm the fact of the message coming—he couldn't confirm who was telephoning—it might have been anybody for all he knew. But I felt certain that she had accomplices—or at least one accomplice. Let us look for a moment at what I discovered at Friningham. You will remember how I spotted the 'patteran.'"

Sir Austin lifted his eyebrows.

"I don't—"

Anthony smiled at him.

"Gypsies leave a trail of crossed twigs or leaves to point the way they have taken. George Borrow calls it the 'patteran.' A gypsy girl is supposed to have instructed him in the art. Her name was Ursula. Don't you remember I mentioned her?" He continued without waiting for Sir Austin's answer. "Anyhow, I put a gypsy on my list and was always on the look-out for one to turn up. It seemed to me as likely that the person who phoned the police station was unused to telephoning. He called them by a number and not by 'police station,' as is usual. Then I got to the bungalow features. We have already discussed several of them—but there are one or two that yet remained to be explained."

"There are," cut in Sir Austin, "who played the violin? Who laughed? Whose hair—?"

"Be patient, sir, and I will endeavour to deal with them all. The violin question puzzled me for a very long time—more so because the violin in the room at Ravenswood was badly out of tune and could not possibly have been the one that the sergeant heard. That violin, on the Chesterfield, I will confidently wager hadn't been played for months. I was very slow over that, Sir Austin—but I got it at last."

Mr. Bathurst took a newspaper cutting from the breast pocket of his dinner jacket and pushed it across to the commissioner. Sir Austin read it and frowned.

"You see," said Bathurst, "London and Daventry—Wednesday afternoon programme—The Derby described by Wallis Edgar as the race is run. 3.30. The 3.30 refers to Kriek. Kriek, comedy violinist with laughing accompaniment.—" The commissioner's eyes almost bulged from his head. He looked up at Anthony, who appeared to be thoroughly enjoying his discomfiture.

"Lee heard the Derby result by wireless as he had been instructed by Dillon, and just as he started to phone the police Kriek started the next item on the programme. Lee had previously seen the violin on the Chesterfield and, phoning had a stroke of genius. He left the receiver off the phone and put the loud speaker against the mouthpiece. He realized how it would puzzle all of us. He was right. It did. All the same, I was off form to be so slow cottoning on to it. Thank you, Sir Austin." Anthony used the ash tray that the commissioner pushed over to him.

"Now we come to the two other points I picked up in the bungalow. The first we will recall the hair symptom. Do you recall me smelling it? For a second or two the odour eluded me. But it soon came to me—that hair was *perruquier's* hair—it reeked of grease paint, the smell of which you can't possibly mistake. It had been in a make-up box with grease paint—and had probably been pulled from a wig. It was false and dark—therefore I looked for a woman the reverse of dark. Mrs. Maitland was fair!"

"A good touch that, Bathurst. One of your best. But who put it—?"

"There are still bills in Latchingford advertising a theatrical performance in which a certain P. W. Dillon recently took part. He had his make-up box in his car—had probably forgotten to take it out—and used it purposely. It would cause another complication. When I eventually found Patrick in the case—and he incidentally offered me a cigarette—I knew I was getting very warm, because I remembered his dramatic activities in the O.U.D.S. His Laertes is still talked about in Oxford. Point number two was the straw in Maitland's trouser turn-ups. I was convinced he had been moved to Friningham and that the straw had probably come from his stable at Queensleigh. Therein I was wrong, because he hadn't been to the Queensleigh stables that afternoon. But the idea served to take us down there—with what result you know. The motorist I felt certain was an accomplice of Mrs. Maitland's—but when we got inside the cowshed I had to remodel some of my opinions. I found evidence there that Julius Maitland might have been killed by a third party.

"Two revolvers had been used and the fatal bullet was nowhere in the dead man's body. I established the fact that it might have been fired through the window space at the back of the shed and gone out through the open door. It might have been fired by Mrs. Maitland, her motorist friend, or perhaps somebody else from outside. And the person who fired it—whoever he or she was—had broken a big cobweb as the arm holding the revolver was pushed through the space to fire. Who might this third person reasonably have been—in this part of the world? I thought of the two neighbouring stables and determined to have a look at each of them. Then doubts began to assail me. Why, I said, should Mrs. Maitland and her motorist go to all the trouble they had done if they were innocent of the killing? Could any set of circumstances justify their actions? I thought and thought and saw a possible answer. They mightn't know! If the two bullets had been fired coincidentally and one of the two from behind them—they mightn't know, especially if this third person slipped away from the back of the shed at once, as was quite easy for anybody.

"Well, we found Pollock and Maitland's first wife, and Nellie King found Dillon for us—or what eventually turned out to be Dillon—and then another idea struck me. It had rained very hard just before Maitland had been killed—and it hadn't rained since that I could remember. We were sitting in Pollock's when I thought of this. Supposing the arm that held the revolver that might have killed Maitland had been in the sleeve of a mackintosh or raincoat? A mackintosh, that in all probability, considering the weather conditions, hadn't been worn since. There might be remnants of cobweb dust still on that sleeve. Anyhow it was worth looking at. Pollock's hall stand yielded nothing. We walked to Cruden's place at Queensleigh. I was by this time on the alert. I contrived to have a look round. A lady's mackintosh hung on the hall stand—a light blue one—and on the cuff of the right-hand sleeve could be easily discovered a filamentous mass of cobweb. I felt that the mackintosh must be Mrs. Cruden's—there was no other woman at Queensleigh close enough to the affair to be implicated."

"But my dear Bathurst—how on earth did Mrs. Cruden come to have a revolver with her? It seems to me—"

"Don't you remember what she told us, sir? She had her son's revolver with her—I rather incline to the theory that he had threatened to commit suicide—he'd make a very poisonous omelette, would Master Cruden. She had been out with him that afternoon and had taken the revolver from him. Now, listen. I felt that Queensleigh might hold the key to the mystery; when I stated to Mr. and Mrs. Cruden that Dick Cruden had gone to town about three o'clock, I did so purposely. Because I knew from what the porter told us that he had caught the five twenty-eight. She—and I say 'she' deliberately—because she knew much more of the detail of his comings and goings than did his father—let my statement pass unchallenged.

"Why? Because she knew when Maitland died. If I believed what I had said, she thought it would prevent me suspecting her precious son if the truth of Maitland's movements ever happened to come out. This came to me like a flash and I felt certain that it was she who had fired the revolver. I don't know that I'm sorry that she did."

"H'm. D'you think Maitland intended mischief to Princess Alicia?"

"Undoubtedly. He was on his way to Queensleigh. He either meant to lame her or put her out of mess altogether. Don't forget the scalpel and the poisoned sugar. Anything else, Sir Austin?"

The commissioner shook his head.

"No! I don't think so! Yes, there is. Why did Maitland phone to Studdenham's? I didn't quite see the force of that."

Anthony smiled.

"He didn't want Dillon to make anything whatever out of the Princess Alicia ticket, or, at any rate, as little as possible. Jealousy's a grim tyrant, you know, and Julius Maitland was suffering under its yoke severely."

He rose and stretched his long arms before speaking again.

"Ah, well, I hope the little lady's second matrimonial venture will turn out more happily than her first. But there—I have no doubt on the point. Why should I have? Dillon's a real good chap. Good night, Sir Austin. You're not coming my way, are you?"

THE END

Made in the USA
Monee, IL
02 September 2023